Y0-EKS-441

Advance kudos for Blind Guys Break 80 . . .

"What a story! I really, *really* liked it. Took *Blind Guys Break 80* on a plane flight from California to England. It was the fastest flight ever. That's my quote!"

- Huey Lewis, rock singer, 10-handicap golfer

"Fred Reiss did for golf what he previously did for surfing—given us a hip, insider's story told with a wicked sense of humor."

- Chris Miller, National Lampoon author of *Animal House*

"Fred Reiss has done something pretty cool with *Blind Guys Break 80*. He's turned a golf course into not just a metaphor for life but an entertaining stage where characters crack wicked jokes and utter deep truths. Imagine teeing it up in a foursome of John Daly, Martha Stewart, David Mamet and George Carlin. Then imagine a 19th hole therapy session with them. That sort of explains what Reiss is up to here—but that doesn't begin to touch on the sweet family drama at the heart of it all. I give this book four strokes a side and four stars out of four."

- Mark Purdy, sports columnist, *San Jose Mercury News*

Here's my gentle tug on the brim of my golf cap to my recently passed and deeply missed Dad (alias "The Mogul") who finished out his back nine at 81-years-old (He finally broke 90!) and to the memory of my Mom, who is two-stepping with him to a Tijuana Brass tune in a distant living room. Now, onto the living, the cast of golfers and surf-hacking deadbeats I grew to know at Valley Gardens in Scotts Valley, California, as well as the golfers that let Fred Single play with them and shared their lives between shots on the courses of Pajaro, Deep Cliff, Poppy Hills, DeLavega, Rancho Cañada, Aptos Seascape, Boulder Creek, the defunct Aptos Par Three, Santa Teresa, Del Monte, the Shorehaven Country Club in Norwalk, CT, and every other offbeat muni track that called me to the tee. Plus, a special extra tug on the brim to Eagle Ridge golf pro Stewart Spence who gives lessons and tales at the Watsonville Airport Driving Range, turf doctor Steve Woodruff, golf rules expert Johnny Arbogast—and, to Freehold, New Jersey, for always being part of me. A thanks to the nice family that gave my brother and myself a tour of our old Stonehurst house and brought our warm home back into our hearts again, which went well with the Sorrento's Subs, Monmouth County Peanut Brittle and Federici's pizza we took back with us, as well as the farewell toast to Dad and Mom with a beer at Moore's Inn.

Kudos for cover by Frank Doyle of Standingstone, as well the editing and design assistance I received from Ken "Where'd my bladder go?" Dixon, font and kerning lessons from New York Times guy and hangover buddy Lee Yarosh and additional mentoring from Beth Regardz of Cabrillo College.

Santa Cruz'n Press. Printed in the USA.

FIRST EDITION

See Fred's movie *Return To Freehold, New Jersey* on YouTube.

Fore *Laurie,*
she makes
all things possible.
Even me.

Blind Guys Break 80

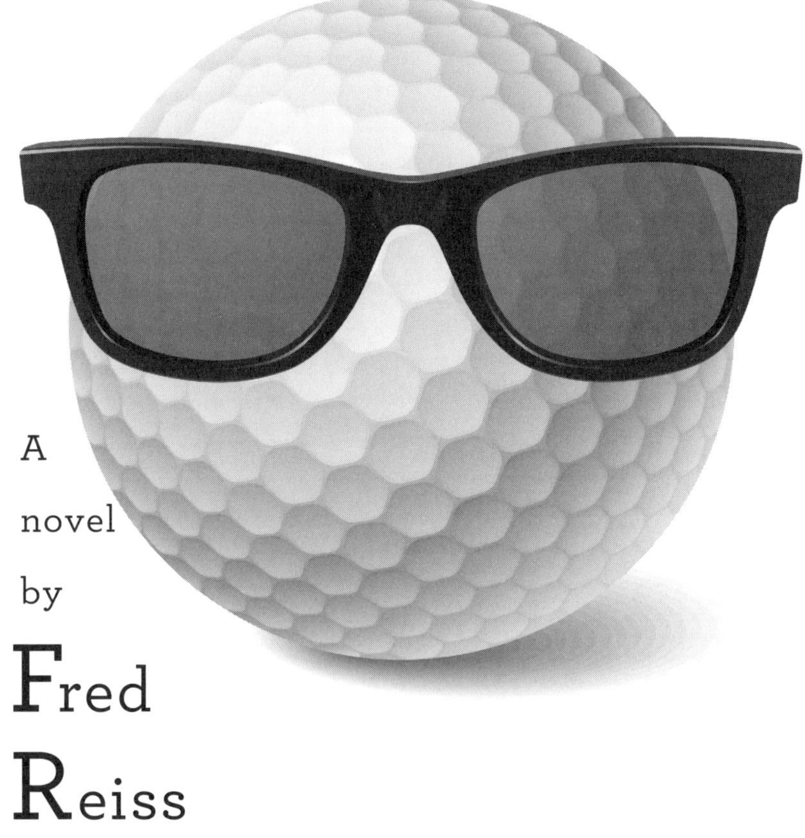

A novel by

Fred Reiss

The story of an underachiever on the *upswing*.
Or, Long Day's Journey on The Back Nine.

"You need to have the proper set up of the true golf position: grip, stance, posture and alignment. Once you have assumed that set up, an early rotation of the body over to the right side allows the hips to turn and keep weight over the inside of the right foot. Let the arms swing completely free from the body allowing them to achieve the proper position at the backswing with a square clubface. The lower body begins the downswing, moving hips slightly laterally, making the club return to its swing plane. From there a free unrestricted flow of energy goes through the hips and arms, releasing the club so it's flying away from you, which allows the weight of the club to pull the golfer into a balanced position on your left side."

– Golf instructional video

"The golf swing isn't that complicated. All you have to do is grip it, turn it, and release it."

– Peter Thomson, five-time British Open champion

On the Tee

Book Course's Slope rating: 223

To The Next Tee

Blind Guys

GOLF RESEMBLED CLOUDY because he played the same way he faced every challenge and break in his 43-year-old life—badly, with a misplaced vengeance.

"Good luck, Cloudy *Junior*," insincerely said Eggplant, jabbing a hand at Cloudy on the first tee of The Gull, the Battleground Country Club's annual member-guest golf tournament. "Your Dad invited you back, huh? Even after how badly you played last year?"

"I'm not a Junior," sharply corrected Cloudy, who kept his hands deeply thrust in his pockets because he couldn't stand Eggplant, whose real name was Tony Anchor. Cloudy blankly stared at his ex-brother-in-law's wise-ass smirk. Eggplant's lips were scuffed and peeling like the mouth of a creature that doesn't use hands to eat. The divorce aged Eggplant beyond and beneath his parts of his 53 years. He put on weight. His face had a puffy booze layer. His hair was grayer, thinner. This pleased Cloudy.

"You're named after your Dad, John Map, so I assumed that here at our club you'll *always* be a junior," said Eggplant. "Just so you know… after I beat your sorry ass, we clinch first and you two finish in last for what? Five years in a row? Why it's a family tradition."

"We can be the spoiler if we win our match," said Cloudy, "and you finish second."

"Ya think?" Eggplant snorted, then shrugged and added cryptically, "And blind guys break 80, what do you want from me?"

"Blind guys break 80? What does that—"

"Give my regards to your sister Wendy," replied Eggplant, relishing the flash of anger he provoked in Cloudy. "I hear she's not doing well."

Cloudy's clenched fists shot out of his pockets. His father quickly came over. He put his arm around his son's shoulder, escorted him away and whispered, "Put a little lavender on it, son."

"Be nice, after what Eggplant *did* to my sister?" Cloudy crossly said.

His father walked back to Eggplant, shook his ex-son-in-law's hand, took in the day and said, "Another beautiful Fairfield County morning. It's going to be a cooker. Typical August weather."

Eggplant signaled his partner over and said, "Don, this is John Map. I gave these guys their nicknames. Members call him 'Clear.' Junior, his pony-tailed son, is 'Cloudy.' Cloudy was a member but dropped out because he couldn't afford it." He paused. "Guys, this is Don Arax."

Arax was six-feet, 225 pounds, in his late forties. He was multi-tiered with body-armor like muscles. His wrap-around sunglasses gave him the appearance of an android. A sloppy goatee and mustache was smeared across his lips like the remains of a whisker milk shake. A disproportionately large crucifix bulged beneath his shirt, as if the cross was a calcium deposit that formed on his sternum.

"Nice to meet you Donald," said Clear, skeptically eyeing the cross.

Arax bridled at the sound of his first name and spat, "Call me Don."

"Where are you from, Cloudy?" asked Arax.

"I'm from Freehold, New Jersey," Cloudy answered.

"You came all the way from South Jersey to play in this tournament?" said Arax. "Freehold is way down where, near Asbury Park?"

Clear said, "He lives in Bridgeport." He became irritated and added to his son, "We've been living in Connecticut how long now? And you still tell people you're from New Jersey."

"Well, that's where I'm originally from—Freehold."

Eggplant said, "Met Don when he put flooring in for my office."

"Just want to wish you guys luck," said Arax, who smiled, rubbed his bulging forearms arms and added, "I haven't played in awhile. I hope I don't embarrass myself."

"Every twosome you played against says you're averaging eight strokes better than your handicap," replied Cloudy. "Hard to play like that without being accused of sandbagging."

"They're sore losers ," said Arax, looking off. "I've been pretty lucky, that's all." He reached into his pocket and produced a roll of candy. "Peppermint Lifesaver, anyone?"

"I'll pass," replied Cloudy. "I'm trying to cut down."

"Check out my new headcover," said Eggplant, chuckling. "A plumber with butt crack. I got a pit bull with hairy balls on back order."

"Man, that's so you," said Cloudy.

There was a long silence. It created a polite but strained distance, which was like the course: filled with hazards. Why, even the wooden white tee markers carved into the shape of armed Colonial Minutemen seemed to standing at their posts to ensure civility,

"You gentlemen have honors," said Clear.

"I'm playing a Titleist Pro VI," said Arax, identifying his ball.

"Me too," said Cloudy. "What number? We don't want to hit the wrong ball by mistake."

"Mine's marked 'Prov: 8:35,'" said Arax. "It's from the Bible."

"Well, mine's marked 'Anti Christ 666,' It's from an Ozzy Osbourne solo album," said Cloudy. "I'm kidding. Mine's a number 4 Nike."

"Ignore him," said Clear. "My son thinks he's funny."

Arax aligned his stance on the tee. He uncoiled a powerful smooth swing. His searing ball spun away, briefly sizzling like an igniting match. The drive stayed low, started climbing, soared and somehow managed to re-enter the earth's atmosphere, swoop down and land 300-plus yards in the fairway's lush crosshatch-cut grass.

"Keep going!" said Eggplant to the rolling ball. Then added 'bitch' but pronounced it. "Beeeee-yatch, keep—"

"Don't talk to my ball!" snapped Arax. He admired his shot and proclaimed, "I can do business with that." He lightly patted his crucifix bulge in gratitude.

"Money," Eggplant said, fist bumping Arax. He turned to the Maps, smirked and added, "If you want to play with the big dogs you have to leave the porch."

Cloudy muttered, "He hasn't played for awhile? Yeah, right."

Eggplant teed up his ball, swung, sliced and pleaded, "Stay in."

Arax stood behind Eggplant on the tee and said, "Your ball is in the short stuff by the 200-yard marker. Near that small shrub."

"I can play either a Maxfli or a Pinnacle," Clear announced. He held up two balls. "Pulled them out of a water hazard. No reason for a 76-year-old hacker with a 33-handicap to play with new balls. I'll hit the Maxfli." He shoved the Pinnacle in his pocket. Clear teed up, swung languidly and asked in amused dismay, "Where did it go?"

"In the rough, 90 yards" sighed Cloudy, standing behind his Dad.

"Another great moment in golf," said Clear. "I'm just bad."

Cloudy lined a tee shot that rattled nearly every branch of a large oak by the low, stone boundary fence along Country Club Lane.

"Outside of that shot, Cloudy," Eggplant cracked. "How's the rest of your life going?"

"Dad, did you see if I went O.B.?" asked Cloudy, turning around. But his father wasn't behind him. Clear sat in a golf cart, scribbling names on the scorecard. "Dad! Did my ball stay in play?"

"See what?" said Clear, looking up, peeved at the interruption.

Cloudy hung his head and glumly conceded, "I'll hit a provisional."

"And just so you know..." said Eggplant, "in golf we call that 'hitting three from the tee.'"

"Thanks for the ruling," said Cloudy, re-teeing. "I'm aware hitting O.B. is a one-stroke penalty and distance."

"Probably because you do it so often."

"Hey Dad, can you watch where this ball goes, please."

"Why? We'll find the first one."

Cloudy laced a 225-yard drive in the rough, close to where his first shot might have gone O.B.. He trudged to the cart, rammed his driver in the bag and said, "Dad, why didn't you watch my first drive? You're supposed to be my partner. Last I checked, that's what partner's do."

"You're talking partners?" Clear said, becoming surly. "Look at me and your Mom. I want to spend next winter in Florida. She doesn't want to leave you kids. Kids! You're both in your forties. Your sister has been living in our condo for six years. No job, going to her AA meetings. And I'm not counting the three days every month she sleeps in her room because she says it's her 'medication.' Who sleeps for three days? Some retirement. I'm living in the Petrified Forest." He added, "Wendy was hanging a face this morning. She was going on about how today would've been her 10th wedding anniversary."

"She'll use it as a frickin' excuse to drink and go off the rails again. Before you left the condo, did Wendy say, 'Oy!'?"

"Oy? Why?"

"She always says 'Oy' when she's been drinking. It's the only time she says it. I don't know why, we're not Jewish. Probably got it from the time she was commuting and working in New York. Why dwell on this crap now, Dad? There are worse places to be."

"Easy for you to say," said Clear. "You don't have to live with it. Golf, drink beer and eat here all day while your Mom is at home afraid to be left alone with her own daughter."

"So that makes *me* the bad guy," said Cloudy. "We're out here golfing. Since we chose to be here, why can't we enjoy being here for now?"

"Our balls are in the fairway," said Eggplant, pulling up next to the Maps parked cart. "Just so you know... the 'Fairway' is the grassy area that's between where you and your Dad's shots land." Eggplant blaaaaaaaaaahed out his fuck-it-if-you-can't-take-a-joke laugh and drove away.

"Nice guy," said Cloudy, wiping sweat from his neck. "It's going to be hot. I'll get some waters from the Pro Shop. I bet Lucy's there. She is!"

"Hurry up," said Clear.

Lucy was crouching on the porch by the cooler. The pro's dog was staring at some crows in the grass near the putting green. She earned her keep by driving away geese and snagging moles. Lucy bolted from the steps and chased the crows off. She scampered to the porch and stretched out at Cloudy's feet to receive a rewarding tummy rub.

"That's so weird," said Cloudy, scratching Lucy's stomach.

"What is, Mr. Map?" curiously asked the club pro, Bobby Mingle, who stepped outside. Mingle was in his forties, courteous—but way too artificially pleasant to be genuinely interested in anyone.

"Lucy didn't bark at the crows," said Cloudy, grabbing a few bottled waters. "Most dogs bark at birds. She doesn't. That's weird is all."

"I *did* hear her bark a few minutes ago, but I'm not sure at what," said Mingle. "Lucy's a runaway I adopted. I think she doesn't bark because her last owner abused her." Mingle pulled a small roll of tickets from his pocket. "Your raffle ticket for the tonight's Gull awards festivities."

Cloudy glanced at the ticket's number: *223*. He had a fondness for the number. And looked at any appearance of the number as a sign of good luck. It reminded him of the Maps' old home address: 223 Stonehurst Way in Freehold, New Jersey. They were happy there. It was a great neighborhood. When his Dad's company, AMF, relocated its headquarters from Manhattan to Westchester County, the Maps corporately migrated to Westport, Connecticut for an easier commute. The transplanted family never recovered from the Jersey-to-Fairfield County culture shock. That was more than 27 years ago. But Cloudy still resented being uprooted. He believed his life would have turned out better in Freehold—or, at least *different.* He'd settled for different.

"HERE LIES MY GREAT OPENING TEE SHOT," said Clear in his submissive tone of self-deprecation. "Buried in the rough. This is going to be a long day, hawkshaw. We don't have a chance against these guys."

"Dad, you're giving up after your first shot on our opening hole? We're still in this," said Cloudy, trying to inspire his father, which rarely worked. "Your handicap gives you two strokes here. This is match play. It doesn't matter who has the lowest score at the end of the round. This is a best-of-9-holes match. It's who has the lowest score on *each* hole. Eggplant can screw up and we can still have a chance take this hole. Use the 8-iron and knock it back on the fairway."

"I'm using my 7-wood," said Clear.

"The rough's too deep for a 7-wood," said Cloudy, but his Dad still pulled out the 7-wood. Cloudy threw up his arms. "Unbelievable."

Clear made a half-hearted slap at the ball. The clubhead snagged the high grass. He topped his shot. The ball rolled a few feet and sunk even deeper into the rough. He walked over, looked at the ball, bent down and picked it up.

"I hit the wrong ball, that's a penalty," said Clear, smiling. "This is a Maxfli. I played a Pinnacle off the tee. I'm out of this hole."

"Dad, didn't you say on the tee you had *two* balls to use?"

Clear plucked the other ball from his pocket and said, "This is a Pinnacle! You're right. I *did* hit a Maxfli. Too late. I can't put the ball back down." He smiled. "You're all alone on this one, son."

Cloudy found his second drive. He swung. His ball hit a tree branch and went O.B. over the stone wall. But then, he spied his first drive, sitting up pretty good, a few feet ahead.

"There's my original tee shot, it didn't go O.B.," happily said Cloudy.

"Pick it up," said Clear. "A group on the tee is waiting to hit."

"No, I'm playing this."

"You can't hit that ball," said Eggplant, who had driven over in his cart. "You already hit your provisional."

"According to the rules," said Cloudy, "after hitting a provisional, I can still play my first ball if I haven't declared it lost or walked past it and hit my second shot. This same thing happened to me last year."

"Rules," gruffly said Eggplant. "What are you some fag lawyer? We're out here to play golf, not follow rules."

"Pick up, son," said Clear, pulling over in the golf cart.

"I'm playing it."

"No one can tell you anything," Clear snapped, driving off.

"What did I do?" Cloudy asked, then reflectively grumbled to himself, "Hello, where's the love?" His frustration with his father's behavior accelerated into rage, then elevated into a calm psychotic moment of clarity. He lashed his 2-iron through the grass. The shot landed by the flagstick. Where did that swing come from? he wondered. He felt nothing—not even contact with the ball. He lost himself in the present. He didn't exist. He *didn't* like it.

Cloudy went down the fairway to his Dad, who parked the cart on a gravel path just off the hole. Clear sat at the wheel and ignored his son. Cloudy went to his bag and exchanged his 2-iron for a putter and walked to the green. Arax's ball was six feet below the cup and Cloudy's rested three feet above the hole.

"You're both on the green in two, putting for birdies," Eggplant said. "I'm was laying four. I picked up." He crouched behind his partner's ball. "Right edge. Breaks a foot left. Don't give the hole away."

Arax stroked his branding-iron shaped putter then cursed, "Hot!"

"Go in!" said Eggplant.

"Don't talk to my ball!" Arax gruffly ordered. "Don't *ever* talk to my ball." The fast putt went a foot past Cloudy's marker, leaving Arax with a longer, more difficult downhill putt and giving Cloudy the benefit of a read. "Shit on my dog," Arax added. "Woof!"

Clear sat in the cart and said to Arax, "Your putt's good."

Arax raised his eyebrows in surprise and quickly pocketed his ball.

"You're away, Cloudy," said Eggplant.

"Wait. You're not giving me my putt? My Dad gave you Donald's. And this putt is *closer* to the hole than his was."

"Ya think?" said Eggplant, smirking. "Golf is a gentlemen's game. Your Dad decided to be a gentleman. I didn't. Why? Because I want to beat your sorry ass."

Cloudy studied his putt and said, "Dad! I need help with a read. You've played here for 25 years, you know how these greens break."

"Just hit the ball," said Clear, dismissively waving off the request. "If it goes in, it goes in."

Cloudy misread the break and missed his putt by a foot.

"Our hole!" Eggplant said, fist bumping Arax.

"How can you win this hole?" asked Cloudy, baffled. "He got a par. I'm putting for a par. If I make this, we push. I halve the hole. We tie."

"My partner strokes here, you don't," said Eggplant.

"I'm giving *your partner* strokes!" exclaimed Cloudy in disbelief. "I have a 25-plus handicap. And this guy's worse than me?"

"We're in with a four, a net-three birdie," clipped Eggplant. "The match is 1-8. We're one-up with eight holes left to play."

Cloudy stomped off the green and plopped into the passenger side of the golf cart, his putter between his legs.

"Well, we're down one," Clear said, driving to the next tee.

"No, they are one *up*!" insisted Cloudy. "We are not down. Down is a negative. We have to be positive."

"So does that change the outcome?" said Clear, parking the cart.

"You gave that frickin' sandbagger a winning putt. You never give away a winning putt—never!" exasperatingly sighed Cloudy. "You're suppose to be *my* partner, not his."

"He would have made it."

"I'm playing against three people: Eggplant, Arax and you," sighed Cloudy.

"I noticed you left yourself out of the mix," said Clear. "Again."

"Lifesaver?" asked Arax, extending the candy roll to Cloudy.

"Yes," replied Cloudy, gazing off at a red-tail hawk circling for gophers and squirrels. "That's not the Lifesaver I need right now."

AS EGGPLANT'S ONSLAUGHT CONTINUED, his partner casually dropped any pretension of being "just lucky." Arax seamlessly striped huge drives in fairways, fired at pins and hit every green in regulation. When he chipped or pitched, his ball looked like it was doing back flips as it tumbled into holes for birdies and eagles. And on top of that, Arax was getting strokes on every hole! Since his Dad wasn't going to be any help, Cloudy gave up and began pounding down beers from kegs placed at each tee box. After all, if the Maps were going down in flames, Cloudy was going crash in blazing inferno— with a solid buzz on. He took risky shots beyond his abilities. He sprayed balls out of bounds and into water hazards or bunkers. He 3-putted every green. Soon the Maps were 5-4 (five down with four holes left to play in their 9-hole match). They were completely closed out. Eggplant's gruesome twosome had easily won. Clear gratefully congratulated them. Cloudy sullenly sat and pouted in the cart holding a broken 8-iron he bent in half after hitting his last approach shot over a fence. He refused to shake hands with the winners. The Maps drove back to the clubhouse. A frayed Cloudy scowled at the passing fairways.

"I'm glad they closed us out after five," said Clear who was smiling and humming. "I pity the guys still playing. They'll be sweating over second place and I'll be holding my nose and diving into a vodka. Getting squiffed." He patted his son's leg and added, "What the hell, hawkshaw. We gave it our best shot."

"No, we didn't," Cloudy burst, his eyes brimming with tears. "You didn't even try to win. You're not even mad at getting snot-slapped by Eggplant and his frickin' sandbagging piece-of-shit crony. Those guys enjoyed humiliating us. It's like you're happy we lost. I don't get it."

"What?" Clear surprised, his grin fading.

"Every time I play in this tournament, I start out trying my best and you don't even make the effort to show me a good time."

"But you don't even play golf that much," said Clear. "You've never taken the game seriously. And I'm terrible. What can you expect?"

"Doesn't mean I'm not trying. Being on a golf course is a great place to be. But you turn it into the worst place on Earth. After we teed up, all you did was bitch and moan about the heat. Gripe about bad shots. Complain about Mom and Wendy and get on my case. It's like you *plan* it. Like you're taking revenge on me. Why waste your money? Next year take me to the driving range, I'll hand you my 2-iron and you can split my head open. Leave me for dead. The crows can eat my brains and call it a day. It would be cheaper."

THE MAPS PARKED in the grass near the Georgian-style clubhouse. The smells of barbecue and cigar smoke altered Cloudy's mood from defeat to beer and meat. The plantation clubhouse setting looked like what would have happened if The South won The Civil War. Red-and-white checkered cloth-covered picnic tables were set up in the grass. Mexican waiters delivered drinks. Black chefs in white double-breasted jackets and red toques sliced roast beef at carving stations or worked flame-throwing grills. Haitian waitresses dressed in a ties, white shirts, black pants and vests strolled through the golfers with silver trays of hors d' oeuvres.

Cloudy sat in the passenger seat, hung his head, looked away and apologized, "I shouldn't have said, what I said, Dad. I'm sorry."

"Forget it," said Clear, getting out of the cart. "Par for the course."

"I'll claim an outside table."

"Outside? Why, it's an oven out here. I'm wetting my pimpled nose in The Grill Room of my club's air-conditioned 19th hole."

"I'll shower first," said Cloudy. "I brought a change of clothes."

"Take a shower at your apartment. We head back after we eat."

"Let's hang, we have an open bar! Why do you want to rush back home? You know what's *there*."

"Fine, why should my responsibilities interrupt your day?" Clear said abruptly, limping away, legs slightly bowed, potbelly leading the way.

Cloudy sighed and reflexively made a beeline to the kegs of beer on the veranda. He greedily scoped out the elegant buffet table lined with silver warming trays of salmon, peanut-sauce covered Satay chicken, corn on the cob, as well as huge crystal bowls with jumbo shrimp hooked along the rims packed with oysters and clams on ice. There were deep wooden dishes with salads and a tons of fruit. The spread even had 5-gallon containers of vanilla and chocolate ice cream—plus, small cups with various toppings to build a sundae. Beyond it was a sushi bar. Not a bad life, Cloudy thought.

"Mr. Map, why we haven't seen you for awhile," tepidly said a Haitian waitress holding a tray of bacon-wrapped scallops. "You play with your Dad every year. Your father looks happier when you're here."

"I bring out the best in him," Cloudy said, inhaling three scallops. "He likes it here. I never cared much for the club myself."

"Well, it's good to see you," she diplomatically replied, withdrawing.

He went to a keg on the veranda and drank beer. Cloudy recognized Kyle, Trent and Todd, sons of members who still belonged to the club. They were fat and smoking cigars. The elite trinity predictably ignored him and cheerfully beckoned to one another at the buffet. Cloudy had long ago categorized this crew and many club members like them as ReRuns because they were assembled from the same box their Dads came in. He was accustomed to their slights. Years ago, when the Maps became members, Cloudy didn't know anyone, wanted to make friends and showed up at the Pro Shop to golf. Mingle said, "Mr. Map, you're a single. A threesome just teed off. I'll take you out." The ReRuns were on the green. Mingle pulled up and said, "Mr. Map is a single. Can he join you?" Without looking from his putt, Kyle sniffed, "We're having a *private* tournament among us." Mingle drove Cloudy back. Who would want to be a ReRun and hang out at the buffet with that unfriendly crew, anyway? thought Cloudy. And why did they feel superior because their family belonged to the club for fifty years, as if they were some form of royalty? If they couldn't pay their dues they'd be kicked out. So what was the big deal?

Cloudy poured beer into two tall paper cups, walked down the veranda's slate steps under a blue *porte-cochère* and along the gravel driveway than ran between the clubhouse and six tennis courts. There were the usual Chardonnay-clutching mothers chattering at a courtside table under a canopy watching their ReRunette daughters thop soulless crisp ground strokes. The compliantly assured women were crop-dusted with make-up. They were over-educated and brittle tongued. Their bodies simmered with perfume. Low-cut blouses revealed tanned sunken rib cages and cleavage that had dropped from top-shelf to the marked-down rack. They had strained expressions, as if their spirits had been broken on Fairfield County bridal trails. No wonder Cloudy's Mom never wanted to come here and avoided all the social events. She wasn't like these women. But over the years, his mother learned how to drink like them.

CLOUDY STEPPED OUT from one of the five spacious rose-marble shower stalls and toweled off by a row of granite sinks. He blow-dried his shoulder-length hair and tied up his ponytail. He shaved, splashed on cologne and patted himself with baby powder. Cloudy furtively glanced around. He quickly stashed two cans of shaving cream and some disposable razors into the folds of his towel. He went to his

Dad's locker and hid the filched items beneath the dirty polo shirt in a gym bag. As he dressed, Cloudy was eye level with the locker's brass nameplate: John Map. When his father was Cloudy's age, John Map was married with two kids, owned a house in Westport and belonged to this country club. He was Director of Personnel for AMF, a major corporation that produced Voit sports equipment, Harley Davidson motorcycles, bowling machines and Hatteras Yachts. Compared to his Dad's achievements, in the Book of Cloudy, what had *he* written about himself? Nothing, really. He never graduated college. Over the years, he'd been fired for lateness at several shipping-and-receiving jobs. Currently, he was operating a forklift in a warehouse and on probation. Why, he didn't own anything. Even the golf clothes he was wearing were purchased with his father's club credits at the Pro Shop. Cloudy lived in the rented first floor of a rundown two-family house in Bridgeport. Sang lead in Mid-Life Vices, a classic-rock cover band. And supplemented his income by dealing weed and coke at The Hugga Mug, a local bar. Not exactly an impressive career run.

Cloudy put on a clean shirt, cautiously looked around, took a bindle of coke from his pocket, tapped a bump on his knuckle and sharply tooted and packed his left nostril.

The locker room door opened. Cloudy put the bindle in his pocket. He quickly wiped his nose. A club member nodded and clomped by him. He was in his late fifties. In shape. Distinguished, gray hair. Attired in flashy clothes. He sat on a bench, calmly removed a golf shoe, stared at it, then violently flung it against his locker door and snarled, "Fuck, my 5-handicap!"

He left the seething golfer to unwind in the velvet-cushioned walls of his members-only inner hell. Cloudy pushed open the door and coasted on his light buzz down a hallway. The walls were lined with shield-shaped wooden plaques engraved with past club tournament winners, Hy Peskin's black-and-white picture of Ben Hogan hitting a 2-iron on the 72nd hole at Merion in the 1950 US Open, and a framed yellow flag from The Masters. Cloudy's nostrils sharply stung from cigarette smoke drifting out of The Card Room, which was off the stairs that lead up to The Grill Room. The smokers were a tight group of Italian members in their eighties. They belonged to the club since Day One: local Norwalk Italians who ran construction firms, auto dealerships and limousine services. They built the course in 1954; in fact, it was a Battleground Club in-joke that you didn't have an official foursome unless it had one Italian. Over time, the dwindling Old Guard was outvoted by newer members who desired a more prestigious club with a challenging golf course. They instituted dress codes, no-smoking inside the clubhouse and gave women equal opportunity to have the same starting tee times as men on weekends, as well as converting the beloved 'Mens-Only' 19th Hole into The Grill Room that allowed women and children. The Old Guards' response to these blasphemous acts? They snatched up their ash trays and dice cups and established The Card Room downstairs. The all-male bunker had a private bar with dark-wood-panelled walls that displayed framed Royal Flushes and below the cards were nameplates engraved with the poker player and the historic date of his hand. Here, they smoked, played cards, groused about the other members or anything new and cracked dirty and racist jokes.

A bald contractor was rolling dice for drinks. He slammed down a leather cup and said, "Sixes all day." He groaned and signed the drink card. "Beaten by a Dago whose neck looks like a roll of dimes."

"My minestrone's on the tab," said his pal, lighting up a cigar. "You don't have to pay for it."

"Screw your soup," the loser said. He signed the tab, and quipped, "Cocksucking guinea."

The men laughed.

CLOUDY RETURNED FROM THE BUFFET to The Grill Room. Eggplant sat at the bar, crowing about his victory and gluttonously and sloppily swigging Tanqueray-and-tonic from The Gull cup. The cup was a large crystal chalice atop the stem of a golf ball balanced on the upraised beak of a ceramic seagull perched on a silver base that had two handles fashioned from the bird's wings. Eggplant's slurping amused his buddies, who were assholes like him. Cloudy noticed established members shot starchy, disdainful glances at Eggplant, which only provoked him to become even more brazen.

"When I tended bar in Long Island," loudly said Eggplant to his drunk cronies. "I'd take a bimbo home every night. I'd shave their pussies. I'd put Hershey's chocolate kisses in their box and eat them out. One babe came back a few days later and said, 'I'm itchy.' I told her, 'You need a shave.'" Eggplant's lewd laugh began as a short nasal chuckle like an evil puppet and peaked into an open-mouthed, fuck'em-if-they-can't-take-a-joke braying haaaaaaaaaaah.

"Young man, put a lid on the language," severely chided The Judge sitting at a table.

Judge Ellis was in his eighties, his left arm partially incapacitated from a stroke. He no longer played golf. He was content to cultivate the stately stature of an accomplished man settled in a comfortable liquored-up groove of retirement. The Judge was a familiar presence, wearing his signature Bermuda shorts, a loud shirt and sandals with black socks. A large glass of white wine in his hand at all times. He often played cards, read the morning newspaper on the veranda, or ambled about the putting green and engaged in conversations with members. When he had a life, he served on the Norwalk bench for 30 years. In the faltering last days of Wendy's marriage to Eggplant, Cloudy's sister was busted for DUIs and evading responsibility after leaving the scene of four car accidents in three towns on one day. The Judge deftly fingered an intricately muted tune on his well-connected judicial strings and her DUI charges were dropped. In the long run this was probably a mistake, thought Cloudy, if Wendy did jail time she might have been better off. So would everyone else.

Eggplant wasn't backing down to The Judge—yet.

"Lighten up, Judge," said Eggplant. "Don't take it personally."

"I do take it personally, because people don't talk to me the way *you* talk to them," evenly fired back The Judge, who leaned on his cane and hobbled past Eggplant. "Remove your golf cap. Tuck in your shirt. Our governing board has a dress code. You're violating it."

"Rules," said Eggplant, bristling. He grudgingly swiped off his cap and tucked in his shirt. "Stupid rules."

In life, like in golf, Eggplant resented rules—any rules. He lived to cut corners. Speed limits? He installed a radar detector in the glove compartment of his dashboard. No smoking in a place? He'd light up a cigar and when told to extinguish it, blow smoke in the manager's face, then put it out. Can't buy liquor on Sunday because of Connecticut Blue Laws? He'd slam two six-packs on the counter of a deli, throw down a twenty-dollar bill and leave. Resent overpriced drinks at the club? Tip or float a few ball game tickets to the bar staff and they didn't accurately record your tab. Have to be on time? Show up late. Fuck'em. But Eggplant was no dummy. Cloudy saw him shrewdly and instantly calculate numbers in his head: inventories, sales projections, point spreads. Eggplant was a successful Snap-On Tools District Manager who was responsible for automotive-shop routes in Connecticut and New York. An ideal job for a dickhead like him. His pushy, intimidating personality confronted and shook down muscular mechanics who fell behind on their installment payments for tools.

Cloudy's tray was loaded with beers and a plate heaped with shrimp, two double cheeseburgers, slices of prime rib and a California roll.

Eggplant snickered at Cloudy's meal and cracked,"Well, look at you. You're on the way to playing scratch—a scratch eater."

On the bar's TV the news showed an arrested child molester.

"You know what they should do with that son of a bitch," said Eggplant. "Stand the prick against the wall and ten feet away have pros tee-up 2-irons and fire shots into his head." He paused. "You're good with a 2-iron, Cloudy. Maybe you can find a career doing that."

"Tell you what, I'll go grab my 2-iron, give you a running start on the 18th fairway and we'll do a dry run," Cloudy replied walked away.

Cloudy joined his Dad, who sat alone at a large walnut table by a corner window that had a panoramic view of the 18th green against a backdrop of the sailboat-flecked Long Island Sound. In a way, father and son were similar, thought Cloudy, his Dad made enemies doing the right thing, while Cloudy made enemies doing the wrong thing, but they still ended up with the same result: unaccepted. His Dad wasn't too popular among the established members. Years ago, the club was concerned about rapid employee turnover and theft. Clear served on the board and used his compensation experience to set up a benefit program for the staff. The result, employees remained in their jobs for years and theft was reduced. But members resented seeing their dues diverted to those who served them (which many members deemed a privilege because it provided their lessers an opportunity to associate with a better class of people).

Clear was happily humming and heavily dusting layers of salt on his Chilean seabass.

A gray-haired member peered over and said in disbelief, "I can't believe how much salt you use."

He kept salting away and said, "I like it."

The member left.

Clear took the last swallow of his vodka and said, "That's Gaffer. He lectures me on salt and then goes outside to smoke."

His son laughed.

"Unlike your Mom, I gave up smoking 22 years ago. You know who steered me down the road to smoking? Bob Hinton. What a sight. Me at seventeen. Six-feet, 118 pounds and smoking a cigarette. Hinton went on to be a sergeant Springfield Police and got arrested for stealing rowboats from Echo Lake." Cloudy laughed. He loved these moments with his Dad. But the vodka would soon spoil the mood. Clear smirked and said in a teasing nasal tone, "Did you enjoy your shower, hawkshaw?" He squinted at his son's face. "Missed a spot shaving under your chin. What a slobberhanus with that long hair. A grown man. I take that back, a man your age with a ponytail. When are you going to chop that thing off?"

"Business in front," replied Cloudy, who smiled, reached back and waggled his ponytail. "Party in the back."

As Cloudy ate, he took in The Grill Room crowd. Very few faces changed over the years. The same members sat at the same chairs at the same tables. "Dad, don't these people ever get tired seeing the same people every day?"

"No."

Cloudy overheard members grouse about government regulations and entitlement programs that provided a level playing field for inferiors in the business world. This always amused Cloudy because those conservative convictions didn't prevent these same members from accepting welfare benefits granted under the USGA's liberal handicap entitlement program that awarded strokes to hackers with below-average games that enabled them to compete and often defeat superior golfers on a level playing field at their country club course.

A black waiter placed a third vodka before Clear.

"Thanks Willie," Clear said to the departing waiter. "Willie knows what I want: a low-density ice cube drink." He patted his son's arm. "I see you've recovered from our debacle. You know, in this short conversation I have spoken to you more than my Dad, your Pop-Pops, ever spoke to me."

"Count your blessings."

"That's good. You have a sense of humor," dryly said Clear, who chuckled and followed it up with a strong slurp that drained half his drink. "You never really got to know your Pop-Pops. He died when you were two. My Dad wasn't highly educated, but he could tell you where the bear ran through the buckwheat. My parents never pushed me like I encouraged you kids. Nobody was on my bag but me. I didn't have a caddie. I went into the Air Force, got out with my GI college loan. It was the only way I was going to get an education. I look at you kids and what have you accomplished?" Oh no, thought Cloudy, here it comes. "What did I do wrong? I send my daughter to Clark University, a good school. She marries and divorces an asshole named Eggplant. And you? The rebel." He paused. "Nobody ever grew up. The simple truth is: you don't become a man until your parents die. That's because nobody is on your bag but you. You have to carry it yourself."

"Now, there's a nice thought," said Cloudy. "By the way do you have a living will? And am I the executor? Do I have power of attorney now?"

"You're a wet fart," Clear, who surveyed the room and observed, "Have you noticed the club is getting more upscale?"

"Maseratis in the parking lot," said Cloudy. "Never saw that before."

"When I joined, it was a golf club for local guys to come here on weekends with families. It was more fun, guys were looser. Now it's more of a tight-white-shoe crowd who decide if they want to spend the weekend at the club, on their boat, or stay at their place in Cape Cod. The waiting list here is twenty deep to get *on* the waiting list. Who know, maybe Harkness and his son might decide to join."

"The Grahams?" Cloudy said. "It was bad enough living next those pompous jerks in Westport. It's hard to believe the Grahams didn't want to stay in touch with you and Mom after you moved into your Bridgeport condo. Isn't it?"

"Yeah, right," glumly said Clear. "They looked down on us for over twenty years." Clear's eyes brightened. He waved. Cloudy turned. Robert Senior and Robert Junior wended through the tables to join the Maps. Junior and Senior were a typical Battleground Country Club Sandwich: an underachieving offspring squirming between thick slices of a dominating father and a bad marriage, obediently held in place with a trust-fund toothpick. Senior was in his seventies, smiling and firm. He was a successful tobacco CEO who still looked like he happily walked away from freshly firing someone. Junior was in his mid-forties. He had a crumpled, strained, caged look. He was a stay-at-home Dad and his wife worked as a stockbroker. The sight of Junior comforted Cloudy. At least he wasn't the only one who came up short on the green of ambition.

Clear's dour mood instantly became cheerful around friends. This predictable vodka-fueled trait of his father's pissed Cloudy off, because he knew after the Nelfords left, his father's charm would evaporate and he'd either belittle Cloudy or instigate an argument so he could rant and list all the disappointments in his life. His Dad never showed that side to his friends. He saved it for family.

Senior introduced himself to Cloudy.

"Robert Nelford," said Senior extending his hand, as if he wasn't announcing his name, but defining the moment.

"Mr. Nelford, I remember you," said Cloudy, shaking his hand. "My band played last summer at your daughter's wedding."

"Robert. Call me, Robert," Senior said, then nodded at the younger, perpetually fading version of himself. "My son, Robert Junior."

"We're the firm of Robert and Robert," pleasantly chimed in Junior. "We promote from within our family."

"Maybe I should have hired from the outside," joked Senior who warmly added, "So did team Map burn up the course today?"

"I couldn't hit a bull in the ass with a bass fiddle out there," Clear replied, beaming with pride. Cloudy rolled his eyes and shook his head. For some twisted reason, his Dad preferred to be seen as a lovable loser instead of a graceful winner. "All that lengthened rough," Clear griped. "They toughened up the course for tournaments. We're showing off the club to guests, it should be a fun time. My tee shots didn't reach one fairway on the par 5's—"

"Your shafts are too stiff, but you won't listen to me," said Cloudy. "Dad, you need to have clubs that are more flexible. You should have ladies shafts on your clubs."

"Ladies shafts on my clubs," Clear said, mulling the observation and swishing vodka from cheek to cheek. He swallowed and slowly added in mock solemnity, "Is *that* the final insult?"

The four men laughed.

"In the match we took against you, your son here was hitting some huge shots," said Senior, who looked at Cloudy. "You could be pretty good at this game if you applied yourself."

"On the 10th," Clear said proudly, "my son here hit a drive past the memory tree Dick Kasmire planted for his wife, TeeDee. He was only 70 yards from the green! I never hit the ball that far. And with a 2-iron? Nobody can hit a 2-iron! Bob, the key word that you said earlier is '*apply*.' Young John doesn't have the short game or the right temperament for golf. Never had those clubs in his game bag. If things don't go the way he wants, my son gets angry and gives up."

"I don't get angry, Dad."

"Yes you do."

Cloudy slapped the table and melodramatically roared, "I said, 'No!' "

They laughed.

"You're a wet fart," Clear said, bemused. "Nitwit."

Senior smacked a waiter's arm and bluntly said, "Two ice teas."

"I could go for a beer," said Junior.

"Two ice teas," Senior stressed with a decisive finality. "In paper cups for outside." Senior stood and announced to the nearby tables. "See, this guy? Clear sold me his Westport house without a realtor. I put in another fireplace, expanded the kitchen and cleared the woods to see the pond out back. It's beautiful! Nicest home I ever had! I love it!"

Junior and Senior turned and walked away.

"Nelford's a dick," said Cloudy, sipping beer. "My band played his daughter's wedding. It was 96 degrees in the shade. Three hours in the sun. He didn't even tip us. We're packing up. He frickin' stands there and goes, 'Thanks.' Duh." Cloudy flapped his lips. "A total dick."

"He's real nice here."

"Yeah, that's the way these guys are, they want to convince everyone *here* they're nice guys. That's the charm of this club, nobody can make you miserable unless you take the time to get to know them. They're not real friends. Sure Nelford will meet you in a neutral corner, like lunch at a restaurant, a club function, or golf. But have any members come to your condo to see you? No. Did Nelford invite you over to his house? No. Not one of these people are like the neighbors we had when we lived in Freehold. That's why Mom never called our place in Westport a home. Mom always called it '*the house.*'"

"Your poor Mom never left Freehold," Clear said, cutting into the fish. "When it came to Westport and this club, Mom did a freeze up. She didn't mix with ladies at the luncheons. Look how popular she was in Freehold. Her women's club. She never got into it with anyone. She loved that Stonehurst house." He sipped his vodka and swished it from cheek to cheek and swallowed. "I was the one who got screwed. Having to take a bus to New York every day from South Jersey. Freehold was great for you kids. It was a perfect place to grow up."

"We needed it," said Cloudy, "for what came *after*." Clear stared at him. "Last night I had a dream about the old Stonehurst place."

"Really, in Jersey?"

"Other people were living in our Freehold home. They were nice and showed me around. I didn't have a memory of what happened in each room. All I knew was that I was happy and the rooms made me happy and I was crying. I rushed back to Connecticut and our house in Westport to tell everyone about it because I felt so happy. I found Mom in the kitchen smashing dishes on the floor."

"At least I have the club," guiltily said Clear, taking a sip of his vodka. "What does she have? Mom spends half the day in her bathrobe reading the paper, doing crossword puzzles and smoking. Before all this happened with your sister, we were having such a nice retirement. Have dinner together. Watch the news and talk. Went to movies. Ate out twice a week. Traveled to London and Paris. And Mommy had such a good time on those trips. We were planning a cruise on the Danube. And that's all gone these past six years. She's a wreck, hunched over from a bad back and belching from bad gas. Won't see a doctor. I'm no help, drinking here. But I shouldn't have to change my way of life." He looked at his glass. "I might have a fourth. I'm half in the bag, feeling good." Clear held up his glass. "This is my cruise on the Danube." He drained his vodka. His face hardened and he sharply added, "So is your friend Pudge still working at Stew Leonard's?"

"You *know* he is, been there for over twenty years," said Cloudy, throwing a flat stare.

"I don't care much for Pudge," churlishly said Clear, "not my kind of guy. He was in your fraternity but *he* graduated. Done well for himself.

A condo in Milford, a nice car. You were both hired at the same time. If you minded your p's and q's, you'd still be at Stews. With benefits and a good salary, a 401k. Pudge stayed in your band and *kept* his job."

"Dad, I got fired years ago."

"Singing in gin mills every night and late for work at Stew's 53 times."

"I wasn't late, they had a 15-minute grace period."

"The point is: you don't come in late for work at *all*," tartly replied Clear. "It's like my Mom, your Nana when she was alive used to say, 'You get nothing from nothing.'" He paused. "You stopped listening."

"Nana," said Cloudy, who couldn't stand his grandmother. "Miss Perfect. Nothing I ever did was good enough for her. She thought Wendy was a princess. She should see her now and—"

"I gave you my old Tercel," grumbled Clear, continuing to list his charges. "You get a DUI, lapse on the insurance. For three years, my old car is still sitting in you apartment's driveway under a tarp. Bet your next-door neighbors love seeing that car every day." Willie put down a vodka and beer. "Another see-through?" gleefully said Clear, rubbing his hands. "Thanks, Willie."

The Gaffer returned from his smoke break.

"There are so few of us left, Gaffer," Clear said, instantly cheering up. He smiled and raised his vodka. "I'm having a Henry VIII meal, drinking. I should have gout, the King's Disease. I'm a lone Democrat living a Republican lifestyle."

Uh-oh, thought Cloudy, another vodka side effect: his Dad baiting people into political arguments, so he could win them.

"Did you see how your great, faith-based President's war took the lives of four young marines today?" said Clear.

"Wrong!" roared The Gaffer. "Those soldiers volunteered. So did the reserves. Better to have the terrorism there than here."

"What do you call 9/11?"

"If an Iraqi shoots an American they should destroy the whole city."

"What about the innocent people?"

"I don't care!"

"Spoken like a true Christian," Clear said gleefully.

The Gaffer leaned over and harshly whispered to Cloudy, "Listen to your father, this is why he's finding less and less people to play golf with." He walked away. "I'm going to play cards."

Clear scooped up a mound of assorted vegetables and grumbled, "The Gaffer never picked up a sport section he didn't like."

"Dad, why did you start on him?" said Cloudy. "These guys don't come here to talk politics. They just want to drink, golf and make jokes about beer farts."

"I'm tired of giving equal time to unequal people," said Clear. "Most of these guys made their money telling people what to do, they can't even agree on how to build a snack shack at the turn—hey!" A man lurched between the tables and Clear was shoved forward. He said,"Hey, how about an excuse me?"

"Excuse *you*," Eggplant replied and drunkenly bumped again into Clear's chair. He held The Gull cup, nudged Arax and pointed from the vodka glass back to the father and from the foamy beer mug to the son and said, "There they are: Clear... and Cloudy."

"We'll be drinking from The Gull Cup next year," Cloudy said.

"Ya think?" scoffed Eggplant. "Like I'm going to lose to a 33-handicapper and a scratch-eating-hothead son who breaks clubs."

"We could. *I* could."

"Yeah and there are blind guys who break 80."

"Again, talking about blind guys. What's that mean?"

"You're mad because we beat your sorry ass," replied Eggplant. "If you want to play with the big dogs you have to leave the porch."

"Woof," said Arax, fist tapping his partner.

Eggplant drunkenly tottered away and said to his partner, "Hear about the girl who went fishing with six guys? Came back with a red snapper." He followed his punchline with his brayed haaaaaaaaaaaaaa!

"That guy goes out of his way to rattle my cage," said Clear, rankled. "It's succeeding." He drained his vodka. "From the get-go, Mom and I should have put the kibosh on Wendy's marriage at Mario's." Here we go, bemoaned Cloudy, taking a bitter tour down memory lane powered by the vodka express. He could recite his Dad's next story with all its dramatic pauses. Clear ruefully continued, "Mom and I were at Mario's for dinner waiting on Eggplant. She was in the rest room. Eggplant was late as usual. Came in drunk as usual. He sat at the table and said to me, 'I want to marry your fucking daughter.' Mom came back and joined us. The waitress returned to take our drink order. Eggplant said, 'Boy, she has great tits.' I stood up and said, 'Pat, let's leave.' Mom stayed seated. She wanted the marriage. Grandchildren. This was her only shot. Wendy was in her thirties. You were singing in bars, going nowhere. I should have got stiff-necked, brought Eggplant up short, sent a message by insisting Mom leave with me that instant. But I sat back down to my everlasting regret."

"Yeah, can you pass me the salt?" asked Cloudy, cutting his steak.

"It's funny how you run into small things and how they put the bigger picture together," said Clear, reflectively nodding. "I played golf with a guy who knew Eggplant as a kid. He told me Eggplant's mother was the one who raised him and let him do whatever her son wanted. He ran wild. The guy told me the Dad was never home and was a rotten prick. Unrelenting on his son. Pounding and pounding. Once when I golfed with Eggplant, we talked about Dads. I said how I loved my Dad. Eggplant said, 'I hate my father.' Just like that. It shows what a parent can do to a kid."

"Tell me about it," said Cloudy, smiling.

"You're a wet fart," replied Clear, who flicked his keys on the table. "Son, you're driving the old man home today." That's me, thought Cloudy, start out as son, then become a vodka chauffeur. This was how their tournaments ended. Cloudy wanting to kick back at the club, drink and hang by the pool. His father ruining it by rapidly pounding several vodkas and insisting on leaving early. "Go to your apartment first and drop you off. I can manage to drive to the condo. And no stops on the way at any bars, we're going straight back."

Cloudy said, "I'll take you to the condo. Pudge can come over and get me. Our band has a gig tonight at the Sand Bar. Mom told me she did my laundry. I have to pick it up."

"Mommy is doing her *sonny's* laundry, how nice," Clear said, teasing, then added, "Have you cleaned your apartment? What a dump. I don't even want to know what the bathroom looks like now. If your Nana was still alive she'd have a heart attack if she saw how you lived. And that car I gave you, still under a dirty tarp in the drivew—"

"Stop," sharply said Cloudy. "Haven't we already picked that scab?" He looked out the window at the 18th hole's green and to the golf course. Somewhere his swing was buried in those rolling fairways, hazards and greens. He'd have to dig in the dirt with his clubs to find it. Why not try? Devote himself to it and see how good he could get at this stupid game. Maybe beating Eggplant and winning The Gull might change things between him and his Dad. Cloudy doubted it, but so far, he lived a life of shallow goals in a world deep with dreams. So why not throw one more on the pile? Cloudy looked at his Dad and said, "You know I think I could get better at this game."

"There are a couple priorities in your life you might address first, like a future," said Clear. "And if I'm still around when that day happens, the darkness will vanish and I will see a light followed by a sucking sound because you finally pulled your head out of your ass."

"Is that any way to talk to the fruit of your loins?" inquired Cloudy.

"The fruit of my loins," said Clear, smiling. "You are a wet fart."

Willie came over and asked, "Would you gentlemen like anything else from the bar?"

"The usual."

CLOUDY DROVE THE CAR into the gated-condo complex. He finished the last of his beer from a paper cup. At least he salvaged the event by ending it with a slight buzz, he thought. His Dad was passed out in the passenger seat. Cloudy's buzz vanished at thew sight of his sister's damaged Camry angled in two parking spaces. The driver side door was crumpled with a white streak of paint across it. She's got into another accident, he thought. The condo door was wide open.

"Dad!" Cloudy said, pulling into a spot. "Something's really wrong."

"What, what?" Clear asked, groggily. "Oh no, what now?"

They got out and circled the Camry. The driver's window was down. An empty 8-ounce bottle of liquid hairspray was in the back seat.

"Help!" Patsy Map cried from inside the condo. "Get her off me!"

Cloudy bolted in. His sister straddled their mother, who was lying on her stomach, her face pressed into the rug of the living room.

"You dumb Polish cunt," howled Wendy, pounding her fists on the 70-year-old woman's back. "You never do anything. You're a drunk, a fucking drunk!"

Cloudy grabbed his thin sister and heaved her across the room. She slammed into an end table. A lamp and a Hummel figurine fell to the floor. Wendy was spread eagle on the rug. Her skirt was thrown above her hips—she wasn't wearing panties. She bounced up, eyes possessed and flung a Hummel at her brother. He ducked. It hit and cracked a framed sketch depicting the Declaration of Independence signing.

Clear protectively held his wife. He turned to Cloudy, helpless.

Wendy shot a withering glare at her brother, charged Cloudy and slurred, "You're all a bunch of drunks!" Cloudy deflected her clawing slaps and threw her down. "You never did anything with your life!"

"Police," said an authoritative male voice at the open front door.

Two young, hardened Bridgeport cops entered. A buff guy with a shaved head and a stocky woman, her hair clamped in a tight bun.

"I'm not going," said Wendy springing up."I hate you fucking people!"

"That's not my sister," Cloudy sadly said to the cops.

Both officers were baffled. The condo didn't profile. This wasn't a section-8 housing unit with low-rent tenants and people doing crack in stairwells. The home was furnished and tastefully decorated in a colonial motif—Revolutionary War paintings, framed profiles of Jefferson, Washington and Lincoln. Shelves lined with history books. A spotless kitchen. And the family? A son in a Battleground Country Club golf shirt. Two shaken, huddling and cowering parents on their knees, ashamed because their living room had become a crime scene.

"Miss, we have some questions," said the male cop.

"Fuck you, leave me alone, you pig!" she said, charging the officers.

The male cop deftly brought Wendy face down to the carpet.

"It's my anniversary," Wendy blubbered, her rapidly heaving breaths separated by deep wet-gulping sobs. She was greedily choking down her favorite form of substance abuse: self-pity. "No one else will have me. I still love him. I tried to make it work. Shoot for the moon. End up in a bowl of green cheese. That prick will pay for what he did to me. You don't know what it's like. "I hate my life."

The female cop's face slightly twitched in recognition, as if she also once uttered those unanswered despairing cries.

"Oy," Wendy said.

"My little girl," sighed Clear. "She was born with a broken wing. She got married and her husband broke the other one."

"Come along," the male cop said, cuffing Wendy.

"I'm fine," softly pleaded Wendy. "Leave me alone. Just please. I'll behave, okay. I'll be good. I'll be good."

"You're going, and you're going to be good," said the male cop. "You left the scene of a crash involving a woman with a two-year-old."

"My God," said Patsy Map sitting on the rug. She shivered and tugged the belt of her blue terry-cloth bathrobe. "Was the baby hurt?"

"No."

"Thank God."

Clear implored, "Wendy, we love you and you do this to us every time. Why do you do this to us? Why? We've done nothing but try to help you. And this is what you do to us."

"Sir, you're not helping," said the female cop, who bent down and asked Wendy. "Have you been drinking?"

"No, let me sleep it off," she said, her eyes distant.

"Sleep what off? You said you weren't drinking so how—"

"My sister drank liquid hair spray," said Cloudy to the cops.

"Liquid hair spray?" said the male cop, appalled.

"Sometimes, it's vanilla extract, Cooking Sherry, cough syrup, or mouthwash," said Cloudy. "She learned all the tricks of the trade from her AA buddies. At least with mouthwash, after she pukes her breath is still fresh."

"Lavender, son," said Clear. "But a little lavender on it."

"I'm going to get sick," said Wendy. "I want to go to my room."

"You can't stay here," the male cop said. "You're in custody."

"Fuck you," she spat and kicked. "You piece of shit."

The male cop dragged Wendy by her ankles to the door. Her dress started working its way up to her hips. She went limp.

"I'll go, okay? I'll go," she moaned. The cop released her. Wendy stood and said, "Dad, don't tell anyone at the club about this."

After she left, the female cop sympathetically studied the shattered family and said, "I'm only writing her up for leaving the scene."

"I know this is terrible for a mother to say," croaked out Cloudy's worn-out Mom, looking down at the broken little-boy-and-girl Hummel figurine in her quivering hands. "But I want that *thing* dead."

The rectangular clock/radio alarm on the floor clicked and played "Spanish Flea" by Herb Alpert and the Tijuana Brass.

The clock's digital numbers changed to 2:23.

Cloudy's Mom remotely gazed into the faint distance to where the Maps veered off course.

She wistfully sighed, "I wish we never left Freehold."

Hacking With The Chops

CLOUDY STOOD IN ONE OF THE MANY STALLS separated by waist-high metal-grill dividers on the driving range at the Ironwoods Municipal Golf Course. He tentatively sniffed the challenging summer air and used his 2-iron to rake one of the many red-striped balls from the plastic tray onto a green spongy tee mat.

"Feet shoulder-width apart," softly said Cloudy, guiding himself with golf tips he gleaned from magazines and videos. "Knees slightly flexed. Never strangle the club—gently grip it like a live bird is in your hands. Swing with a waltz tempo. Uncoil like you're standing in an imaginary barrel without your hips touching the sides. Tempo: 1-2-3 waltz. Never pull the club—let it lag behind. Continue at impact. Only hit with 75 percent of your strength. Follow through to your natural height. Finish in a reverse-K. Visualize a perfect shot."

Cloudy swung. It was a terrible. The shot banged against his stall's metal divider. Reverberating clangs embarrassingly echoed throughout the range as the ball went back and forth between Cloudy's legs and ricocheted off the dividers.

"I know what I did," he said, evaluating his finishing position. He slowly retracted his swing plane to the specific point in its radius where it strayed from perfection, then diagnosed the problem. "Didn't end in a Reverse-K. I should..."

His voice sullenly trailed off. Cloudy tugged at his ponytail like it was an emergency brake. He sighed and tilted back the brim of his blue New York Yankee cap. His arms went slack. His club felt heavier than a sledgehammer. He'd been practicing and playing for a year but wasn't even close to finding a swing. If he didn't slice, he hooked. And, if he didn't hook, he sliced. He hadn't improved. He had gotten worse! Every swing today felt like a pang. He brooded over the remaining range balls as if they were a pile of stones.

"Hey, Chop, you happy hitting the ball like that?" asked Buttons, the Ironwoods pro. Buttons was in his early fifties. He had thatched hair that resembled a dried patch of rough. His blue eyes looked like they were comfortably set within a benign piece of ice. Sun-engraved wrinkles carved a sling for faint smile. He gave off the bemused but submissive expression of a man who had numerous disappointments and was resigned to settle for par.

"Do I look frickin' happy hitting a ball like that?" Cloudy said, completely spun. "I suck! Why am I trying to swing with a waltz tempo? I never waltzed. I hate stringed orchestras! I rock. Golf has turned me into a freak show act. Watch the amazing, Reverse-K Man rotate his hips inside a barrel and strangle birds with his loose overlapping grip!"

"Is that right?" dryly queried Buttons. "You're playing *against* yourself. That's your mistake. This game is hard enough. Golf is like life."

"Well, if I wanted golf to be like life, I wouldn't play it."

"Golf is like life. You have to confront your bad habits to get out of your own way before the quality of your life can get better and improve. Same holds true in golf, you have to get out of your way to find the true bottom of your natural swing arc. That's how blind guys break 80."

"How do blind guys break 80?"

"There are two reasons," chirped Buttons. "First: they get out of their way to find the bottom of their natural swing arc. And the second: no one really tells them where their shot actually went."

"Bada-bing," said Cloudy. "I'll be here all week, try the veal." He paused. "I've been working on muscle memory."

"Is that right?" said Buttons. "Muscle memory, huh? There's only one activity where I have muscle memory—and, it's not golf."

Cloudy laughed.

Buttons looked disparagingly at Cloudy's clothes."I've seen you on the range all year, beating balls—even in the winter when we had heated stalls. You've logged a ton of rounds here. But look at you, Chop. No one would ever know you cared about the game. People judge you by your appearance. So dress like a golfer! Take pride in how you look. Don't show up in a stained T-shirt and jeans with a beer like some half-drunk roofer when our afternoon rates drop. So, besides your personality, what's your handicap, Chop?"

"Don't have one—a handicap. I just play. With personality, of course."

"Get a GHIN number."

"A Chin-number? What's that? The salted prawn special with fried rice and egg rolls at the Great Wall Chinese Palace?"

"G-H-I-N: Golf Handicap Index Number. Join the men's club here. You get a USGA card with a GHIN number. Then after you play your rounds, start recording your scores."

"Why can't I hit the ball and have a good time?"

"A handicap defines who you are in golf. It's what your game really is. You play against your handicap, not the course," said Buttons. "But the core is this: golf is a one-ball game. When you chunk a shot you don't drop another ball and hit again. There are no mulligans. No fluffing up lies. No lift, clean and placing the ball. Anyone can play their best shots. The point is you have to play *all* your shots. You can't cut corners. You not only obey but *respect* the rules. Play any other way, you're only hitting the ball for fun. And there's nothing wrong with that. But you're not golfing."

A Camero squealed into the parking lot. The stereo loudly played Metallica's 'Enter Sandman.'

"Yo, Dawg!" said Pudge, stepping out of the car. Pudge wore a sleeveless shirt, cut-off bluejean shorts and a Mets hat with the brim backwards. Dragon tattoos were on his calves.

"The rest of the guys in the band showing?" Cloudy asked.

"Turdle and Schultzie are coming," said Pudge, opening his trunk and putting a Budweiser 18-pack down on the asphalt. He dropped a bag of ice near it and stuffed the cans and cubes into the pockets of his golf bag. He smiled and added, "Stocking up on swing oil."

"You guys are in a band?" Buttons asked.

"A classic-rock cover band," replied Cloudy. "Mid-Life Vices."

"What 'Vice' are you?"

"The Vice with the voice."

"Is that right?" observed Buttons, who chipped a disparaging glance at Pudge. Buttons walked away he added to Cloudy, "If you're with that guy, you're not golfing, you're a Chop with a beer."

"You called me a Chop again," said Cloudy. "What's a Chop?"

"Golfer on the first tee is a Chop," said Buttons, pointing.

The Chop addressing his tee shot was in his waist-expanding forties, disproportionately attired in bright, tight-fitting clothes. When the guy started his backswing, he snatched the club over his head like he was going to split a log, then chopped down and plowed the clubface deep into the ground. The ball bounced a few feet and a green scalp of turf flew three yards past it like a badly tossed salad. The golfer retraced his swing plane and said, "I know what I did."

"Oh no, that *is* me," Cloudy lamented. "I am a Chop!"

"Believe it or not, that guy has taken six lessons with me."

"You're not instilling me with much confidence, Buttons."

"I'm not supposed to give you confidence."

"Hey, I meant confidence in *your* abilities as a teaching pro."

"Don't look at me," said Buttons. "I give a Chop a lesson. They complain I changed their swing. Then they go back to his old habits and do the same thing over again and expect a different result. They call it golf. I call it insanity. You can't talk to them. The dumbs ones believe they know everything. The smart ones think they can figure the game out by themselves. Chops should take lessons in *how* to take a lesson. A lot of people remain Chops their whole lives."

CLOUDY STOOD ON THE FIRST TEE with his bandmates, Turdle and Schultzie, who were in their late-thirties. Turdle played bass. Schultzie was a drummer. The two had shaved heads. They wore baseball caps backwards and were attired in sleeveless shirts and low, baggy, Hip Hop shorts with boxer underwear that rose higher than the waistline of their pants. They had sneakers instead of spikes. Pudge stood by his golf bag. The bag's pockets dripped water from melting ice and formed a puddle around his sandals.

Turdle stepped up to the tee, put his 24-ounce beer can down and set himself over the ball. He leaned over. His weight was completely on his heels. He started his downswing and...

BLEEEEEEEAAAAAH! blasted an air horn.

Turdle jerked backwards, swung and hit a low liner that banged off the ball washer on the tee box. His shot rolled between a few startled people standing on the nearby putting green.

"That was funny as shit, Turd," said Pudge, holding the air horn, which was the size of a small, aerosol canister. "I'm such a pissah!"

The band laughed.

"Gentlemen we have two groups waiting," sternly said Buttons, leaning on a railing in front of the pro-shop/19th hole, which was a trailer with white aluminum siding surrounded by a wooden deck and positioned between the first tee and 10th hole.

"Back off, you/re not my boss," said Pudge, who was instinctively hostile to any authority—especially if he was drinking.

"Just hit the frickin' ball," said Cloudy, cracking his second beer.

"No, dawg," Pudge indignantly said to Cloudy. "I'm here to kick back and chill, not to get hosed with buzz kill and power-trip bullshit. I get enough of that at work."

After Turdle hit again, Pudge took the tee. His loose body stiffened over the ball. He didn't turn his hips. He used his arms and swung.

"Fire in the hole!" shouted Turdle.

"Booyah!" cheered Schultzie, admiring his drive.

Pudge belched the words, "Not too shabby."

As Cloudy chugged his cold beer, he felt Buttons' reproachful stare. But it was an embarrassment he couldn't own up to. He quickly teed up and drove his shot into the pond.

"Hit another one," said Pudge. "Fuck him. We paid to play."

"No, let's go," replied Cloudy, glancing back to Buttons. "It's a lateral hazard there. I'll drop a ball and play my shot."

"What are you, turning pro or something?" huffed Pudge who picked up his bag, hawked up mucous and shot an arcing wad of snot. He defiantly glared at Buttons and said, "Peace out, Dawg. I'm gone."

THROUGHOUT THE ROUND, Cloudy's hapless cover band of brothers slammed down brews and expelled more marijuana smoke than a touring reggae group. Every third shot they hit was either a hook into a hazard, worm-burner, a 20-yard pop-up or an out-of-bounds slice landing in the mobile home park that bordered the course. They gave themselves mulligans, improved their lies and didn't take penalty strokes for hitting O.B. or into lateral hazards. By the 15th hole, Cloudy's buddies were toasted beyond recognition. Turdle and Schultzie absently left half-filled beer cans where they took their last swing or forgot wedges by bunkers. Several times they searched too long for a ball, then when they found it, felt they had the wrong club, wandered back to their bag and couldn't remember where their ball was. Pudge swore, chucked clubs and spit sunflower seed shells on greens. Cloudy stopped drinking an the 8th. He cleaned up after them—replacing divots, raking sand traps and repairing ball marks on the green. His pals were defiling the course. It disturbed him.

"Yee-haa!" said Schultzie, straddling a pull cart as he ran down the fairway, smacking his butt like he was riding a bucking bronco.

"I hit my shot in the water," drunkenly blurted Turdle, reaching for the ball retriever in his bag. "Time to take out my Jewish 1-iron."

"Yo, Turd," Pudge said, "twenty bucks if you jump into the pond."

Without hesitation, Turdle ran and shouted, "Cannonball!"

"Fire in the hole!"

"Booyah!"

Turdle kablooshed in the lily pads. He staggered out of the pond. Mud streaked across his shirt. His wet socks squished in his sneakers.

"Pony up the bucks," said Turdle, patting his drenched pockets.

"We didn't shake on it, Dawg," said Pudge.

Turdle's face blanched and eyes bulged as he said, "Shit, my cell phone!" They laughed. "It's not funny, man," Turdle drunkenly blurted, jabbing his finger on the dead phone's screen.

"Hawk action, center stage," said Schultzie, pointing in the tall grass by a maintenance cart left at a Porta Potty between the fairways.

A hawk was trying to fly off with a mourning dove in its talons. The dove resisted, clinging to the grass. Cloudy shooed the hawk away. The battered dove fluttered its wings but went nowhere. The grounded bird was injured, confused and terrified. The hawk casually perched above the scene on a branch, confidently waiting atop his secure and predatory roost for his inevitable due.

"She can't fly, poor thing," Cloudy sadly said, looking at the dazed dove. He pointed at the hawk. "He broke her wing."

"Would you rather have an eagle or a birdie, dawg?" Pudge said, then smirked. "Hawks got to eat. It's nature being nature."

"I'm part of nature too," said Cloudy, taking a plastic pail from the maintenance cart. "I decided to get involved." He draped a golf towel over the quivering bird and gently put it in the bucket. He walked away pulling the golf cart and holding the bucket in his free hand.

"Where you going?" asked Pudge. "We're not done."

"There's a shelter a couple blocks away."

"It's nice, what Cloudy's doing," said Turdle, who furrowed his brow and added, "I think I left my hash pipe on the bench at the last tee."

Pudge staggered to the Porta Potty and said, "I have to take a Deuce."

"Booyah," said Schultzie.

"Fire *in* your hole," said Turdle.

THE ANIMAL SHELTER was on a dead-end road. It was depressing. The square, puke-yellow, cinder-block building had a rusty cyclone fence around it and a cracked asphalt parking lot with tufts of weeds and patches of dirt. Cloudy opened a thick unpainted metal door. He heard growls, yips, squawks, meows, barks and yelps. He smelled wet fur, kitty litter, poop and urine. The dingy lobby had cheap wood paneling and a grimy linoleum floor missing a few tiles. The place was dimly illuminated by intermittently flickering ceiling panel lights. One wall had a peeling cork bulletin board plastered with pictures of missing animals as well as flyers for free spay-and-neuter clinics.

A dreary, pear-faced lesser light of a woman sat behind an L-shaped counter. She didn't look up. She was texting on a cell phone. She was overweight, bored, had oily hair parted in the middle, a purple swirling blotch of a tattoo on each arm and a silver-hooked piercing in her upper lip. Her butt looked like it melted over the chair, hardened like wax and was the only thing that kept her upright. If her picture was posted beside the lost dogs and cats, Cloudy figured he'd be hard pressed to tell the difference between her and the missing.

"Yeah?" she indifferently said and kept texting.

"I have a bird I found on the golf course," he said, putting down his golf bag and tilting up the bucket. "I think her wing is broken."

"What do you expect me to do about it?"

"This is a shelter. Aren't you supposed to take care of hurt animals?"

"With birds there's really nothing we can do."

"If she heals, she might fly again."

"They're dirty, lice-ridden and have a lot of diseases," she said, then coughed and added, "They can infect the other animals."

"Obviously they make an exceptions, you're here," said Cloudy, who decided she was an asshole zone and there was no reason to be polite."So what's up with your lip piercing? Swallow the bait but kept the hook?" He put the bucket on the counter. "She's yours."

"Don't dump her on me. Why don't you heal her?"

"I'm not the one who's supposed to—you're the one that's a shelter. I didn't break her wing."

When the sludge of a woman grudgingly rose, her butt made a sucking sound as it released its prehensile grip on the chair. She sniffed and disapprovingly said, "Have you been drinking?"

"You talking to the bird or me?"

"Want the bucket back?" she said, reluctantly taking it.

"Yes."

She dragged her feet through the swinging doors to the kennel.

He picked up his golf bag and left.

CLOUDY WALKED FROM THE SHELTER to Ironwoods. He entered the pro-shop/19th hole. It was divided in two sections. The Pro Shop consisted of a meager selection of golf caps and shirts, knock-off clubs on racks along the walls, used drivers in a barrel and a fingerprint-smeared glass counter with golf balls, tees and gloves. The 19th hole began halfway down the counter at the draft beer taps and hot dog broiler spike rotisserie. There was also a candy display shelf, a rack of peanuts and potato chips and a small fridge with sodas, bottled water, microwave burritos and energy drinks. The lounge area was occupied by golfers sitting around three folding tables, who drank beer, shared open bags of junk food and watched golf on a wall-anchored corner TV. Below the set was the clubhouse computer where players entered GHIN numbers and posted their scores.

Buttons was at the counter, explaining the cash-register codes to a baffled, open-mouthed teenage employee.

"Do you have time to schedule a lesson?" Cloudy asked. "Now?"

"Is that right?" said Buttons, giving him a token for the driving-range ball machine. "Loosen up by hitting a few from a bucket and I'll see you over at the range, Chop."

ON THE DRIVING RANGE, Buttons twisted, tugged and stretched Cloudy's body into the contorted golf position professional instructors define as a "relaxed, natural stance."

"Are you torturing me?" Cloudy asked, his usual stance grappling against a coiled backswing and a chin over a rotated left shoulder. His lower back muscles tightened. "I'm not made of rubber."

"You don't have a swing, Chop," replied Buttons. "You have a bad habit. Bad habits are comfortable. That's why the correct way to do things hurts. What you have right there is a fully loaded backswing. Now, let it go!"

Cloudy uncoiled. The club seemed to be going too fast and flying away. He followed through and watched the ball go.

"Smoked it. 300 yards. Lights out," said Buttons. "How did it feel?"

"Um, I didn't feel it."

"It's because you got out of your way."

"The swing did feel a little gay."

"Hitting a shot like that is enough to keep you coming back. Isn't it?"

"That's bullshit," crisply snapped Cloudy. "Hitting one good shot isn't enough to keep me coming back. I'm not a battered woman like my sister, taking abuse to hear one 'I love you.' That's not me."

"You don't want to be battered? Who are you kidding? All golfers are battered!" said Buttons, slapping his leg and laughing. "You're a Chop with issues, I'll give you that. But don't confuse issues with depth."

"I'm not here for one good shot," Cloudy continued. "Out on the course every time I swing I'm going for I-love-yous the whole goddamn round. That's what I'm shooting for."

"Chop, if you're looking for love out there," said Buttons, who gestured to the course and ominously added, "you might not like what you find out about yourself."

AFTER THE LESSON WAS OVER, Cloudy hit through the remaining balls on the range. He went to the bus stop, sat on the bench, took a small brush from his bag and removed the dirt caked in the grooves of his irons. If his Nana were still alive, Cloudy thought, she'd approve. She often stated her most distinctive traits, "I can always see two things: money and dirt." Basically, she was a perfectly decent person who was a royal pain in the ass. She valued family above all else. "The only thing a stranger's hands are good for is taking a hot coal out of your fire." Her broth of values was drawn from a stern, unforgiving immigrant stock. In the early 1900s, she left a farm in Poland and came to America in steerage where she got her first taste of life's fruit. "Someone offered me a lemon, I was six. I had never seen one before. I thought it was going to be sweet. I bit into it. I'll never forget how sour it tasted." And odd. She and Pop-Pop ran a Bakery and had a small farm. "I looked outside in the yard. This rooster was bothering the hens. I went outside and chopped his head off. Fixed his wagon." She laughed. When Pop-Pops died face down in his dinner at age 56, she was only 50. But Nana never expressed an interest in a man for her next 43 years (Once he overheard Nana on the phone with her say, "Who wants to see Mr. Ugly again?"). Cloudy's Dad was her only child. Nana's social life revolved around going on vacations with her numerous sisters, working in the Lamp Department at Bambergers in Eatontown and picking up extra cash catering. She made a big show of going to church every Sunday and spent holidays with the Maps (Every birthday or Christmas, she gave Cloudy clothes he'd never wear, or socks and underwear. She explained the gifts were meant to help save his parents clothing money.). And she actually had a lot of friends and maintained those friendships, but if somehow a friend got her angry, she wouldn't talk to her for years. When Nana got up in age and was no longer able to live on her own, his Dad made a huge blunder. He didn't consult his wife or anyone else and moved Nana into their Westport house. His wife never forgave him for it. Wendy and her girlfriend had an apartment so Cloudy's sister never had to deal with it. But Cloudy was in his mid-twenties and still living at home, working a day job, going out every night and playing in a band. Nana took an exception to his carefree existence and embarked on personal crusade to reform him, which was easy for her, because she never respected anyone's privacy. After Cloudy's parents left for work at seven in the morning, Nana came upstairs, poked her cane to pushed open his bedroom door and woke him up. Cloudy was usually hungover after a late-night gig. She chastised him, "Wasting your life in bars. You're too old to be living at home. You should have a house and a wife. Just look at this filthy, disgusting mess of a room." 'Filthy' and 'disgusting' were her two favorite words besides 'money' and 'dirt.' And throughout the day, she'd make an issue out of everything he did. She defended her harsh criticism of her grandson by saying, "It's the truth." Once at noon, he barbecued a steak. As he ate it and watched The Three Stooges on TV, she lectured, "That's not lunch food, that's *dinner* food." Nana didn't understand anyone who wasn't devoting their spare time to work and earn money or improve the value of the house. If Cloudy listened to music, watched TV or read a book, she'd lecture him with her motto: "You get nothing from nothing." And she was right. When she died, Cloudy felt nothing except anger. After all, he reasoned, Nana lived into her nineties, always did what she wanted to do, never approved of him and often said it to his face. So after playing golf, why had her deeply interred cane of 'nothing' somehow found another way to poke open the door of Cloudy's scattered and fragmented and jagged-edged recollections of her?

CLOUDY WAS THE ONLY WHITE GUY ON THE BUS—and definitely the only one with golf clubs. There were Puerto Ricans, Mexicans and blacks. He sat by a large black woman who was dressed in a pink pants suit adorned with a huge white flower. Cloudy fidgeted in his seat, wincing from a sharp, lower intestinal pinch that signaled the incoming coordinates of a fart powered by chili dogs armed with a warhead of onions and sauerkraut he ate at the Ironwoods 19th Hole. He slightly raised his right butt cheek to ease out the pressurized and hot SBD (silent-but-deadly) gas.

A few seconds passed.

The woman in the pants suit sharply sniffed the unpleasant odor, twisted her face and said, "What's that smell?"

"Maybe it's the clutch or the exhaust," Cloudy unconvincingly said. "Or the diesel engine exhaust?"

"I've been riding this bus for 17 years and I ain't never smelled nothing like that!" she firmly stated. She sharply fixed her prosecutorial glare at him and accusingly added, "You know, I think it was *you*."

Cloudy ignored the her. Besides, he never minded the smell of his own farts. He looked out the window. How many times had he driven on The Post Road from Norwalk to B-port? Over the years, industrial plants like Exide Battery, Handy and Harman, MLK Labs and Bullards were replaced with malls, cineplexes, fast-food joints, factory outlets, superstores. The local stores faded away—The Paint Bucket, Barry's Shoes, Schafer's Sporting Goods, Izzo's Hardware, Bill's Smoke Shop, used book and record stores. All gone. In came the chains: Blockbuster, Starbucks, Home Depot, Barnes & Noble and Pottery Barn. Many of the stores that survived were just weird. In Westport people shopped at places like The Age of Reason, Nine West and Anthropologie. What did places with names like that sell? With increased property values came higher commercial rents and those hikes squeezed out family restaurants like Porky Manero's, The Clam Box, Circus Big Top, along with 99-cent breakfast nooks, luncheonette hangs and cool diners. They were replaced by 4-star eateries with foo-foo names like The Aqua, Chez Pierre, and Jasmine. The next step was killing live music. For years, Cloudy's band had tons of one-nighters at places like the Surfside, The Fore and Aft, Player's Tavern, but those local joints along with many bars became frame shops, galleries, realtor offices, nail parlors, investment firms or antique stores. The winners who profit from transitions defined it was "progress," concluded Cloudy, and the losers were forced to accept it as "change." He didn't belong to either view. Cloudy never liked living in Fairfield County in the "before" or the "after,' but now the musical life he pursued to escape his unhappiness was slowly disappearing. He turned away from the Post Road and spotted the bus number above the windshield: 223. He smiled, closed his eyes and tuned-in the soothing 223-soundtrack of his past: the three-valved trumpet call of Herb Alpert & The Tijuana Brass playing 'Whipped Cream' returned Cloudy to the soft spot where he first caught the beginning half-formed notes of the person he was intended to be …

IT WAS A CLASSIC FREEHOLD PARTY at 223 Stonehurst Way in the Map home. The impossibly happy, upbeat and downright sexy melodies of Herb Alpert and the Tijuana Brass stretched and bounced out from the living room's Admiral Stereophonic Super-20 phonograph speakers housed in a wood cabinet. Cloudy and Wendy were in pyjamas and sat on the steps that led upstairs to their bedrooms. They pressed their heads against the thin, twisted, white wooden balusters, fascinated by the smoke-filled ice-cube-clinking adult world of Saturday night. Their Mom banned John and Wendy from ever eating or drinking in the living room. But not adults! Tonight every table was loaded with food and snacks in trays, chaffing dishes, saucepans, fondue pots, bowls and Tupperware. There were Charles Chips, dry-roasted Planter's peanuts, Tom's Bugles, rumaki, Vienna sausages, Dipsy Doodles, Swedish meatballs, tuna-noodle casseroles, Bachman beer pretzels, cold cuts, deviled eggs, Kraft Old English cheese spreads, stuffed cherry tomatoes and mushrooms, pupu platters and glass dishes with containers of clam or spinach dip in the center encircled by Ritz crackers. And the adults who were so serious all week were laughing and being weird and silly! Lots of laughs!

Mr. Gallagher wore a turban and blew a three-foot long plastic horn along with Herb Alpert. Mr. Dubonowki was dressed as a pregnant woman, splayed on the couch and going through labor. Mr. Ruhl wore a stethoscope and a toga, stood between Mr. Dubonowki's spread legs and acted like he was delivering a baby.

"It's a boy!" declared Mr. Ruhl, pulling out a basketball from beneath the folds of Mr. Dubonowki's dress.

"I wanted a girl," sighed Mr. Dubonowki, shamefully turning away.

Mr. Gallagher went outside, stood on the front steps and celebrated the birth announcement by blowing his plastic horn. There were cheers and laughs from the wives who had bouffant-styled hair and were all dressed in Hawaiian muumuus.

Young John and Wendy couldn't wait to grow up. These people were having fun! They happily watched their parents bounce a two-step polka to the thumping beat of 'Butterball' through the dancers and drinkers, who were knocking back Whiskey Sours, Old Fashions, Vodka Martinis, Brandy Alexanders, Grasshoppers or a Tom Collins.

"John," said Mr. Ruhl, chewing rumaki and pointing out the living room window. "Your neighbors across the street, the Brunettis erected five-foot marble statues of Jesus, Mary and Joseph on their front lawn."

"Yeah," replied John Map as he danced. He was shirtless, wore a beaded gold necklace and a sombrero. Their Mom Had on a toga, black wig and sunglasses. "If those statues start to move every Catholic in the world will be parked on my yard."

"John, you know what the problem is when you have neighbors like that?" asked Mr. Ruhl, studying the marble trinity.

"No."

"They never *move!*"

Men laughed and clinked cocktails and Ballentine beer cans.

Then the party was interrupted.

A foot kicked the metal panel below the house's screen front door which led to the living room. The person growled, "What's going on with blowing that horn at this time of night?"

It was Mr. Fozberg. He was a retired army officer. He viewed the entire neighborhood as a military base and treated everyone as enlisted men under his command. Nobody liked him. He lived in a ranch house. He didn't try to get along with anybody. He lived to keep his lawn perfect—it looked like a green baize gaming table, but he was bordered by neighbors who didn't care about crabgrass and rarely mowed their grass, which was mainly weeds and dandelions. He thought everyone was an idiot. When his son came home from college with long hair, Mr. Fozberg slammed the door in his son's face. The kid moved to Montana. The guy was cheap too. Mr. Fozberg was a customer on Cloudy's Freehold Transcript paper route. He insisted on getting his paper early and never tipped. When blacks rioted one night in downtown Freehold and smashed storefront windows, Fozberg tried recruiting men to drive down there and "take care of things." Nobody went but him.

The music stopped. Mr. Straw who was in a Batman costume, lifted the hi-fi needle off Herb Alpert.

Mr. Fozberg pressed his square face against the screen, his flesh oozed out in a tiny pattern of miniscule squares of the mesh. He barked, "Do you people realize it's 11:30!"

In response, Mr. Gallagher pressed his long plastic horn against the screen in front of Mr. Fozberg face and blew out one long foghorn-like ba-waaaaaaaaaaaaaah.

"What are you doing, a moose call?" said Mr. Fozberg, holding his ground. He lived to argue.

John Map said, "Yes, and it looks like we flushed one out."

The partiers laughed.

Mr. Fozberg glowered, turned and indignantly marched off. Mr.

Gallagher opened the door and celebrated the Fozberg's retreat by blowing out of sustained fart from his horn. The hi-fi needle dropped back with a bounce and scratch into Herb Alpert and the Tijuana Brass' 'Third Man Theme' and everyone clapped and the floor thumped and the walls pulsed with the beat of dancing feet.

When Mr. Gallagher returned, John Map saluted with an upraised martini and warmly said, "Bill Gallagher, there are so few of us left."

"More power to you, John," replied Mr. Gallagher to the toast.

In 1964 STONEHURST BEGAN as a single-family development with 256 homes in Freehold, New Jersey, a 38 square-mile Monmouth County town promoted by realtors as the "midpoint between New York City and Philadelphia." Freehold was divided into two areas: Borough and Township. The Borough side (known as the "boro" to locals), included the downtown area, and was largely populated by blacks, people who wanted to move somewhere else and old-time locals who once worked for the Karagheusian rug factory until the plant closed to escape the unions and relocated the company's looms in North Carolina. Stonehurst residents were untouched by the "boro" and its racial and economic issues because the Township side was west of Route 9, north of 534, a dividing point where the housing development was built on 230 acres of farmlands, orchards and forests. The average age of the families moving into the newly constructed homes was in the mid-thirties range. Nearly everyone was white, made close to the same income and had two or three kids. There was even a New York commuter bus route that wound through the neighborhood and picked up Dads. As the development expanded block by block, everyone got to know the new people. The men made friends on their way to work or as they mowed their lawns, which led to arranging Saturday penny-poker nights and weekend golf dates, placing bets for each other at the Freehold "Trotters and Pacers" Raceway and meeting up with their wives at Moore's Tavern on Fridays. Very few of the Moms worked. After the kids were sent off to school, the women went to each other's kitchens, drank coffee, smoked, planned social events, gossiped and laughed. They rotated turns picking up each other's kids at ball games and school events or babysat so their girlfriends could shop. If any kid was walking home, other Moms stopped and offered them rides—but, they'd also tell your parents if you were doing something you *weren't* supposed to be doing. It was a wide open neighborhood, really. Kids cut through everybody's yards. The only people who fenced-in their property had pools, were retired seniors or came from Long Island (the Long Island people usually staked out their turf with ugly, cyclone metal fences and kept to themselves). Parties rotated every Saturday night, as well as on Memorial Day, Labor Day and The Fourth, where horseshoes clanged in sandy pits and beer spilled from paper cups on the grass in backyards. Most families joined the Stonehurst Swim Club, which had a large Y-shaped pool with three diving boards of different heights in the deep section. The club had asphalt tennis and basketball courts, shuffleboard and a picnic area where adults drank and barbecued in the evenings. And kids were all over the neighborhood! Teenagers shot hoops in driveways. Girls rode bikes and flirted with guys, practiced cheers on lawns, listened to records in each other's rooms, and made necklaces out of gum wrappers and pop-top tab from soda cans. Little kids played kickball, Wiffle Ball, freeze tag and touch football in the street and stopped their games by chanting, "Car, Car, C-A-R, stick your head in a jelly jar." Then waited for the car to pass and resumed their games. Large vacant fields throughout the neighborhood became makeshift playgrounds for older kids to shoot off plastic rockets and fly gas-powered airplane models or choose-up sides and play tackle football and pick-up baseball games. The land bordering the growing development was laid out for future streets and had a network of underground sewage pipes and manholes. It was the ideal battlefield to play army. Boys formed platoons and threw crab apples and dirt bombs at each other, crawled down the pipes and popped out of manhole covers they pretended were machine gun nests. There were woods and fields of knee-high weeds with pheasants, rabbits and woodchucks. The kids explored the creeks, caught frogs, tadpoles, catfish, carp, salamanders, box and snapping turtles— sometimes they spotted muskrats and slithering water moccasins.

For a happy, isolated place, Stonehurst had a lot of death. The Map family got the first dry, dark chalky taste: a crib death. They lost 36-day-old Matthew David Map. Cloudy took the only picture of his baby brother with a Polaroid Swinger camera. Little Matthew flashed a gummed smile, a tiny hand curled at his lower lip, his tiny soft head wrapped in a white blanket. Then there were others. Mr. Weber and Mr. Giselmen dropped dead from heart attacks in their late thirties. The 9-year-old McCauley boy was struck by a car and died after his head hit against the curb on Avon Drive. The four-year-old Perry kid snuck into the Shiebels' swimming pool and drowned. After a high-speed chase, 17-year-old Michael Dicanto got killed in a head-on collision on Shanck Road. Young Tony Lobianco became a doctor, got drafted, went to Vietnam and was killed in a Viet Cong hospital raid. And one of Cloudy's closest friends, Frank—well, his mother, Mrs. Doyle, a wonderful lady who when kids came over to play made sandwiches and Kool-Aid, died from stomach cancer. There was a suicide. A homely kid. Leon Case. High school kids (including Cloudy) relentlessly teased and ridiculed Leon's simian-shelf forehead, heavy beard and pimpled face. One day, Leon pulled down the garage door, sat in a running car and died from carbon-monoxide poisoning.

There were dramas, too. Kids decided Mrs. Hill was an ex-Playboy bunny because she had huge breasts and wore a tiger bikini at the swim club—it was a widely held belief her second husband limped because he was caught in bed with Mrs. Hill by her *first* husband who shot him. The Bibbs boy got punched for trying to play with Bruce Urban's dick in a tree house. The Barry girl was prematurely bald, wore a wig and became pregnant at sixteen. Keith Ashworth and Skip Brodnick got arrested trying to "hock" batteries from cars in auto dealership lots. Tim Boyle got in trouble for egging Mr. Fozberg's house and waxing up car windows on Mischief Night. Mr. Denneck was removed as a Little League manager because he told the Warner boy not to play too well during team tryouts so he could to pick him for his team. Roger Corless drove too fast in a souped-up, mag-wheeled 1955 Chevy through the neighborhood (His car was "boss" because it had a Hurst shifter and STP stickers on the rear bumpers.). Bob Everett blew off his left hand trying to make a pipe bomb out of matches and gunpowder in his basement. Mr. Louro almost got sucked down into the sewer system during a torrential rainstorm when he used a crowbar to pry a manhole cover to drain the water flooding Hampton Drive. Neighborhood women shunned Mr.

Cuneo because when he got off the commuter bus he was greeted at the driveway by his Asian wife holding his slippers (John Map later told his son, "All the wives made fun of her and hated Mr. Cuneo But he was the happiest guy in our neighborhood."). Then there was Mrs. Black who got plastered at the American Hotel, danced on the bar and was hit in the back of her head by a ceiling fan and knocked to the floor. Mr. Farley was sent to prison for embezzling (Cloudy played with the Farley kids and was always puzzled by the numerous jars of change in their closets.). Gunner Mariano's German Shepherd attacked Tommy Fucarino. Marty Rowe spray-painted the word "Shit" on the aluminum siding of the Wilhelm house—and Mr. Wilhelm surprised everybody by not pressing charges. When Joe Deblasio stole Bob Verling's 10-speed bike, Verling's mother went to the Deblasio house and got it back (By the way, the Deblasio's were from Long Island and had a cyclone fence. Joe claimed he was "borrowing the bike.") One winter, Mrs. Williams called the police because when she driving with her two-year-old she almost got into an accident after a group of kids snowballed her Chrysler New Yorker hardtop station wagon. The Brace boys were banned from open-gym night basketball for smuggling in beers. Vandals flattened tires and put sugar in the gas tanks of several Freehold Regional High School buses that closed school for the day. Teenagers set brush fires in vacant fields, burned down abandoned farmhouses, formed garage bands, regularly shot out streetlights with BB guns, blew up frogs with cherry bombs, broke windows at construction sites or stole plywood to build "make-out" tree houses with dirty, torn mattresses. In the winter, the "greaser" teenagers who always wanted to look cool, froze in their leather jackets and walked around throwing slush balls with rocks in them. They were the same guys who chased younger kids with dog shit on the end of a stick. Every kid seemed to go through a period where they were "a problem." The neighbors tolerated the flaws and rebellions in each other's children and adapted to the needs and losses of families and shared troubles and stuck together because these Stonehurst events *happened* to everyone. It wasn't only Cloudy who saw it this way. Over the years, if he accidently bumped into a person from Freehold, they agreed it was special time and unique place they never experienced anywhere else—even the ones who were parents back then loved it. So

Freehold wasn't in Cloudy's imagination, it was alive and shaped him every day. So he kept its taste close.

In the early '70s, the Maps' Freehold world ended. After Cloudy finished high school, his Dad's company moved out of New York City. John Map uprooted his family from Stonehurst and replanted them in the focused, deceptively upscale potted soil of Westport, Connecticut... it was the biggest mistake of his life.

"THAT'S GRAHAM NOT CRAM, Harkness Graham the III. And this is my bride, Mary Beth," their new neighbor stated as he stood beside his wife in the Maps' white gravel driveway. He extended a welcome basket of flowers as if he was also using it to keep the Map family at a polite distance. The reserved Grahams were in their forties. Their cheeks, chins and lips looked like they had been designed and snapped into place so anyone who dared to face them on an equal level had to look into the pink heir-lined nostrils of their upturned noses. Did this snothead really say his name was Harkness? thought Cloudy. And then said he was The Third? Cloudy felt he was meeting Mr. Howell from *Gilligan's Island.* And Harkness? That's a name for a horse not a person! But, it was Mr. Graham's real name. And he was the Third one! Cloudy wondered if the other two were nearby, hiding in the woods as reinforcements, just in case the Maps caused trouble.

"I'm John, this is Patsy," said Clear. "My oldest here, Johnny, has finished high school. My daughter, Wendy, will be starting as a junior."

"Our boy, Tucker, isn't home at the moment," said Harkness. "He's a year younger than your son. He's at summer football camp. Tucker is punter on the varsity team and holds the record for the longest punt. He's a team leader in the high school opera club and our church choir."

Cloudy imagined Tucker in a clown outfit, punting on 4th down as he cried and sang "Vesti La Guiba" from *I Pagliacci.* He hadn't met him yet, but Cloudy knew they'd never be friends.

"Hark also mentors youth at our church," said Mary Beth. "So what school are you attending, young John?"

"Western Connecticut in Danbury."

There was a shifting patronizing silence—after all, WestConn was a *state* school.

"Do you commute to New York?" Mary Beth asked Clear. "We have an apartment in The City. Hark stays there when he's tired from working late." Harkness shot a cutting glance at his wife. She noticed. "I use it when I take in a matinee every other Wednesday."

"My company, AMF, relocated from New York to White Plains. Too far a commute from South Jersey. We're best known for manufacturing automatic bowling pin-setters. AMF stands for American Machine and Foundry. Bowlers think it means 'Another Mechanical Fuckup.'"

Clear chuckled but the Grahams seemed to retract, nod and arch their eyebrows in suppressed shock at the remark.

"I'm highly familiar with your firm," Harkness clipped. "We handle advertising for AMF's Voit division. I'm with Gray."

"Would you two like to come over for coffee?" asked Patsy Map.

"That would be nice," eagerly said Mary Beth. "Harky and I—"

"We have to get back," Harkness crisply said, pivoting on his polished white shoes, crunching the gravel in the driveway. "Tah."

Mary Beth lingered. She looked like she wanted to get acquainted, but when Harkness emitted a partially submerged explosive glare, it had the power to jerk his wife toward him. The couple held hands and left through the thick tall fir trees separating the properties.

"If that guy has to make a show of holding hands with his wife, he's cheating on her," whispered Clear, amused, eyes glinting.

"They're different," said his wife, amused.

In that brief meet-and-greet, Harkness appraised, undervalued and dismissed the Maps. For the next 20 years, he never invited the Maps over for drinks, dinner, a barbecue or to watch a game on TV. Harkness did everything for appearance and it was never a convincing performance. When Harkness made his traditional visit on holidays to the Map house, he never ventured beyond the welcome mat, and if he did go beyond it, he never took off his jacket or sat down. He'd ceremoniously hand off a box of candy or poinsettias, woodenly utter some platitudes, stiffly clear his throat and depart. The Grahams never came over as a couple to the Maps or anyone's house because it provided them with a convenient excuse to avoid a prolonged visit. Harkness' most visible activity was yard work. The Graham property was manicured—even the forest floor didn't have a broken branch, leaf, or underbrush, and the neatly arranged woodpile looked varnished and dusted. On many weekends, Clear observed the firm of Harkness & Son performing their yard chores and once commented to Cloudy, "Harkness is trying to IBM me. He wants my property to look like *his* property." And Harkness was active in his church—*very* active. Clear was right about the hand-holding Harkness. When the wife and son were away, Hark hosted candlelight luncheons in a darkened dining room and mentored various women in his church group; and, at night, he restlessly prowled the neighborhood with champagne to check on the wives whose husbands were away on business trips. It was obvious what activity Harkness engaged in at his Manhattan apartment when he was working late and "too tired" to pull out his commuter pass and board the New York-New Haven train on its burdensome track of tears to Westport.

The Grahams were one of the many reasons there was no *connect* in Cloudy's Connecticut. On the surface, the Map house in Westport seemed like a step up. It was three times the size of their Jersey home. The back yard had two acres of forest with 20-year-old maples and oaks, and a large pond with trout and bass fed by the Saugatuck River. There were only eight homes on the block separated by tall fir trees and low stone walls. Every other house had a pool or a tennis court. The wide streets didn't have curbs or sidewalks. There was even a zoning ordinance against clotheslines and burning leaves. It wasn't a neighborhood—it was a "community," which meant everyone wanted to be left to alone. Cloudy spent that first friendless summer waiting tables and helping his mother plant hydrangeas along the house. He wished they stayed in Freehold. He felt cheated. If they were still in Jersey, he'd be sharing a Fed's pie with his Freehold buddies at Federici's pizzeria, stopping for subs at Sorrento's on the way to the shore, or going to Asbury Park to hear bands at The Stone Pony. And what about the girls he had been getting to know in his senior year? Who was Cheryl Gettmenoff seeing? Once Cheryl came to English class wearing a white blouse with a red bra. Her blouse was too small and the opening between its buttons revealed her taut bra cups. And Cheryl was attracted to him! In high school, she proved it to her girlfriends by sneaking up behind Cloudy during passing and yanking the cloth loop off the back of his shirt (The loops were called "fairy hooks" and if a girl took yours it meant *really* she liked you.). A summer with Cheryl at the shore, riding waves on air-mattress rafts, playing Skee-Ball, miniature golf and pinball in the arcades and finishing out their day in Freehold eating soft-serve cones at Jersey Freeze. That's what Cloudy wanted his 17th summer to be! He and Cheryl would probably make another date for the following night to see *The Godfather* at the Shore Drive-In and park in the back of the lot. This summer was lost. But Cheryl wasn't here and Cloudy wasn't there. All these disappointments were playing in his head as he left the family room, slid the glass door and walked onto the screened-in patio deck. His Dad sat on a cushioned metal-framed lawn chair, sipping a martini and looking through the trees into the pond, enjoying a beautiful summer evening. The deck was his father's favorite part of the house, where he had coffee in the morning, read history books and the newspaper. His Dad loved Westport, his upcoming membership at the Battleground Club, and his easy commute to work. But at this particular moment, Clear looked more conflicted than pleased.

"Son," said Clear, holding his martini. "I have to eat a lot of bullshit at work, but sometimes it tastes sweet."

"I'm glad everything's working out so well for you," said Cloudy, who turned and went back inside the house.

"What'd I say?" asked Clear, baffled. "Really, what did I say?" He sighed. "What's the matter with everybody?"

Years passed before Cloudy got a clear glimpse into the shallow bottom of Harkness' personality. Cloudy was casting a lure in the pond. Harkness & Son were doing weekend yard work, scouring any sign of life from the forest floor. The Grahams were welcomed to fish there too, but never deigned to dip a rod.

"He's got one," excitedly blurted Tucker, walking over.

Cloudy hooked a trout. The rainbow jumped to shake the hook. He lowered his rod to slacken the line, then slowly raised it.

"Tucker," admonished Harkness, clenching his rake, as if he felt any social contact with a Map would contaminate his son.

"But he's got a fish," Tucker sputtered in brief defiance. "He—"

"Tucker!" Hark angrily commanded.

The house-broken Tucker obediently returned to his father's side and dutifully wheel-barrowed the brush away. Cloudy unhooked the trout. He wasn't surprised by Harkness' outburst. He was offended.

Harkness knew it but tried to smooth over of the roughness of the moment to conceal his contempt.

"Nice fish," Harkness said, but he didn't budge. He contented himself to teeter on the manicured tightrope of his property line, holding the rake upright to balance himself.

"I keep the bail loose, if you give a trout any tension they shake the hook," explained Cloudy, putting the struggling, two-pounder on a chinging metal-clipped stringer. "There are fewer trout every year." Cloudy pointed out the weeds tips sticking up in the middle of the pond. "The water is silting up from dirt carried downstream. Pickerel and bass are taking over. The pond is turning into a swamp."

"Maybe you'll catch a striped bass," Harkness said.

"If I do hook a striper, I'll be surprised."

"Why is that?"

"A striper is a *salt* water fish."

Harkness pressed his lips, perturbed because his fishy faux pas dropped him down one rung of the social ladder closer to a Map.

When Cloudy's parents sold the Westport house and retired to a condo in Bridgeport, Cloudy returned to fish the pond one final time. On his first few casts, the Mepps Black Fury treble hook got tangled in weeds or snagged decaying leaves. After cleaning off the hook, Cloudy cast the lure where the stream flowed into the pond. The spinner glittered. A pickerel quickly darted from the shadows and chomped down on the Mepps. The lure popped out of its mouth. The fish missed. It clamped down on the lure and incredibly avoided getting hooked again. The pickerel made another run. When its jaws opened to engulf the lure, Cloudy tightened the line and flicked up the rod. The spinner flipped out of the water and shot past his ear and into the weeds. Why hook a fish that couldn't tell the difference between hunger and food? thought Cloudy, there's no challenge to catching a fish that caught itself. He placed the spinner's treble hook onto the rod guide, tightened the line and left.

The pond was a swampy, pickerel world—they could keep it.

Cloudy never visited or drove through the neighborhood again.

HERB ALPERT AND THE TIJUANA BRASS' TRUMPETS FADED. The driver called out the Black Rock bus stop. Cloudy opened his eyes, reeling from dream withdrawal. He was loggy with harmony and top heavy with melody and awake again in a tone-deaf world. His brain dilated and half sloshed with a soothing overflow of Freehold flashbacks that were drained away by Westport feedback. Why were these memories breaking to the surface so quickly? They were suddenly more powerful and their impact hit him with a fresh velocity he never experienced before. They were angry. What exhumed them? Cloudy uneasily rose. He lost his balance and dropped back into the seat. When he left the bus he briefly glanced over his shoulder.

The regal black lady shook her head at him and disapprovingly said, "And you appeared to be such a young man."

Cloudy walked a block to his place. He rented the first floor of a dilapidated two-family house in a generally well-maintained residential section of Bridgeport known as Black Rock. More and more upper-middle class couples renovated houses in Black Rock because it was one of the few areas left to buy an affordable house in Fairfield County within commuting distance to New York and Stamford. Throughout Black Rock restaurants opened, followed by ice cream, antique shops, delis and small retail stores. Residents never admitted they lived in Bridgeport. They said "Black Rock" because B-port was notoriously renown for its farm system of crack addicts, a government run by a corrupt political machine, rough sections with tough cops or "inner-city at-risk" youths with "anger management issues." You have to understand, Bridgeport was well known for inexplicably placing its dump near a main beach. Still, with all the tony improvements to Black Rock, the hard-core element of B-port wasn't going to go down easily. Less than three blocks away were two strip clubs, three biker bars and a massage parlor called The Tokyo Health Spa. And often, close to the curbing in the street were remnants of tiny bluish-green shards of glass from car break-ins, these scattered fragments were derisively described by locals as "Bridgeport emeralds."

Cloudy went into his place, put his clubs down, flipped his sneakers off and flopped on the living-room couch. He was about to pick up the TV-remote to catch an old *Seinfeld* on the 36-inch plasma screen. But instead, he coldly appraised his living space. If Nana could still use her cane to poke open the front door, she'd dismiss his place as a "filthy, disgusting mess." It was furnished with scuffed chairs, faded rugs and a sagging couch. Every table had single-guy residue: empty beer bottles, pizza cartons, golf tees, scorecards and hamburger wrappers. The walls were adorned with posters of Springsteen, the New York Yankees, beer advertisements with busty women and a Budweiser bar light he kept from his frat days. In his bedroom was an unmade mattress on the floor. It's only distinguished piece of furniture was stereo system atop a steamer trunk beside a wooden cabinet with alphabetized rows of several hundred classic-rock CDs. There was a week's worth of laundry piled in a corner by the closet. The kitchen had a folding table and two white-plastic chairs. The drawers and cabinets were made of cheap wood and glopped with layers of white paint. The sink was stacked with dirty pint glasses lifted from bars. Cloudy became consumed with an unexplainable urge to clean everything. He put his laundry into the washer. Did the dishes. Scraped off layers of burnt cheese inside the oven. Mopped the kitchen and bathroom floors. Plucked hair out of the shower drain. Cleaned the toilet. Vacuumed. Dusted the furniture. Tossed out the beer cans, newspapers and pizza cartons. Cloudy wiped off the windows—and didn't leave streaks. His finishing touch: brush stroking spider webs out of every ceiling corner. Cloudy put fresh sheets on his bed, showered, shaved and changed into clean jeans and shirt. He ironed, folded and put away his laundry. Cloudy plopped back on the couch and felt lighter, like he peeled away a filmy layer from himself. He felt pride. What inspired all this? He didn't clean the place. He attacked it. Why? The mess never bothered him before. The urge's origin came from beating range balls for two hours. And where did that discipline, persistence and focus to work on his game come from? Descriptive words that never appeared in any of his job reviews: Discipline. Persistence. Focus. But a feeling of pride? Then he flashed to one of Nana's stories. She and Pop-Pops owned a bakery in Springfield, New Jersey. During the Depression, she was on her knees scouring the floor and a rich woman in town entered the bakery, looked down at Nana and said, "Stella don't you feel bad having to clean the floor on your knees?" And Nana replied, "No, I'd feel bad if I had to clean *your* floor." Until now, the only thing Cloudy thought he had common with Nana was their extreme dislike for Eggplant—the food, and the man. One evening in the Westport house, Nana and Cloudy were finishing their dinner on tray tables in the family room and watching *60 Minutes* on TV. Nana was waiting for Wendy to bring her after-dinner glass of white wine and a slice of apple. Eggplant barged in, late for supper and drunk after two rounds at Battleground. He said, "Why you watching this? The game's on." He changed the channel and sat on the couch. Wendy came out, kissed him, set up a tray table and poured Eggplant a frosted mug of beer. She left to warm up dinner for him. Nana barked, "You should get off your lazy behind and make your own dinner." Eggplant's eyes glazed over. He smirked and replied, "You know, your granddaughter sucks a great cock." Nana stiffened. Cloudy was aghast and said, "Don't talk to her like that. What's the matter with you?" Eggplant replied, "She didn't understand what I said because she never did it." Then he blaaaaaaaaaaaaaaaah-ed out his fuck-the-world laugh. The next morning, Cloudy came downstairs and saw Nana at the kitchen table. Her hands were limply folded across her lap, shoulders slumped, as if she had bitten into another piece of promising fruit that had turned sour like her first trusting bite into that lemon in steerage. "I don't like that man," she firmly said to Cloudy, gazing sadly out the window. "I should have never come to this house. I'm seeing too much. I think I've lived too long." It was one of the few times Cloudy allowed himself to understand her. He cheered Nana up by making her banana pancakes, then he went in the back yard and refilled the bird feeder because she enjoyed identifying various birds and watching their fluttering and territorial antics. Fortunately, there were no roosters.

Is that what was driving him when he got out of his way to get better at golf? Nana and her poking cane? So what else was lying in wait for him at the bottom of his swing arc?

The House of Denial has many rooms. Throughout his life, Cloudy built a mansion. There was only one escape route left for him to still enjoy its unobstructed views.

"BECAUSE TRAMPS LIKE US," Cloudy drunkenly belted out his Bruce Springsteen impression to the cheering crowd of 40 people at the Hugga Mug's karaoke night. "Baby, we were boooooooooorn to run!"

When Cloudy finished the South Jersey anthem, he drew a huge ovation by slamming down a shot of Jagermeister. He left the stage, sat at the bar and was greeted with free round by the owner. Cloudy briefly pinched his nostrils together and kneaded his lower teeth into a numbed upper lip. He and the bartender were still buzzed after doing a rail of coke off the men's room sink. Cloudy did all his dealing at The Mug because he didn't want cars pulling up to his place at all hours of the night. He kept his customer base small, steady and local. He stayed low-key, never really let on to his parents or anyone he had money. He lived like a bum, he never wanted a mortgage, car insurance, or taking the bus. He didn't even have a checking account. In the past ten years he collected unemployment four times and always got a tax refund from his short job spurts. On the bar, his cell phone vibrated by his beer. Cloudy looked at the screen. A Florida area code. Wendy was in a rehab there. He left and stood beyond the cigarette smoke of puffing pale patrons on the sidewalk. He took the call.

"Yeah, Wendy."

"It's your crazy sister."

"Well, not too many people call me from Florida."

"I'm doing fine. My counselor said, 'You're a shining star,'" Wendy said, then paused for Cloudy to respond. He didn't. "Oy, I fucked up," she continued, crying. "I want to come home."

"Wendy, it's not your home. It's Mom and Dad's condo."

"I'll get my own place. But I'm not going to take just any job."

"You're lucky right now to take whatever job you can get. That's what happens to people who live off their parents, drink for six years and don't work."

"Let's not go there. It's history."

"History? I don't think we're in the past yet."

Wendy said, "Remember in Freehold when we were kids and got in trouble because I told on you for taking Tastykake Butterscotch Krimpets from the bread box, and so you told on me for taking a Yoo-hoo? We thought Mom was going to send us to our rooms. But instead, she took us to Jersey Freeze."

"Yeah," said Cloudy, smiling. "Jersey Freeze off the traffic circle. The ceiling lights above the order window were always packed with dead gnats and moths. I always ordered a large, soft vanilla cone dipped in 'crunch coat,' which was chopped up peanut brittle. Yeah, I remember the ice cream, the brittle."

"Mom treated us and said, 'You two should never tattle on each other. A brother and sister should stick together because no matter whatever happens in life you always have each other.' But when we were kids, you made fun of me in front of your friends. Said I was skinny and called me 'Bone Bones.'" She expected a response. Cloudy said nothing. "When your friends picked on me, you joined in. You never stood up for me."

"Well, like you say, that's *history*."

"Easy for you to say, you were always Mom and Dad's favorite."

"Say what?"

"Every year Dad takes you to play in the golf tournament but not me."

"You don't play golf."

"I want to come home. I'm not one of these people!"

"You threw a carving knife at Dad on Thanksgiving. You called our Mom a 'cunt.' You damaged almost every appliance in their kitchen. I cleaned out your room and found 14 empty bottles of liquid hairspray hidden in the bottom of your closet. You *are* one of those people."

"I can stop drinking hair spray anytime I want to."

"That's assuring."

"You haven't told anyone at the club where I am?"

"The country club? I don't go there. Why would I? What does that have to do with anything? You don't belong anymore."

"I love you."

"Have you been drinking?"

"No it's my medication. I'm bipolar."

"Everyone's bipolar when they can't get what they want."

"Oy."

"Who do you think you're fooling?"

"Fooling? What does that mean?"

"You're drunk."

"Fuck you," she said, hanging up.

Cloudy shut his cell phone. He listed slightly, adrift between forgiving and forgetting. How could tough love be the best way to treat alcoholics? It was Eggplant's abuse and neglect that drove his sister to drink. So, how would tough love's indifference to Wendy's pain *stop* her from drinking? But being sympathetic to her was useless. He heard her false promises and stale apologies too many times. Forgiveness went nowhere. He tried all buttons to take her somewhere else, but Wendy was an elevator that only stopped on one floor. Then, Cloudy spied the glittering lightning bugs dappling the backdrop of the evening's purple sky. He enjoyed the way the whirring-winged bugs' lime-tail bulbs sprayed a handful of harmless splintered cinders. The coolness in the air meant rain. He smelled roasting coffee down the block from The Same Old Grind on the corner. Coffee. Sign of rain. Lightning bugs. They sparked him back to Freehold. As a kid, he knew when it was going to rain because the air became heavy with the deep aroma of coffee roasted at the town's Nescafé plant. It gave Cloudy enough warning to get home ahead of the approaching storm. But the pleasant memory was interrupted.

"The prick bastard is gonna pay for what he did to me," grumbled a homeless woman, glaring at Cloudy. "I'll get a lawyer."

The derelict bore a disturbing dehydrated resemblance to Wendy on a five-day binge. Is this how Wendy was going to end up? The skin on her hands looking like dried jerky? No shoes or socks? A four-inch dirty, bloody divot of open flesh gouged in her right foot?

"Did you marry and divorce a guy named Eggplant too?" he asked.

"Marry an eggplant? What the fuck are you smoking?"

"Just curious," Cloudy said, shrugging. "It's an inside joke that even I don't find funny."

"Go ahead and ignore me, everybody else does."

"They're avoiding you," he icily replied, "I'm not ignoring you."

"I'm wearing gloves so I don't get cut," she said proudly, reaching into a trash basket for empties. "The prick is gonna pay."

Cloudy went inside The Same Old Grind. He stood at the counter and studied the coffee menu board. His sister tapered down his buzz. He could use a hit of caffeine to power up. John Coltrane played on the speaker system. Actually, Cloudy didn't know if it was Coltrane or not. All jazz sounded like Coltrane to him: a saxophone going off on interminable and frantic chord-changing solos, drums without a steady beat accompanied by thumping bass runs and guitar licks that combined to produce a song without a single note resembling a hook or a melody. But skittish bebop perfectly meshed with the tone of this coffee shop where people read books and newspapers, high school kids flirted, church groups met and nursed one coffee for hours, students discussed the meaning of films and unemployed guys took advantage of the "Free Wi-Fi" to surf porn sites on their laptops.

A woman waiting for her order spoke on her cell phone, "I was late because I had to drop my daughter off at dance class. I'm sorry. Bye"

Cloudy stood in line and said, "Don't ever apologize for being a good Mom. Moms don't ever need to apologize for being Moms."

"You're right. Thank you," she replied, leaving with her latte.

He noticed a cute female barista overheard his comment. She flashed a smile. *The Feel* visited him. The background behind her seemed to recede. She was perfectly defined against a blurred world. Her green eyes had stopping power. His back ribs quivered. His blood pumped. His brain fishtailed on emotions. He turned into the skid. He was no longer Cloudy. He was a lost Map.

The barista placed her hands on the counter's edge, stretched in a bouncing, leaning pose and said, "Do you know what you want?"

"I used to," he stammered.

She was cute, in her thirties, thin, small breasted, shoulder-length black hair. She wore a Same Old Grind purple polo shirt that stopped above her belly button, which was pierced. Her nose looked big but it was small. Her eyes seemed to bulge but they glowed. Her forehead was wide and curved but it was banked. She radiated so much enthusiasm her flesh stretched out a vibrant, trampoline-like tautness that bounced off him off her world and tossed him into a weightless universe. He had never floated like this!

"A Grind Mocha Espresso Cool Chip, I think," said Cloudy.

"Single?"

"Yes, I am," said Cloudy.

There was a pause. His remark made a connection.

"Would you like some mint in that?" she asked, then added 'darling' but pronounced it with a Russian-spy accent. "*Dar*-link?"

Dar-link. Her foreign inflection jellied-out Cloudy.

"I always try to make what people ask for better," she cheerfully said.

"If someone asks for a caramel, okay, I say why not try some chocolate on that? I've done the math and 99 out of a 100 are nice and open to it."

"Can you guess which one I am?" replied Cloudy, smirking.

"It's a mystery to me, *dar*-link."

"Mint? Sure, I'll take a hit."

"Name?" she asked, poised to write on a paper cup.

"It's Cloudy—er, John."

"Cloudy? Who are the others in your family? Hot, Hazy and Humid?"

"My Dad likes vodka so he got nicknamed 'Clear.' I got 'Cloudy' because I like beer. But my real name is John Map."

"I'm Penny. Thanks for asking, *John*," she said, smirking. "I'm willing to bet your father is a John too."

"My Dad told me, 'Your name is John. My name is John. My father's name was John. If you have a kid, you know what his name is going to be?' I said, 'What?' He said, 'John!'"

"Your Dad is a funny guy," she said, laughing and patting his hand. Her soft touch jolted him. She crossed his power lines. She pointed outside. "Check it out," she said. "The fireflies in the trees. I love it when spring jump-starts summer."

"When I was a kid in Jersey," Cloudy said, "we'd catch lightning bugs and put them in jars with holes punched in the top. One time, I turned off all the living room lights and released them. The lightning bugs were so beautiful outside I wanted them to be beautiful *inside* our home. My Mom came in and saw all these flashing lightning bugs in the living room she freaked! She was yelling, 'How did all these bugs get in here? Maybe there's a nest!' I thought she'd like it. I knew I was going to get in trouble so I didn't say anything."

"Ka-yikes, lightning bugs in a living room," she said, laughing. "You're a hoot." She smiled. "So, you're a guy from Jersey?"

"Grew up in Freehold," replied Cloudy, adding. "Exit 123."

"Springsteen-ville. The Boss is from Freehold, right?"

"Yeah, Bruce lived on Randolph Street in the 'boro.' I was on the other side of town, but for awhile, I went to Freehold Regional. Same school. Colonials was our football team. Bruce graduated before me. He was a couple grades ahead of me. Still is."

"I like his early stuff. He's too depressing now."

"Yeah, it's called: 'growing as an artist.' His music used to speak to me.

Now it speaks to him. Bruce outgrew his early stuff. I didn't. I guess I never *grew* as a listener."

"Your drink will be up in a few. With tax that'll be a ginormous $2.77."

"Whatever works," he said, paying with a five.

"Your change: $2.23," she laughed. "Ka-yikes, that's my birthday. 2/23. February 23rd. You know: 223."

"In Freehold we lived at 223 Stonehurst Way. I've always liked that number. Because it was so great growing up there. I mean I even like saying it: two-twenty-three. Once I had a chance to rent a place with a 223 number, but I didn't take it. Wonder what it would have been like?"

"Wow 223," she said. "Worlds collide."

Cloudy smiled. Her reply reminded him of a phrase George Costanza used in a *Seinfeld* episode. He didn't mention it, because every time he pointed out connections from the popular TV show to life most people didn't get the reference, or thought he was weird.

"What are you smiling about?"

"Oh, nothing."

"Don't forget the receipt. You might need it for tax purposes."

"Won't pay much this year, I lost my job."

"You didn't lose it, you got rid of it."

"No, they got rid of me."

"Who knows? Losing that job might turn out to be the best thing that ever happened to you."

"Yeah, people with jobs always tell me that," said Cloudy. "I bet someone is telling my old boss the same thing."

"Stay positive. When one door closes another opens."

"When a door closes it means they locked you out."

"But you scored unemployment, right?" she said, smiling. "It's the Summer of Johnny. Just like 'The Summer of George' in *Seinfeld*."

"I'm way into *Seinfeld*."

"Me too! I'm beginning to base my life on it. It's scary."

They rapidly traded off catch phrases from the TV sitcom.

"You double dipped the chip!"

"No soup for you!"

"Sponge worthy."

"Close talker."

"A Festivus for the rest of us."

"Yadda yadda."

"Not that…" said Cloudy, imitating Jerry.

Penny finished the line, "there's anything *wrong* with that!"

A young yuppie couple walked by the shop, talking on cell phones.

"Look," sarcastically whispered Cloudy. "There goes Bill from Human Resources with Beverly from Accounting. They have to be from frickin' *Waste*port. You can see there's something about them that isn't right, but it's *just* right enough for them."

"My best friend does nails in Westport. Has heard all their stories over the years. The women give their kids everything. Send them to college. The kids drop out. Do drugs. If they graduate don't amount to anything. Parents feel they failed. Drink too much."

"Maybe their kids weren't loved."

"Are you kidding? They were given too *much* love."

Cloudy remembered the black woman's scornful glare on the bus. He imitated her voice as he vaguely said to himself, "'I think it was *you.*'"

"Where did that come from?" asked Penny.

"I'm a ReRun, I've been one of them the whole time," Cloudy confessed, grasping yet another decomposed and bloated truth that detached itself from the bottom of his swing arc and surface in his face. "Me, I never knew. A ReRun. I've always been one of them."

"A ReRun? What's that?"

BLEEEEEEAAAAAH! blasted an air horn behind Cloudy.

Cloudy jumped. The patrons stopped talking and stared.

"Dawg, wassssup?" said Pudge, maliciously laughing at his stunt.

"It *was* all good," said Cloudy.

Pudge was wired and drunk and feeling no pain and said, "I'm such a pissah." He held up the air horn and said to Penny, "I honked this horn on the golf course when my bro Turdle was teeing off. He swung and his shot hit the ball washer."

"Was the ball washer hurt?" Penny asked.

"A ball washer is a *thing* not a person, stupid," said Pudge.

"Let me get this straight," said Penny. "You treat people like that on a golf course where men are armed with clubs and you're still alive?"

Cloudy laughed.

"Pardon me for existing," said Pudge, snorting.

"You're don't want a pardon," said Penny, "you want a reprieve."

Cloudy laughed and said, "You're feisty!"

"What can I say?" said Pudge, smiling. "I'm an acquired taste."

"Yeah, like vomit."

"Double feisty," said Cloudy, laughing. "With some mocha on it."

Pudge turned on Cloudy. "Nice shirt, is it yours or your Dad's?" he said, resentfully thumping his flicking finger on the Battleground Country Club logo of Cloudy's polo shirt. "Golfing with Dad in the member-guest tournament this month?"

"No, they're holding it in September not June. The old-fart members bitched that it was too hot when they held it last summer."

"Battleground Country Club in Westport no less," Penny said, raising her eyebrows. "Ooooh, la la. Very swanky franky."

"Cloudy doesn't belong to Battleground, his Dad does."

"I didn't say *I* was a member," said Cloudy.

Penny said, "My Dad plays golf. I swear golf is the only sport where a guy acts like a woman because he accessorizes. When he dresses up for the course I can actually hear him thinking, 'Will these shoes go with my bag? Does this shirt and these pants match?' Then he puts on orange socks!" She laughed. "Whatever blows up your skirt."

Pudge said, "Dawg, the B-port All Stars are playing at The Cove. Ace will let us jam. You can sing. They need a guy who can do Springsteen covers."

"You sing?" said Penny, impressed. "Not many people have a voice."

"Yeah, but mine is someone else's."

"After we play, let's hit up the Tokyo Health Spa," said Pudge, who shifted into a Japanese woman's voice. " 'Fifty dollah for tug and rub.' " He leered at Penny. "Not that *we* would know." He left and said, "Peace out, dawg. I'm gone."

Cloudy was pissed at Pudge's crude crack but covered for his friend's rudeness by explaining to Penny, "That's Pudge being Pudge."

"That's a shame."

"Seinfeld line," said Cloudy, smiling. "Well, Pudge can't help who he is. It's how he was raised."

"He wasn't raised."

"Cloudy single," shouted the barista who prepared the drink.

"What?"

"Your mocha's up," explained Penny. "I'll get it for you."

"Thanks," he said. "'Cloudy Single' is how they call me to the tee."

"Don't lose the cup. My phone number is on it."

He turned to leave.

"*Dar*-link!"

He stopped and said, "Yes?"

"You'd be a lot better looking without that long hair."

"Business in front," replied Cloudy, who reached back and wagged his ponytail at her. "Party in the back."

"Ka-yikes, you're a hoot, you are."

"And you're the reason I believe in lightning bugs and rainbows," said Cloudy leaving. "Feistiness helps too." He glanced back. Penny was still checking him out. He turned away, smiling, pumped.

When he got outside, Pudge was getting into his parked Camero. He said, "That coffee girl is hot, next time ask her to leave room for cream." He leaning out the passenger window. "Yo, Dawg, let's rock!"

"I'll pass," said Cloudy. "I have an early tee time."

"What are you, in training?"

The homeless woman walked between them and muttered, "He'll pay, he'll pay. Oh how he will pay."

"Shut your pie hole, you played-out tard," said Pudge. "Here's a buck." He flicked the bill on the sidewalk. She bent over for the money.

BLEEEEEEAAAAAH! blasted an air horn.

The woman jumped and ran away.

Pudge brandished the air horn and said, "I am such a pissah."

"That was O.B., man. There was no call for that, Pudge."

"Ya think?" his buddy said.

When Pudge countered Cloudy's objection with Eggplant's patented "ya-think" comeback, Cloudy saw the connection between his friendship with Pudge and Wendy's marriage to Eggplant. Wendy never understood why Cloudy hung with Pudge. Cloudy never got why she married an asshole. During her marriage, Eggplant refused to make any improvements to their home, alienated all her friends and nagged her for spending money on shopping or home improvements, but treated himself to 36 holes of golf at the club on Saturday and Sunday, and kept his season tickets to the Giants, Jets, Mets, and Yankees. Eggplant never changed one aspect of his lifestyle. He was a single guy who just happened to also be married. And by the time he got through with Wendy, his poor sister was reduced to a hollow shell with her yolk blown out. That being said, why *did* Cloudy hang out with Pudge? How many times had Cloudy apologized for Pudge's obnoxious behavior? What about the way Pudge claimed a higher percentage of the band's money because he supposedly set up their gigs? And there were Pudge's self-indulgent guitar solos that drove dancers off the floor. And how about what he did to the homeless lady? Pudge always had a mean streak. In their frat house days, Pudge thought it was hilarious to leave pennies in the urinals for the cleaning woman to find. And he was always thinking about himself first. No matter what they did together, Pudge had to have more than anybody else, whatever it was. When they split a pizza, he took the biggest slice. If there were five pieces of candy left, he took three. Even if they were just shooting hoops, he had to take one more shot than you. But when Pudge maliciously downgraded him to Penny with that crack about the Tokyo Spa and he went out of his way to point out Cloudy wasn't a Battleground Country Club member, a switch clicked off inside him. Cloudy bottomed out on Pudge.

"Let's go and jam."

"I'm outta our band. It's a glorified hobby."

"A hobby, what do ya call golf then?"

"The band's not going anywhere. I'm a ReRun doing covers. There was a time I thought the music would take me somewhere, but it's not."

"Speak for yourself."

"I thought I did. And, I did it quite well."

"So that's it? Nice way to talk to a friend."

"I guess you could say that."

"Go ahead and be that way, Dawg. That girl back there has already got your cream whipped and you haven't even started going out with her yet," said Pudge. He flapped his lips. "Peace out, dawg. I'm gone."

Pudge drove off. The Camero's spinning tires laid patch and sounded like an injured puppy's yipping.

Cloudy finished his cold coffee drink. The mint did add flavor. He saw Penny's phone number on the cup.

"Where's the love?" he said, pantomiming a golf swing and lit off and launched an imaginary ball into the lightning-bug spangling night.

Snowman In August

"CLOUDY SINGLE ON THE TEE with Ernie-and-Pete twosome," Buttons announced on the Ironwoods PA system. Single was Cloudy's new last name. Throughout the summer, he Singled himself out at Ironwoods. Single wasn't trying to turn pro, he was trying to go Cloudy. Single clipped off Cloudy's rock-poseur ponytail. Single overcame Cloudy's tardiness habit and arrived promptly for tee times. Single was shaved, neatly dressed, had shined shoes. Single stopped Cloudy from taking mulligans, fluffing up lies, giving himself three-foot putts or removing a ball from a shallow grave of a divot. Single made Cloudy hunker down, learn and respect the rules of golf and call penalties on himself. Cloudy's game was still erratic and fibrillated from the mid-90s to over 100. But he freely accepted the burden and fluctuation of his 25-handicap and gradually lightened its load by staying within himself and grinding out every shot.

Ernie and Pete were hyperactive testosterone-bursting 15-year-olds. When Cloudy Single joined the attention-deficit-disorder poster children up on the tee, they were competing to see who could bounce a golf ball off their wedge clubface the longest.

Ernie counted each of his golf ball bounces aloud, "45, 46, 47."

Pete tried to mess up his pal's concentration by counting his bounces even louder but adding, "48, Ernie's gay. 49, Ernie sucks."

"50—dang!" said Ernie, who missed. His ball hit the grass.

Pete mocked Ernie's loss by continuing to bounce the ball off his wedge and saying, "51, I'm great. 52, Ernie's a dickweed. 53..."

Ernie playfully shoved Pete to prevent the 53rd consecutive bounce.

When the lanky dingleheads realized Cloudy was on the tee, the two surprisingly stopped their clowning and politely introduced themselves. Cloudy jealously noticed they had the latest and most expensive set of clubs in their bags, along with golf balls that cost

$50 a dozen. They weren't walking either. The kids dropped $20 apiece for a cart. But they weren't Chops. They turned out to be great sticks. Throughout the front nine, they consistently laced huge drives. Invincibility saturated their abilities. The closer they got to the hole, the more fearless they played, taking full swings with lob wedges and sticking balls with backspin near the cup. They effortlessly carded birdies or pars. Cloudy rarely reached greens in regulation, but two-putted and one-putted. He bogeyed the par-4s, but parred the par-5s and par-3s. After they finished the turn, Cloudy totaled his scorecard: 41. His best front nine ever. And his first legitimate shot to break 90!

AT THE 10TH TEE, THERE WAS A BACK-UP OF THREE FOURSOMES. Ernie and Pete decided to get food. Cloudy tagged along with them to the clubhouse. When they entered, Buttons was pouring a draft beer. Regulars kicked back at tables, shared snacks and brews and watched the Golf Channel on TV.

"Three groups are still waiting to hit on 10," said Cloudy.

"Yeah, it's slow, there was a tournament earlier," replied Buttons. "Hey Chop, want a tubesteak on the house? I have three Polish and a regular. They've been on awhile. I'm only going to toss them."

The overcooked hot dogs were impaled on a pronged rotisserie spike and rotated under red heat lamps in a glass metal-framed box on the counter. The shriveled meat looked like the remains of a World War I soldier left for weeks on barb wire in No Man's Land.

"Thanks, I'll pass."

"We'll chow down those meat puppies," eagerly said Pete.

"Score," added Ernie. "Dang."

The teenagers also purchased chips, soda and Snickers bars. They sat at a table, devoured the dogs and washed their meal down with two Mountain Dews.

"Man," said Cloudy to Buttons as the teenagers pigged out. "You should see those two move on the ball. *In*credible."

"You can never tell with kids," said Buttons. "I coached a high school team. Promising kids, but when puberty, beer, girls, and partying hits, I lose them. The next time I see'em, they're 31, have tattoos on their elbows, divorced, and driving a pick-up with a dog."

"So what's so wrong with that?" brusquely grunted a man behind Cloudy. "I'm divorced and have a pick-up truck and a dog."

"Is that right?" dryly said Buttons, smiling.

The indignant voice was Donald Arax. He held a first-place trophy from the day's tournament. Arax was sweaty and reeked. His damp goatee looked like it was smeared on. He wore drawstring black shorts and shirt with a large crucifix beneath it. A bulge in his left sock held his wallet—or, perhaps concealed a house-arrest bracelet.

The three men turned to the golf on TV. A gallery of spectators reverently stood behind white ropes against a backdrop of the Pacific coastline. A pro was on the tee. His downswing was a blur of elbows and knees. After his club went past his hips and lashed through the back of the ball, the whipping flex of the shaft echoed within the narrow corridor of cypress trees.

"I'd give anything to hit a ball like that," Arax said longingly.

"You wouldn't give *anything* to hit a ball like him," Buttons said with an uncharacteristic sharp edge. "That pro's divorced. His son is on drugs. The guy's in debt up the ying."

"So, I'm divorced twice," replied Arax, shrugging. "My two kids are on drugs. My life has turned out worse *trying* to hit a golf ball like that guy! Why wouldn't I want to play like him?"

"Last I checked," said Buttons, "the rules in the pro circuit don't allow Peppermint Lifesavers."

"Bite me," huffed Arax, abruptly leaving.

Buttons wiped down the counter, smiled and said, "Calling Donald on his shit is a tap-in." He shook his head and added, "Peppermint."

"Why'd he get so pissed at your Lifesavers crack?" asked Cloudy.

"Arax cheats with candy. It's his secret go-to mulligan. Why I don't put anything past that guy. I wouldn't be surprised if he had holes in his pockets to could drop a ball down his pants leg so he wouldn't have to declare his ball lost."

"How do you cheat with Lifesavers in golf?"

"When Arax plays he always has a Lifesaver in his mouth. They're white, right? He sucks them down until they get paper-thin. When his ball is in a tough lie, that's when he uses them. No one expects you to cheat with candy. He covers his mouth, slips the Lifesaver into his hand and says he has to identify his ball. He picks up the ball, declares it's his, but when he replaces the ball there's a thin Lifesaver beneath it. He uses the Lifesaver as a tee to make his shot easier."

"Arax is only lying to himself. What does he really gain?"

"Don't you get it, Chop? Cheating is the *only* way some people can *ever* be number one at anything," said Buttons. "They won. That's all they care about. Doesn't matter how they do it as long as they win." He paused. "It's how they go through life: 'I got mine, you get yours.' They eat everything on the forest floor and leave nothing for anybody else. You know, assholes."

"My ex-brother-in-law is like that. So, what's Arax's story?"

"Lives in a trailer park or something, installs flooring for a living. He's active in his church. It's how he hustles up flooring jobs and free rounds of golf. Arax thumps The Bible so a paycheck pops out. The crucifix he wears is a tool on his belt. Really, it might as well be a corkscrew. When it comes to accounting for himself, Arax keeps two different sets of The Good Books: in life and golf."

"Not telling me anything I don't know. Arax was ex-brother-in-law's partner in a member-guest tournament. Sandbagged me and my Dad last year. Decimated us. Closed us out in 5 straight holes. And, Arax *did* have Lifesavers. And Arax is playing in it again."

"Is that right?" said Buttons, coming around the counter. "Walk with me, but don't talk to me, Chop." They went to the computer where players entered their scores to maintain accurate handicaps. Buttons hit the keys and searched through a list of golfers on the screen. "Here he is. Donald Arax." Buttons examined Arax's rounds. "He's posting big numbers to inflate his handicap. Arax is definitely is single-digit in every way—IQ and golf. Believe me, I should know, we competed against each other as kids. When he was 17, Arax was riding his bike to get his pro card when he was hit by a car and broke his wrist in two places. His game was never the same. When I got my card and turned pro, he was furious."

"What was it like playing on the tour?"

"Being a pro? It's no walk in the park," said Buttons heading back to the register. "The game I needed never came. I couldn't cut it inside the ropes. Burned out, dropped out. Took me 10 years to like golf again." He paused. "There are a ton of up-and-comer kids today who are plus-2 handicaps, but no college coach is interested in them. They're searching for something extra. They're looking for the extra something I finally realized I didn't have in that hotel room in Carlsbad when I didn't make my fourth cut in a row. And you know who I think had it? That all-consuming drive to win at all costs and take no prisoners. Arax has it, but he doesn't have my swing."

"Are you're talking about character building?" asked Cloudy, wincing. "Man, I hate character building."

"I don't know about golf building character. For some, maybe. On the tour, I'd call a penalty on myself when no one was around and cheat on my wife that night. If you really want it, the closer you get to the hole the more you see who you really are. You might get bigger but sometimes the hole gets *smaller.*"

"Hey, I have a chance at breaking 90!" said Cloudy.

"Those who live life by the numbers don't add up to anything," said Buttons, nodding in the direction of the course. "No Lifesavers out there, Chop. Stay humble. Remember, you don't have a good round, you rent it."

ON THE BACK NINE the snack food took its toll on Ernie and Pete. They pushed shots left, came up short with lob wedges and blew easy putts. Their mental games were like a building without fire stops in the walls. Whenever a small flame of disappointment flared, there were no safeguards in place to prevent the structure of their entire game from being engulfed in an adolescent blaze. They threw clubs, took impractical, low-percentage shots. After they double bogeyed four holes in a row, they stopped recording their scores and abandoned their game. They clowned around, nearly flipped their cart driving too fast down the side of hills and left skid marks on gravel paths. Single saw a lot of his former Cloudy in them. Before he became Single, if golf didn't go Cloudy's way, he'd swear, have a tantrum, lose interest, pop beers and smoke dope. But Single had a mental game that could go the distance of 18 holes. He didn't give up, he endured the lulls. Even throughout the back nine, Cloudy made his usual bad shots, but scrambled to make some gratifying recoveries. After he holed out a 12-footer for a par on the 17th, he checked his score: 84. He not only deserved the chance to break 90—he was *entitled* to it. After all, Cloudy logged in 53 rounds and spent hours on the range, putting green, and chipping area. He played in the rain, on windy or humid days, often stayed on the course until dark, then dropped extra balls and hit pitch shots to the green under the rising moon.

When he stepped on the tee of the last hole, the green looked like the oasis he reached after a long trudge through muddy fairways, deep rough and parched land of watery bogeys. The 18th at Ironwoods was a 345-yard par-4. It had a wide-ass fairway with trees to the right. The large green was guarded by bunkers on each side. It was the easiest hole on the course.

Just as Cloudy set up over the ball, Ernie and Pete began wrestling behind him. He stopped his backswing and said, "Hey guys, come on. Don't make me become the adult. I'm not good at it."

They surprised him and stopped.

"How old are you, sir?" asked Ernie, drinking a Red Bull and stuffing a handful of M&Ms into his mouth.

"Sir? Sir is 44."

"You're 44, dang! So you're old. You don't look it," said Pete. "My Dad is 40 and he's fat, grouchy, bald, yells at the news and traffic and glares at Mom a lot. She doesn't glare back at him though."

"Gives you a good idea of what raising a kid like you can do to a man," said Cloudy, smiling. "I know what I put my Dad through."

The teenagers didn't grasp his insight, weren't paying attention—or, through the miracle of youth, accomplished both at the same time.

Cloudy ripped his best drive of the day, a 275-yard shot down the middle of the fairway, 70 yards from the pin. Ernie and Pete tried to kill the ball and sliced their drives into the trees. Cloudy went to his tee shot, took out a wedge and patiently waited for the teenagers to hit. Pete swung and was on the green. Ernie's shot nicked a branch and rolled deeper into the woods.

"O.B., dang," said Ernie, flicking his club up at the offending tree. His 9-iron got stuck in the high branches.

"Nice dickweed," observed Pete. "Your best iron of the day."

The teenagers started wrestling again.

Instead of becoming a referee for their misplaced testosterone-laced bout, Cloudy decided to play his shot. He had a perfect lie. A routine pitching wedge to the pin. Just get on the green, he thought, even if you three-putt you can still break 90! He took a few practice swings. D*on't* hit it in the trap, he said to himself, *don't* hit it in the trap—*don't.*

He swung and beckoned to his ascending shot, "Be *right!*"

The ball made a depressing, flat, wet thud in the sand trap.

Cloudy consoled himself with the fact he was only lying two. He whispered to himself, "You can still get up-and-down with a bogey and get an 89." He went to his shot. He slowly ground his spikes in the sand, as if he was stamping out two lit cigarettes. *Don't* scoop it, he thought, hit behind the ball with the wedge's flange in the sand. *Don't* stop your follow-through. He swung, scooped and stopped his follow through. The ball smacked the trap's lip, rolled back and settled into a footprint he left in the sand. "Cloudy!" he yelped, then angrily swung again and again the ball. He was lying 6—and, still in the trap.

Ernie and Pete laughed. Cloudy turned to the kids, infuriated by their rudeness. Their laughter had nothing to do with his tantrum. While Cloudy had been concentrating on trying to break 90, the two dingleberries were completely absorbed in the task of tossing clubs at Ernie's 9-iron to dislodge it from the tree. But instead of knocking the club loose, all Ernie's irons were tangled in the limbs. The boys found this hilarious. Cloudy shook his head and shrugged. He regained his composure, laughed, relaxed and took an insignificant seventh swing.

"Golf shot," Cloudy said to himself, nodding as the ball seemed to softly float from the puff of sand into a short, tight, high arch from the trap and flop an inch from the cup. He raked the trap as if he was covering up a turd, went to the green and tapped in his putt. An 8. A snowman in August. He penciled in 92 and studied his scorecard like it was a traffic-accident report. He was the victim in a hit-and-run that only involved himself. He had gotten in his way by attaching a scorecard to the club shaft.

A chorus of loosing howls came from a group on the nearby 9th hole.

"Fire in the hole."

"Booyah!"

"I'm such a pissah!"

Cloudy saw his former Vices: Pudge, Turdle and Schultzie. Pudge was parading on the green and chugging a beer because he holed-out a chip. His Vices were drunk and having fun and playing, but they weren't *golfing.* Cloudy was no longer hacking with the Chops. He was a golfer. A sulking, reluctantly, humbled, defiled, frustrated, thwarted, twisted, battered pissed-off golfer standing next to a snowman on the 18th green with a 92. A goddamn useless, piece-of-shit frickin' muthafuckin' 92.

INSTEAD OF LIPPING OUT over a beer mug at the 19th hole because he chunked breaking 90, Cloudy communed and commiserated with his putter on the putting green. Between putts he watched an endless procession of swithering Chops hitting off the first tee. The longer each Chop hunched over the ball, the more they stressed out. Their loose bodies hardened into crunched statues. Cloudy could hear Don'ts rampaging through their swings thoughts: *Don't* sway your lower body too much. *Don't* drop your shoulder! *Don't* get ahead of yourself so you stay behind the ball. But the Chops swayed their lower body, dropped their shoulder and weren't behind the ball. When Cloudy had his chance to break 90 and nailed his great drive on 18 and stood over his second shot, he did the same thing. Just *don't* hit it in the trap. He did. Once in the sand trap, *don't* scoop it, *don't* stop the follow-through. He scooped and stopped his follow through. Why bother fighting The Don'ts? Didn't every club in his bag have the potential to cause a meltdown? So, let The Don't Gallery heckle all they want through the ropes until their don'ts were no different than the croaking frogs or chirping birds on the course. They merely came with the territory of each shot. Cloudy dropped a few balls. As he drew his club back they said, "*Don't* leave it short. *Don't* push it right. *Don't* yip!" Cloudy closed his eyes and got out of his way and dissolved into the pendulum rock of his shoulders. His putter never wavered. It dropped to the bottom of its arc. *The Feel* visited him. He listened to the ball rattle in the cup.

He opened his eyes.

Oh no, he thought. It can't be. But it was.

Another figure unmoored itself from at the bottom of Cloudy's swing arc to testify against him as a character witness... in the flesh.

"THAT'S GRAHAM NOT CRAM," said Tucker as Buttons snapped a photo. Tucker had his arm on his teenage son's shoulder then spoke like he was puffing a pipe between words. "It's the boy's third hole-in-one. Takes after me. I still hold the longest punt record at Staples High in Westport. Do I take it upon myself to report his achievement to the Darien News or task that due diligence to you?"

Tucker Graham's hair was brown, gray at his temples and full. He was heavier in the face and had over-the-pants-belt gut overhang. He wore the same preppie body armor that never goes out of style for his pedigree: polo shirt with a club insignia, khaki slacks and tasseled loafers. Tucker's son was a dutiful replica, thought Cloudy, a molded ReRun entitled to a first-class country club membership in New Canaan, or some other upper-class, East-Coast shithole. After Cloudy left Westport, there was no reason for him to stay in touch with Tucker, who never introduced Cloudy and Wendy to his friends or invited them to his parties. Throughout the summers, Cloudy remembered hearing Timothy's soulless baritone voice belt out boring arias through the open screen windows of the Graham manse. In fall, the arias were replaced by the leathery thump of a football as he practiced punting for his college team.

"Tucker?" said Cloudy standing on the putting green.

"Why, yes," Tucker stiffly replied, trying to maintain distance while remaining in one place.

"John Map."

"The Maps from *Jersey* who were our neighbors for twenty years," said Tucker, as if he was reading a label on a jar.

"Yes, that's what we did."

"I assume this day finds you well," he said, extending his hand to keep Cloudy at arm's length.

"Another day older, another Bud*wiser*," said Cloudy. "So what brings you out this way?"

Buttons sensed the stare-down on the putting green. He walked to the deck, leaned on the railing and took in the show.

"Wee Burn, our Darien club hosted a shotgun fundraising event for the pro's autistic daughter," said Tucker. "The boy and I here couldn't set up a tee time so we decided to *take in* a muni."

"Does 'the boy' have a name?"

Tucker clipped to his son, “Hark, put the clubs in the car.”

Oh no, another Harkness! thought Cloudy. The Graham family firm had grown another branch office. Harkness To The Fourth Power complied, taking his cushioned and casual steps on the commuter most traveled by: 1.) Graduate Ivy League. 2.) Live and work in New York. 3.) Intermarry within their elite-petting zoo. 4.) Move to Fairfield County to raise a family. 5.) Lay their eggs die at Cape Cod.

They didn’t have a tradition, they had a migratory pattern.

“Tuck, or should I say Frair Tuck because you’re carrying some extra poundage,” said Cloudy, patting Tucker’s overhang. “Do you still sing?”

“I dabble,” Tucker said, slightly taken back by his bowdlerization of his name—and worse, being *touched.* “I’ve always considered my voice an instrument.”

“Do you now? What band do you sing with?”

“I don’t.”

“But you said you still sing. What’s your band’s name?”

“I’m not a member of a band. I’m choral director in our church.”

“So you never really did *anything* with your voice,” said Cloudy, who paused. “You punted it.”

A taut restrained low flame of a gentrified glare crackled within Tucker’ patrician pupils.

“I have to toddle along.”

“Where you toddling’? Is the cravat outlet is having a sale?”

Tucker wasn’t accustomed to getting his yacht rocked in the marina. But formality was the weapon his father passed down to him.

“Our family is going to visit Mother and Father Graham at the Cape. Father’s retired from Gray,” replied Tucker, as he was reading cue cards held by a servant.

“So did Father pass down his apartment in The City to you?”

“Why, yes. It’s still in the family.”

“For when you get too *tired* to go home?”

“Tah,” Tucker clipped, abruptly, turned and departed.

“Don’t tah, me,” sharply said Cloudy. “Your Dad tah-ed my family to death and we didn’t deserve it. And you’re not going to continue the Harkness family tradition and tah me now or ever again! So just get tah fuck out of here.”

Tucker briskly walked off.

"Yeah, that's right, keep going. Maybe you and little Harkness can do some yard work at your house and trim a hedge fund together. Just keep going. Don't say anything, no last words from you or I'll punch you in that frickin' pompous-ass mouth of yours."

He grimly watched the Grahams quickly cram golf bags into a Volvo.

Buttons laughed and said, "Hey Chop, where's the love?"

"He doesn't take it personally. I'm confirming his father's opinion of me," Cloudy replied. "Nothing touches people like him because they never touch anybody else—unless you're *like* them."

Cloudy resumed his putting drill. The Don't Gallery was replaced by Grahams behind the ropes. The Grahams backs were turned away from him because they weren't concerned whether he sunk the putt or not. The Grahams said to one another: "*Don't* give him the time of day." They weren't roped off from Cloudy—he was roped off *from* them. He shut his eyes and stroked the putt. The ball rattled into the cup, but it felt more like a hollow achievement that echoed within him. He opened his eyes. The gallery was gone. So were the Grahams.

The cell phone vibrated in his pocket. Cloudy answered it.

"Hey—"

"Son," solemnly said his Dad.

Oh no, thought Cloudy. Something's wrong. His Dad rarely greeted him as an object. Was it Wendy? Did she overdose again? Did she…

"I had to take Mom to the doctor this morning," his Dad flatly said, mechanically and slowly. "She was—"

"Mom?"

"Her heart rate was 155," continued his Dad in an even steady tone. "They also found a hard-like tumor near her stomach. The hospital is doing a series of tests to find out about her heart." He paused. "I think Mom knows more than she's telling me."

"Okay."

"You should come home." His Dad paused. "I haven't told Wendy yet. I think we have enough on our hands now."

John Map Junior helplessly looked upward to the useless clear blue sky and softly croaked, "Mom."

Single's last remaining comfort zone was burned off: cloud cover.

O.B.
Without A Drop

HIS SLEEPING MOTHER WAS RESTLESS. Cloudy sat by her bedside at the St. Vincent Medical Center in Bridgeport. The monitor screen displayed a child-like lime scrawl of her vital signs. Above her lap was a suspended tray that held a sealed juice cup, a plastic-wrapped sandwich and a jelly doughnut with one bite out of it, which was the only piece of food he managed to get her to eat. Two weeks ago, he brought Fig Newtons, her favorite cookie, but the package remained unopened on a nightstand, along with the box of soft-centered chocolates beside her unread Get Well cards stacked by a vase of fresh flowers. Cloudy came every day. She'd be here for me, he thought, she'd be here for me.

"Oh, Mom," Cloudy quietly sighed, covering his face with his right hand and breathing in quick, sharp, mucous-snapping snorts. He ground his palms into his eyes and wiped streaks of tears down to his chin. He exhaled a prolonged mmmmm-groan. When he was sick, his mother selflessly pressed her soft cheek against his warm one to see if her son had a temperature. She never feared catching his cold. What could he do to ease her suffering now? Nothing. Why didn't he pick up the warning signs? But how could he? Death doesn't have a motive.

"I'm so thirsty and it hurts," she pleaded. "Help me, help me."

Help me, help me. Her plea lacerated through Cloudy, he shivered from the shock. *My mother said help me.*

"Nurse!" Cloudy cried, bolting from the room.

"Help me, help me."

Cloudy returned with help. The nurse's arrival infuriated his mother.

"Get that horrible bitch away from me!"

"Hello Mrs. Map," said the nurse, injecting drugs through the I.V. drip. "Let's see how you're doing."

"Go away," she said, then whispered to Cloudy, "Help me."

"There you are," said the nurse, who somehow tenderly added (minus the empathy) to Cloudy. "She's had *episodes* before. I see it a lot."

"Episodes?"

His mother scrunched her eyes and snapped, "Go. Kill someone else."

The nurse left. Cloudy followed her into the hallway.

"I wanted to thank you," said Cloudy. He lowered his voice. "My mother doesn't act like this to people." He paused. "That's not her."

"I can see by you who your mother really is," said the nurse. "Some women get mad when they're forced to leave their family unfinished."

"Unfinished?" said Cloudy, briefly confused. But he knew what the nurse meant. The Mom who gave her children so many chances was denied *her* second chance to sit down at the dining room table, read the Daily News, do a *New York Times* crossword puzzle and be there for her family.

A FEW MINUTES LATER, his mother opened her eyes, smiled at her son and said, "You look so much better with shorter hair. It brings out your blue eyes more. And you're dressed in pressed slacks and a nice shirt and shoes. As a kid you never liked clothes. All little kids like clothes but not *you*. I got you all dressed up on your 5th birthday party and you disappeared. All the kids came over. You come down the stairs, naked. So pleased with yourself, doing a funny dance with your head wobbling, shaking your shiny dupah. Always had to be the center of attention, my little rock star." She smiled and looked upon him with a quiet wonderment. "And you haven't changed, you or your sister. Wendy was born crying and hasn't stopped since. When she was little, the women in our apartment complex thought I was a terrible mother, until they got to know how Wendy was. Remember Dr. Caligaro in Clifton? Dr. Cal said to me, 'You can try to shape your children or you can let your kids become themselves.'"

"So that's why we're dysfunctional."

"You always have to get in the last word. Nobody could ever tell you anything unless you did get it in. You could dish it out but you couldn't take it. You've always been so thin-skinned." Cloudy sucked in his lips. Her remarks cut and stung. But they were true. His mother never judged or categorized people, Cloudy did. His Mom always looked at other people with a half smile, wondering what made them. Even when people got angry, she was quietly amused. And if they were difficult, she'd shrug and simply say, "That the way they are." And leave it at that. But Cloudy would have an opinion and dismiss them.

"Johnny," she said, looking inconsolable and frightened. "I didn't think it would happen this fast." He hung his head. His stomach seemed to fold over like a burnt tripe omelet. His bones felt heavier than the rest of his body. "I can't eat my lunch." She pointed to the tray. "You probably haven't had anything. I ordered ham with mustard on a poppy seed roll today." She pushed the meal toward him. "It's for you. I know you don't like mayonnaise. No pickles. I asked them to hollow out bread inside the roll too. I always loved to watch you eat, it made you strong." She closed her eyes.

While she slept, Cloudy ate the sandwich. He savored each piece in his mouth until it softened, then dryly swallowed. As sick as she was, his mother was still feeding him. Cloudy guiltily reviewed the times he hurt her. When he was seven, he wanted to buy baseball cards and she caught him stealing change from her purse. When he was thirteen, he was arrested for shoplifting a James Bond 'Dr. No' paperback at McCory's. In his sophomore year, Cloudy got thrown out of WestConn for partying in his dorm. His mother managed to get him back into the school. He lived off campus in a frat house. He gave his parents the impression he was going to graduate, but throughout the semester he partied and never cracked a book. When Graduation Day came, the family got ready to leave for the ceremony. Cloudy stood in the driveway, wearing a jacket and a tie. He hung his head, crunched the white gravel under his polished shoes and said, "I'm not graduating." His mother's face drooped as she said, "Thanks, John." He promised to never disappoint her again, but he did—and, often.

Car keys jangled at the doorway. Cloudy looked up. His distraught Dad shuffled into the room, hands in pockets. He winced as he looked at his wife and forlornly said, "My lady." He paused. "Last month, your mother insisted we fly down to Florida to visit Wendy. Before all this, I think she knew then." He looked down. "Mom decided against chemo. I agreed. I hope we made the right decision." He made a tight smile, nervously jangled the keys in his pocket again, looked at his wife and faintly added, "51 wonderful years..."

Well, the years weren't wonderful in Westport, thought Cloudy, the longer the Maps lived in Fairfield County, the earlier and longer his parents drank and bickered. A typical summer evening had Clear, Cloudy and Nana in the family room watching TV. Nana made a point of finishing her dinner first. Clear and Cloudy hadn't eaten yet. They sat behind wooden tray tables and drank. Clear was working on his third vodka. He was in his Battleground golf clothes. Cloudy had finished his shipping and receiving shift at Stew Leonard's and was into his second beer. The air conditioner was going full blast.

"Turn the TV up louder for my old ears, please," said Nana. "Does the conditioner have to be on? It's so cold in here."

"It's 90 degrees outside," said Cloudy, getting up for another beer.

Wendy stuck her head into the room from the kitchen and said, "Nana, do you want your after-dinner glass of white wine and apple?"

"I'm not helpless," Nana snapped. "I might be in a walker, but I can get my own wine and apple." She paused. "Patsy?"

There was no response.

"Patsy!" shouted Nana, her voice rising.

"What?" his mother sharply countered but remained in the kitchen.

"Do you need any help?"

"No!" she barked.

"Your wife won't let me do anything," crossly muttered Nana to her son for sympathy. "I always offer to help make dinner before she comes home from work at Clairol to make it easier for her. She won't let me. On Thanksgiving your wife wouldn't let me peel potatoes. On Easter she wouldn't let me make my split pea soup from the ham bone. I made my barley soup yesterday, she got mad at me. Said it was salty."

Cloudy returned with a beer.

Nana glared at Cloudy, and said, "Oh, so I guess, I'm *nobody*."

"What Nan?" said Cloudy, sitting down, puzzled.

She snapped, "You could have asked me if I wanted anything."

"Nan, Wendy just asked you if you wanted something and you got mad. And if I don't ask you, then you still get mad."

"I'm obviously in everyone's way so I'll turn in," she pouted, uneasily rising on her walker to leave. "Maybe I won't wake up in the morning and you won't have to burdened by my presence any longer."

The phone rang. Wendy rushed to answer it. She was dressed to meet Eggplant for dinner. Their relationship was in its early stages. Eggplant had come over a few times for meals, but he was on his best behavior. Why wouldn't he be? Cloudy thought much later, after all a spider doesn't paint its web.

"Who could that possibly be," said Clear, rolling his eyes. "Eggplant?"

"Hi, honey bunny!" Wendy said cheerfully answering the phone and smiling. "I'm leaving now." She hung up. "He always calls me. Calls to make sure I get home. Calls me at work. Calls me at lunch. Always wants to know where I am and what I'm doing. He's even getting me one of those new cell phones! I'll see you later. Bye."

Wendy turned and walked straight into the closed sliding door that led to the screened-in patio deck. Her head banged against the glass, rattling the frame. She staggered backwards.

"Jesus, what was that?" said Clear, startled.

"What do you *think* happened?" asked Cloudy, clapping his hands and laughing. "She did it again."

"It's not funny!" said Wendy, holding her head. "You and Dad are always making fun of me." She pointed at the sliding door. "When the windows are clean, the door looks open. And it's not just me, before we screened-in the outside deck birds flew into the door all the time."

"Yeah, birds!" said Cloudy. "Birds have brains the size of a pencil eraser. When you leave a room that has carpeting, a couch, a TV and air conditioning then head into a different place where there's grass, sky and squirrels, don't you think there might be *something* separating those two worlds? Like maybe... a thick layer of glass attached to a door in a wall of a house?"

"Well, that's you, that's how you think," Wendy said, going through the kitchen door. "Now I have to redo my makeup."

"Oh, I bought these today at Caldor's, but forgot to put them up," their Mom said entering the family room. She held up colorful bird stickers and started putting them at eye-level on the glass door. "See? Now you can tell if the door is closed or open."

Clear sighed in mock dismay, "Stickers on the windows to remind my daughter she's leaving the house." He paused. "A college graduate."

"I don't like this sticker. It's a crow," said their Mom. "Crows ate the ducklings in our pond. Oh! Here's a toucan. They're cute." She put the last sticker on the door, went in the kitchen and returned to put plates of spaghetti and meatballs on the tray tables. She said to Cloudy, "I made the special *thin* spaghetti you like, brat. Here are three paper napkins to wipe your spoiled fat lips."

"Waiting on her *sonny*," said Clear, teasing.

"Since I'm up, Father," she said, "do you want a beer with dinner?"

"I'm fine," Clear replied, his eyes widening as he rubbed his hands. "Oh, look at this meal!"

"There's some garlic bread in the oven," she said, leaving.

Clear lowered his voice and confided to his son, "Your mother's *not* going back in the kitchen to get garlic bread."

His Dad was right. Cloudy heard the opening freezer door's sticky peeling suction followed by her digging out ice cubes. She returned with bread, her plate and a bottomless glass of scotch. She sat on the rug by a low table in front of the couch and lit a cigarette.

Clear fanned the air and said, "Cigarettes are what now? Four dollars a pack?" He coughed, over exaggerating the smoke's effect.

"It's out," his Mom snapped, twisting the cigarette in the ashtray, which was next to a boy-and-girl Hummel figurine.

"Outdid yourself again Patsy, wonderful," said Clear, returning to his meal. He glanced at Cloudy's frosted mug. "That beer does look good."

"I'll get you one," his wife sighed, slowly rising.

"Patsy, you just got comfortable," Clear protested. "I'm fine."

"You know you want a beer, so eat your dinner," curtly said his wife, who brought back a frosted mug and a can of beer.

"I'm heading out!" excitedly said Wendy bursting out of the kitchen and through the family room.

"Watch the door!"

She banged into the glass again.

Cloudy laughed.

"I can't believe you did that!" said Clear.

"Maybe I should buy some more bird stickers," their Mom said, clicking her thumbnail with her teeth, pondering. "Or bigger ones."

"I'm so useless," said Wendy, leaving.

They ate and watched the end of the news.

"I've never trusted Walter Mondale," said his mother staring at the TV. "He looks like my sister Bunny's first husband."

"Is it tomorrow or next Sunday we have that wedding in Jersey?"

"The invitation has been on the fridge for a month. Tomorrow."

"Tomorrow?" he griped. "I'm dragging my ass on a beautiful summer day to Jersey? Can't we send a check? I get soaked for every baptism and marriage in your family. Who has a wedding on a Sunday? Most people work Monday. We'll hit shore traffic going down. The bridge traffic coming back will be murder. A long drawn-out ordeal—"

"Fine, we won't go!" she testily said, grabbed her dinner, stamped into the kitchen and snarled, "Fuck you!"

"What did I say?" said Clear. He simmered then dourly grumbled to himself, "Jesus Christ, I ask a simple question and this is how people in my own house talk to me. Swearing. Smoking." He shuddered. "Goddamn it. I'm only talking and everyone explodes!"

"Like what you're doing now?" Cloudy asked.

"Another country heard from," replied his Dad. "I'll call the embassy."

"The Yanks are on," said Cloudy, hitting the TV remote.

"You call that team Yankees?" said Clear, flapping his lips.

"This game is dedicated to the late great Thurmon Munson!" said Cloudy, intentionally baiting his Dad. "Cut down in his prime."

"He was a bum," said Clear, who listed the years *his* Yankees won the World Series. "1937, 1938, 1939, 1941, 1942. Tommy Hendrick, Red Rolfe, Lefty Grove, Frankie Crosetti. Hall of Famers all and you hear nothing about them. Back in the twenties, can you imagine seeing Babe Ruth in a chinchilla coat, in a Ben Hogan hat, driving a Stutz Bearcat down Fifth Avenue? How can anyone tell me he wasn't the greatest ballplayer of all time? That's a Yankee!"

"Yeah, but what about Gene 'The Stick' Michaels'?" said Cloudy, running through the Yankees' mediocre roster during the sixties. "Stan Bahnsen, Fritz Peterson, Horace Clark, Roy White, Bobby Murcer, Jerry Kenney. And let's not forget: Roger Repoz." He paused. "I think I still have those baseball cards somewhere."

"Please, those are not *my* Yankees," said Clear. "Stop."

"Ron Bloomberg, the first designated hitter."

"There's a distinction! Being good enough to bat for a pitcher."

The men silently finished their meals and watched the game. Clear closed his eyes.

"Dad, why don't you go to bed?"

"It's too early," he said, nodding off.

Cloudy heard the freezer door open again. The metallic clink of ice in a glass. He gathered up the dishes and went into the kitchen.

"Leave them in the sink," his Mom said, sitting at the table with her scotch, lighting up a cigarette and listening to the portable radio play 'The Night The Lights Went Out In Georgia' sung by Vicki Lawrence.

"I like this song, it tells a story," she said, nodding.

A sleepy Clear padded in his socks past them, uttering mock groans of pleasure from the meal. He went down the hallway and said, "Time for the old man to turn in. Dinner was another winner, Patsy."

His wife didn't reply, she looked off and said to her son, "Sometimes I think your father would have been happier showing off how much he knows by being a professor and teaching history at a college and not having any kids. He gets up early to read his paper before Nana wakes up so he can avoid her. Then he goes off and always leaves me with her. As he's getting older, he's getting more selfish. He was raised an only child and he's becoming one again. Weekends all he cares about is the club, the club. I can't stand going to those club functions. The husbands only talk to each other and drink too much and won't dance with their wives. The last time we went, a couple at our table argued and swore at each other all night. No one acted like that in Freehold. Maybe a person in the couple might be in a bad mood, but nothing like *that*." She exhaled. "We danced together more in Freehold."

The move from Jersey was hard on his Mom. During their first summer in Westport, Cloudy helped her plant a mimosa tree in the center of the front lawn and hydrangeas along the foundation below the street-facing windows of the house like they did in Freehold. In Stonehurst, they struggled to dig through the orange hard clay because the developer took out the topsoil and sold it before he built the houses, but Connecticut ground was different. They quickly realized why there were so many low stone fences and large boulders placed on every residential street corner in the Fairfield County. With every shovelful, Cloudy hit and unearthed and scraped out several French-roll sized gray rocks in the dark, rich soil. In the first couple years, his mother joined the Westport Young Women's Club, did volunteer work, built floats for parades (and used her own money to purchase materials for decorations). After she participated in these events, she was stunned none of the women invited her over to their homes for coffee.

She threw a housewarming party. The Grahams were "unable to attend." The rest of the neighbors came. They brought less than they took, drank the liquor cabinet dry, name-dropped, argued with their spouses and when his Mom went into the kitchen a husband grabbed her ass. She decided to live for her job at Clairol and provide for the family. Here she was, Cloudy thought, alone at the kitchen table on a Saturday night with a scotch. She spent so many evenings staying up late, watching TV, drinking and making long distance calls to her friends in Freehold or sisters in Lyndhurst. For her, trying to recreate a Freehold life in Fairfield County was like planting hydrangeas by the house—it wasn't worth the effort to sift through the rocks.

"Do you want dessert?" she asked Cloudy. "I went shopping and bought some Yodels. They're in the freezer—and brat, I also picked up Chocolate Chocolate Chip Häagen-Dazs ice cream for you too."

"Thanks. Maybe later. I'm playing a gig with Pudge."

The patio door slid back.

"Yo, Dawg!" said Pudge, strutting into the kitchen. He tried to look casual and relaxed in the Map home, but couldn't conceal his jealousy: he viewed anything others had through the bars of caged resentment. "Hey, Mrs. M., smells good in here."

"Did you eat yet, Pudge?" she asked, getting up.

"I'll grab something at the club They have good nachos."

"I put extra spaghetti in Tupperware for you, it's on the counter. You can take it with you."

"Yeah, I could use the roughage after the gig," said Pudge.

"The only reason we even have leftovers tonight is because Eggplant took Wendy out instead of having dinner here. That man can eat. He inhales food. I don't think he even tastes it. Shovels it into his mouth. We never have leftovers if he's here, ever. He never leaves anything, even dessert." She paused. "Don't forget to bring back the bowl."

Pudge said, "I'll meet you out in the car, Dawg."

Cloudy watched Pudge go and said to his mother, "He never says, 'Thank you.' Kiss that bowl goodbye. He doesn't return anything."

"He wasn't taught how to behave, his parents weren't there for him. Never hurts to be kind," she said. "Where are you two low-lifes off to?"

"Who knows, Mom?"

"Johnny, do you need any money?"

"No, I'm fine."

"Get Dad's wallet."

Cloudy took the wallet from the kitchen counter.

"Have a good time," she said, handing him a twenty. She perked up. "Maybe there is a scary movie I can watch on TV tonight."

Cloudy grabbed the entertainment section. "Yeah, *The Birds*. Hitchcock. You like Hitchcock."

"That's a good one," she said, then added in a concerned tone. "You sound stuffy. Like you a still have a touch of a cold. Come here." He bent over. She pressed her warm, soft cheek against his. "You're still a little warm."

"I'm okay," Cloudy replied, standing up. "Mom, why not invite people you work with at Clairol to the house some weekend?"

"I can't have them come here. If they saw how we lived, they'd never talk to me again," she said, taking a sip of her scotch, the ice cubes rattled and Cloudy imagined the booze slithering down her throat like a poisonous snake.

"Mom, do you need anything?"

"Bring the phone over."

"MAYBE MOM WAS RIGHT, we should have never left Freehold," Clear said in a faltering voice at his wife's hospital bed. His shoulders shook as he blubbered, "Why did I move our family here? I could have found another job in Jersey. She's my lady, I should have taken better care of her. She's my lady." He gulped and recovered. "I thought the move would be good for us." He sliced away his tears with the edge of his hand. "Son, when you were in college and Wendy was looking at schools and we were living in Westport, Mom saw our bills and without me saying anything, she went out a got a job. I always admired her for that. My Patsy could see numbers. A lot of women can't. She was proud of her customer service job at Clairol too. Look how good she did as a high school graduate. They sent her on business trips. She supervised people. She was popular at work. She worked hard. Then the bastards laid her off and kept all the dead wood. That's what they did to my Patsy. She never got over that." He regretfully added, "And...leaving Freehold. She loved that Stonehurst house.

She was so happy there. What is wrong with me?" He reflected for a moment, then looked bewildered. "I searched for some papers in the house. I found letters that I wrote to Mom when I was in college. She kept them! I never knew they were there." Clear jangled the keys in his pocket. "In one letter I was asking for a picture of her in a bathing suit." He paused. "She saved them, she saved them all."

"Father?" plaintively said his wife, weakly turning toward him. "What do you want me to do?"

His Dad looked away. Cloudy studied his parents. They existed in a plane beyond their arguments, disappointments, dancing and laughter—and beyond Cloudy. Growing up, he never overheard their private conversations, financial worries or intimacies in bed. The only time Cloudy was in a hospital room with his parents was in Freehold, when little Matthew was born. Cloudy was nine. Wendy stood next to him. Their Mom cradled her new son. She sat up, propped against a pillow. She wore a blue nightgown. She smiled, radiant, victorious. More beautiful than he had ever seen her. Dad humbly reverent at the foot of her bed like it was an altar, admiring her. It was the first time Cloudy saw the love that united them. *The Feel* was real.

And now, as he Dad jangled the car keys in his pocket, Cloudy felt that love again. Its force overpowered him with a sense of loss and left him wanting less of himself and more of them.

"When was your first date with Mom, Dad?"

"I don't know," he said indifferently, shrugging.

She said, "My cousin Terry was going out with a guy she didn't like and asked me to go along on the date with her cousin John."

"Whatever," said his Dad.

"That night we went to this place, off Route 33, it was..."

"Whatever."

"I forget the name."

"Rudy's," affectionately added his Dad with emphasis. "Rudy's."

"So how was the date, Mom?"

"Well, we had a second one. So, I guess it was good."

"Dad, where did you ask Mom to marry you?"

"Whatever."

"Seaside Heights by the beach," she softly replied.

"Worked all summer for that ring," he added, looking at his wife.

Cloudy's Mom held up her bruised hand with the I.V needle and said, "When we lived in Clifton and Freehold, I added you kids' birthstones to my wedding ring. There's you, Wendy, and baby Matthew. You know, when we were at the cemetery, our neighbors in Freehold cleaned out our home of all his baby things. Mr. Louro took the crib back to Britts Department store and said, 'It's new. The crib's got everything on it. I don't have a receipt. Their baby died.' And the store took it back. But they did miss something. When we got home from little Matthew's service, I went through the dryer. There were his little baby clothes." Cloudy expected her to cry, but she didn't. She weakly smiled. "You and Wendy's birthstones stayed in my ring, but little Matthew's stone always falls out. Makes you wonder doesn't it?"

"Poor little guy," said Clear. "His tiny white marble casket. All closed at his grave. I'll never forget that sight."

"Dad, I still know our old phone numbers from Clifton and Freehold."

"You do?" said Clear, surprised and curious.

"Clifton was Gregory-2 1974."

"Gregory-2 1974," said Clear, pleasantly. "Pat, Gregory-2 1974!"

"What?" she asked.

"Our number in Clifton, when we had an apartment."

"The apartment in North Jersey," she said. "Before we moved to Freehold. Remember when we drove down to look at Stonehurst. I saw those beautiful model houses and huge yards. I couldn't believe my family could live like that. It was a dream, a dream."

"Freehold was 462-5343," added Cloudy.

"462-5343," Clear fondly said, as if the numbers were a combination to a vault from the past filled with laughter, music and friends.

"Father, I was thinking about Martha. She was a good cat."

"Martha," his Dad said, as if entering a guilty plea. "Martha. That damn tramp of a cat we had in Freehold?"

"Martha was a good cat. She always had her kittens in the bathroom. I fixed up a bed of towels for her under the sink. I'd pet her tummy until a kitten came out. Then she looked at me because she wanted to be alone to clean her baby. I said, 'Okay Martha.' Then I'd leave. After Martha cleaned up her first kitten, she come out and meow for me. I'd go in. She'd lie down. I'd pet her again. She'd have another kitten. And I'd leave. She'd come out and meow. She and I had five that day."

"You said it would teach me about life," said Cloudy.

"That's why I had to take Martha to the pound. She kept getting knocked up," said Clear. "When I brought her there, they told me *I* had to put her in the cage. I did. Martha scratched me." Clear rubbed the top of his right hand and looked down. "I deserved it." He paused. "I wouldn't do that today." He smiled. "Our dumb Freehold cat."

"I think there's still some Yodels in the fridge," she said to Cloudy, then closed her eyes. They waited for her to speak. She was asleep.

"She's somewhere else, that's nice," said Clear, who looked crumpled, as if his body was on a hanger instead of a skeleton, his clothes loosely draped over him. "Yodels," repeated Clear, shaking his head and stared at her with admiration. "My Patsy was always about you kids. She is all Mom. Back in Freehold, she won $75 at St. Rose of Lima's Bingo. She was all excited! She got you the baseball glove you wanted, Wendy a nice pair of shoes, a steak for me and an oil painting for the living room. She never spent a dime on herself. We came first. That's my Patsy, my lady."

The monitor beeped and pumped medication into her.

"Hey Dad?"

"Yes, son."

"Little Matthew. His middle name was David. Who was David? We don't have an Uncle David. Mom didn't have a brother David. Nobody I know in our family is a David. So why was his middle name David?"

"I don't know," said Clear and jangled the keys in his pocket. "Later today they're placing her in the hospice they took Nana years ago. They said it's 'palliative care.'"

Cloudy dialed back to Nana's funeral. He didn't cry or offer any sympathy to his father. Wendy placed a plastic-wrapped glass of white wine and an apple in Nana's coffin. His Dad watched her and sadly noted, "At least I know someone in my family loved my mother." And now, Cloudy was losing *his* mother and his Dad was losing his wife. Cloudy didn't want to be *that* cloudy anymore.

"Dad," blurted Cloudy. "I'm sorry about Nana and how I acted at her funeral. I didn't appreciate her like I should have. I was wrong."

Clear was taken aback, but deeply touched and said, "Just when I think you're going to crash into a mountain on takeoff, you clear it. You've always surprised me. Always have. Always will."

"What I remember most about Nana," said Cloudy. "She was big on taking pictures of the family. She had that Kodak Instamatic camera and nearly every time she gathered the whole room together the flash never worked."

"That did happen a lot didn't it? Your Nana, when you think of all the things she accomplished and didn't even have a high school education. No grass grew under her feet," said Clear smiled. "Your Nana, she thought you were *her* kids. I wish she and Mom got along better. Yet, those two went to church every Sunday, but God was never able to build a big enough kitchen for them to get along in." He paused. "You've been here all day, why don't you take a break, I'll sit here with Mommy and read the newspaper."

"If that's okay," Cloudy said, remaining in the chair. "I might hit a few golf balls."

"Golfing? You? Since when?"

"Surprise," said Cloudy. "Just cleared another mountain on takeoff."

He kissed his sleeping Mom goodbye.

On his way out, he looked back. His Dad stood at the foot of the bed, jingled the car keys in his pocket once, looked at his wife and smiled and reflectively said, "Gregory-2 1974. 462-5343. Huh."

"CLOUDY SINGLE TO THE FIRST TEE," a disembodied voice announced on the Ironwoods golf course PA system.

On the first four holes Cloudy felt he was suspended in a stinging, syrupy haze. It was 90. Humid. He licked his lips and tasted salty sweat. He enjoyed the discomfort and the edginess. The sun glared off the grass. The course was in a soft focus, as if filtered through cheesecloth. He was disoriented. Above him, two Red-tailed hawks glided lazily for gophers and feral kittens. On the fairways there was no mother in pain. Just a tee-to-green world sedative. He got out of his way. He no longer existed. He didn't want to. As Cloudy played, he lost himself in the motion of his club as it dropped into the bottom of its arc and connected him into the sweet spot of the present.

But when Cloudy got to the 5th tee, the spell broke.

An abandoned infant in a plastic carrier was on the grass between the 5th tee-box markers. Who left this child here? he wondered. What if the baby had crawled from the carrier into the nearby water hazard and drowned? He reached for his cell phone to dial 911.

"Hey Don Junior, miss your Daddy?" said Arax carrying his clubs. He knelt down, picked up a rattle and put it into the boy's small hand. Then he spoke to Cloudy, "The kid has a strong grip."

"Oh," said Cloudy, numbed. "That's *your* son?"

"Until the good Lord comes down and tells me otherwise," said Arax, who shouldered off his golf bag. He was wearing sweat pants, a black shirt, and white socks. The sock on his right leg had a bulge in it.

"Two foursomes ahead of us," said Cloudy. "Might as well join me."

"Yeah, I guess I have to," replied Arax. "I got tired of waiting behind two groups so I replayed number 2. No point in lugging the kid the whole way so I left him here." Arax casually swung his club at a flower, decapitating the bud from the stem with a crisp snap. The purple petal puff sailed into the pond. He chortled. "I'm Don. Want a Lifesaver? They're Peppermint."

"Thanks, I'll pass," replied Cloudy, realizing Arax didn't recognize him without his ponytail.

Arax pointed at the floating flower on the water and gleefully added, "Hey check out the carnage: pickerel-and-duck action."

"Where?" said Cloudy who walked over and saw a pickerel closing in on the stray duckling. The clueless bird had fallen behind its mother. The rest of the brood trailed her and safely waddled out of the pond. Cloudy chucked a golf ball at the charging fish. The water splashed. The pickerel darted into the lily pads. The frightened duckling squawked and scrambled up the bank and rejoined the family.

"Go little guy. Go back to Mommy," urged Cloudy, smiling.

"Why'd you ruin the show?" said Arax, snorting. "You're no fun."

"Nobody eats ducklings on my watch," said Cloudy, who set up over his ball and hit a drive down the fairway.

"Looks like you barely went 225," said Arax, popping a Peppermint Lifesaver into his mouth. "Does your husband play golf too?"

"It'll play."

"This hole cries out for a draw," Arax noted, teeing up. He added, "Damn course has more dog legs than a Korean Restaurant."

Arax pulled his drive. It was going O.B..

"Stay in," said Cloudy.

"Don't talk to my ball!" growled Arax. His drive flew over a fence and clanged against the wind chimes on a mobile home's patio deck. "See what you did?" said Arax, slamming his driver down. "Shit on my dog. Woof! I'm not starting off this hole like that. No way."

"So you're taking a mulligan?"

"You can have one too."

"I don't take mulligans."

"Then you only have yourself to blame," Arax said, teeing up another ball and giving himself a pep talk, "A gak drive with a draw on the screws. Followed by a solid wedge to the left of the pin. Roll a putt one-ball left of the cup for the bird." His downswing grated the earth. The ball shot out like a flushed quail and wrapped around the dog-leg fairway. "I can do business with that." He patted the crucifix bulge like it was a pet and nodded. "Roped it 300 yards. In the short stuff." He studied the driver's clubface. "That was a lower groove shot."

"You want me to keep score?"

"I keep score in my head," Arax firmly said. He shouldered his bag, grabbed the baby carrier and strutted down the fairway.

"Fore right!" hollered a golfer from another tee.

A golf ball bounced to Arax's left and narrowly missed the baby's head. Cloudy cringed. Arax didn't react or break his stride.

"Don Junior didn't even flinch," Arax said proudly. "Kid's a gamer."

THROUGHOUT THE FRONT NINE, Arax unleashed mondo drives that split tight fairways, reached par-5 greens in two and set up birdies on par-4s by aggressively hitting wedges to sucker pins tucked behind sand traps. In comparison, Cloudy's play was uneventfully precise, hitting fairways with drives that put him within 160 yards of the pin. He got on a few greens in regulation. Other times, he'd land short, chip up and stroke several perfectly, placed putts for par. He didn't think much about it, but knew he was scoring well.

On the 9th hole, Arax sliced his drive.

"Stay in," said Cloudy, smirking.

"Don't talk to my ball!" strenuously objected Arax, scowling as his shot skittered into deep rough. "Didn't I tell you not to talk to my ball!"

"My bad," replied Cloudy. "I was trying to be supportive."

"I don't need it."

When they got to Arax's shot, he cheated with candy.

"I have to identify my ball," Arax said. He covered his mouth to conceal ejecting a slimmed down Lifesaver through lips into a cupped palm. He reached down and picked up his ball. "'Prov: 8:35.' This is me all right." Arax furtively slid the white round-holed candy beneath the ball and replaced it in the rough. He swung. His shot landed on the green. He crowed, "Own it!"

"Impressive hit from a tough lie," said Cloudy, amused.

"Let's make it interesting, back nine for a beer?" said Arax, sucking a another Lifesaver between his lips. "Spot you a stroke on each hole."

"Sure, Donald."

"That *Don*."

"Bill," said Cloudy, who didn't want Arax to remember him.

"Huh, Bill. What's your last name: Past Due?"

"Yeah, I guess you can say that."

WHEN TWO COMPETING RIVALS reached the 18th green, Cloudy didn't know his exact score, but he was clearly beating Arax, who was well aware of it, simmering and ready to explode.

Arax lined up a three-foot putt. He stroked it.

"Go in!" said Cloudy.

"Don't talk to my ball!"

The putt spun around the rim of the hole but didn't drop.

"Shit on my dog, woof!" Arax grumbled. "I'm lipping out more than a gynecologist at rush hour in free clinic." He snatched up his ball and walked away adding, "I'm giving myself a four on this hole because I always par it. So you can—" He was interrupted by a 'Braveheart Theme' ringtone in his right sock. "Gotta be the War Department," Arax muttered, peeling down his sock and pulling out his phone, which was wrapped in a rubber band around a wallet. The rubber band broke. The wallet's contents spilled out the high grass near the green. Arax answered the phone, "I'm in the car now." He shut the phone, quickly swept the contents of his wallet and grabbed his bag. "Have to bolt. The wife. I'll get you back on that beer."

"You forgot your baby."

"Thanks," said Arax, who returned for the carrier and stamped away.

Cloudy spied the sun reflecting off a forgotten plastic card that fell from Arax's wallet. It was Arax's USGA card with his GHIN number. Cloudy deviously smiled. He had an idea. He tucked the card in his pocket and went to his ball. He closed his eyes. The Don't Gallery pressed against the ropes and taunted him: "*Don't* leave it short. *Don't* yip. *Don't* push it." He firmly stroked the putt. The ball rattled in the cup. He opened his eyes and totaled up his score. An 89! He couldn't believe it. Cloudy reflected on his play. He didn't hit long drives. His approach shots were good but nothing fantastic. He got up-and-down one-putting most of the greens. That was the key. Cloudy replaced the flagstick like an explorer planting a flag to claim a new land. The cell phone in his front pocket vibrated. He pulled it out and looked at the screen. A Florida number. Cloudy's career high vanished. The call transformed him back into his original form: an unemployed guy in his forties with an alcoholic sister whose mother was dying from cancer. Not a good way to end a round.

"Hello, Wendy."

"Dad's flying me home in couple days. Mom's going in a hospice?"

"Yes."

"My friend Sue is picking me up at the airport. You've met her before."

"One of your AA-people, right? Who live off each other's dramas like vampires? Don't you have any normal friends with *real* lives?"

"She's meeting me at the airport. You aren't."

"You're a big girl."

There was a pause.

"Where did Mom go to high school?" Wendy asked.

"Huh?"

"I asked where Mom went to high school. You don't know do you?"

"No."

"When is her birthday?"

"February something."

"Her wedding anniversary?"

"You always told me when it was coming up."

"September 10th."

"Good for you."

"What's her favorite food?"

"Fig Newtons."

"Those are cookies. I said food. What about food?"

"Uh, I know what she cooked best."

"You don't know, do you? I do! Because I shopped and cooked with her. Mom likes peanut butter from a jar, macaroni and cheese, cracked king crab, mayonnaise-and-banana sandwiches, ribs, liver and onions."

"God, liver and onions! That's right. I couldn't stand watching her eat that stuff."

"And what perfume did Mom use?"

"Was it Channel?"

"She never used perfume. Mom said she liked the smell of perfume on other women, but not on her."

"I'm losing you. You're breaking up," he lied, shutting his phone.

Why wasn't he able to answer his sister's questions? The pathetic answer: Cloudy only knew what his Mom had done *for* him. How long had he been taking those mulligans?

AFTER BREAKING 90, Cloudy left the bus and went into the Super Stop & Shop, carrying his golf clubs. He walked down the aisle with a 30-pack of Budweiser and a frozen Tree Tavern Pizza. A young mother wheeled a shopping cart past him. She was in her crisp twenties with a whining 10-year-old son and a sulking 7-year-old daughter.

"Ice cream," the boy demanded greedily. "Chocolate Ripple."

"We get ice cream last so it won't melt in the basket," the mom said.

"I want Strawberry," said the girl.

"Strawberry's stupid! Chocolate Ripple," the boy insisted, sharply thumping a fist in the middle of his sister's back. "And you're ugly."

"Ow! He hit me."

"Don't hit your sister."

"It didn't hurt," said the boy. "She acting."

The woman was the same age as Cloudy's Mom when he was ten and Wendy was seven. Cloudy wondered how many times his Mom circled aisles like these. And here he was, amid all these shelves of food and what was he making for dinner? Beer and frozen pizza. He never learned to cook. Growing up, he polished off his plate, left it unwashed in the sink and waited for dessert. That was it. A slightly bowed Cloudy threaded down the aisles among the Moms wheeling shopping carts who were trailed by their insatiable children. *The Feel* visited him. It pinned him into an unfocused awe of these ladies. These wonderful women. It was like he had never seen them before and they had been around him his whole life. They were gorgeous. No centerfold could capture their beauty. Their tasks didn't have a checkout line. How many school lunches had these Moms made? How many clothes had they ironed and folded? How many dishes and pots and pans had these Moms washed? How many pieces of furniture had they polished? What about the diapers they changed? The spills they wiped off counters? The toilets, sinks and bathtubs they scrubbed. The floors they mopped and waxed. And the jobs they took to support their kids. These women. His mother was one of them. Her hospital pleas haunted him. *Help me.* He choked up. *I didn't think it would happen so fast.* Cloudy slogged along, as if he was up to his hips, bogged down against a current. He was drawn back to those Freehold holiday meals. How he was embraced by the kitchen's warmth. That warmth! Pots simmered atop every blue flame on the stove. The smell of biscuits in the oven. On the counter, trays of kielbasa, kabusta, pierogis and a tin-foil covered bowl of home-made eggnog. His Mom always left two detached mixer beaters covered with mashed potatoes on a cutting board for him to lick. He picked up a beater and ran his tongue along the curved steel prongs, licking off hot clumps. His Mom stood by the fridge behind Wendy, carefully combing her daughter's luxuriant brown hair. Nana wasn't living with them, she was up for holiday. Outside Cloudy saw Nana's car parked in the driveway, a Plymouth Valiant its back seat loaded with Christmas presents, a box of Kleenex by the rear window. Nana sat at the table and hand rolled pierogis with her 80-year-old hands. She smiled at the two women. He'd never enter that kitchen again. Cloudy leadenly dragged his feet down the aisles as tears dribbled down his face. Those women gave him the gift of love and he didn't have the sense to unwrap it until his mother was dying.

Cloudy sat on the couch, watched *Seinfeld*, polished off the Tree Tavern pizza and drained his fourth Budweiser. He went into the bedroom, slid back the steamer trunk and lifted the piece of flooring beneath it. He pulled out a small metal box that had over $16,000 in envelopes, a set of scales and a plastic container of weed and packets of cocaine. It was time for a clearance sale. Cloudy broke his dealer's rule. He impulsively contacted customers and told them to come to his house. He sold the last of his stash for $3,750 and tossed his scales into a neighbor's dumpster. Cloudy yanked the mildewed and muddy tarp off the Tercel. The car was coated with grime. It had three flats. He washed it. He vacuumed the interior. When he was finished, he sat behind the wheel. He looked down and found a perfectly preserved French fry lodged under the emergency brake between the seats. Just for the hell of it, he turned the key in the ignition. The car was dead. He decided to tow the Toyota to a garage for new tires, a battery and a tune up. It was 8:30. A Wednesday night. If he was going to go out, he definitely smelled a little ripe and needed to wash up.

In the shower, Cloudy kneaded shampoo into his greasy, dirty scalp. He imagined his fingers were scrubbing out his mother's cancer cells. Cloudy toweled off, went into his room, pulled back the clean sheets, fluffed up a pillow and lay naked in bed. He felt a cool breeze through the screen window coast over his body. He heard the calming sound of a rotary lawn sprinkler metal-plate flap click against the shooting stream of water. It tapped out a metronomic ssst-click-ssst-click-ssst code that dialed Cloudy back to a Freehold summer. He was tooling down Stonehurst Way on an AMF Stingray bike that had a banana seat, a 5-speed stick shift, shoulder-high raised handlebars and streamers dangling from hand grips. He weaved up a driveway curb cut and onto the sidewalk in front of a neighbor's house and sped through front lawn sprinkler's spray. The water cooled and dampened the back of his T-shirt, invigorating him. He weaved down the next driveway to the street, popped a quick wheelie, went up another driveway onto the sidewalk and through another sprinkler shower. Every rubbery cutting turn of his front tires flashed with thrill and drive. He wasn't Cloudy back then. His top concern in life: getting home in time for dinner.

I didn't think it would happen so fast.

He buried his face into a pillow and muffled a groan, "Oh Mom.

Mom. You don't deserve what's happening, you don't deserve it."

Cloudy made short, jagged coughs and cried. His throat ached. The pollen of grief hit him hard. His eyes stung. He ground the heels of his palms into his sockets and smeared warm wet tears in streaks across his cheeks. He thought of his mother being put in a hospice bed, held in place by tubes. She couldn't leave. He could! He shivered, sprung up, dressed and bounded towards the scent of roasting coffee in the lingering trails of the summer night.

"DOUBLE MOCHA WITH WHIP CREAM—and some mint, please," said Cloudy, nervously standing at the Same Old Grind's counter. Penny's back was to him.

"I predicted you'd like it. I'm addicting," said Penny, spinning around and smiling. "You cleaned up your act. The guy from Jersey *sans* his ponytail. I thought you blew me off."

"I'm sorry, when I get caught up in stuff, I lose perspective. All I was thinking about was myself and golf and nothing else. That's the way I was in music too, with anything I wanted," said Cloudy. "It's not something I'm proud of." He paused. "But, it got me this far."

"At *least* it got you this far," said Penny, searching his face. "*Dar*-link, you're not right. Look at you, all peekid."

"My Mom's dying," Cloudy said softly, looking down, shifting his feet. "It's not fair for me to lay this on you. You don't know me and all."

"Barb, I have to leave," said Penny to a barista coworker. "We're slow here, anyway. I mean who wants a stale croissant at night?"

"Just the junkies," her friend and said, "Cover my morning tomorrow."

"Yeah," said Penny, who hooked her arm around Cloudy. "Guess you need a drink. Never been to the Hugga Mug. I hear it's a dive."

"Let's hit The Castle. You know, the Irish pub across the street."

THE CASTLE WAS DEAD. At the rear of the place, a waitress and two middle-aged barflies sang along with Bruce Springsteen's 'Thunder Road' on the jukebox. The long-haired drunks had beer guts. They were in jeans and faded rock concert T-shirts that were ten years old.

"Cloudy, my man, nice to see you dating women again," said one of the singers, who was missing teeth and not concerned by it.

"And she's white!" added his equally dentally-challenged bud.

Penny whispered in disbelief, "You *know* those guys?"

"I know guys like that in every bar," said Cloudy, who waved at the two drunks but remained seated by the bar.

"Go ahead, be anti-social," said one of the drunks and sang Bruce's lyrics, "'Roll down the windows and let the wind blow back your hair.'"

Cloudy passionately belted out the song's next lyric, "'Because the night's busted open and these two lanes will take us anywhere!'"

"Wow, you have pipes. I mean really good, really," Penny said. She rested her chin on his shoulder. Cloudy enjoyed her warm breath against his neck. "I'll get us some brews."

She brought back malted-scotch beers. The smell was toxic. He coughed and fought a sudden spike of gut-piercing nausea.

"I can't drink that stuff," said Cloudy, shuddering and pushing the mug away. "It smells like scotch. That's what my Mom drank." He coughed. "Scotch. That's a poison to me." He paused. "I'm sorry."

"I'll get something else," she said.

How many nights had he smelled scotch, watered-down scotch and rug-soaked scotch? It didn't matter how many nights, because all those nights were the same long night....

THERE WERE MANY OF THOSE LONG NIGHTS. Every time Cloudy came back from a gig and turned into the gravel driveway of the Map house in Westport, he dreaded the familiar sight of the TV's flickering blue light glowing from the dark family room's windows. He quietly drew back the sliding porch door. Mom was on the couch in her bathrobe, snoring and grinding her teeth. She wasn't sleeping. She was passed out. All she had beside her family was this. Cloudy took an afghan from a rocking chair and covered her up. He sighed and sadly gazed at her. When he was a kid in Freehold. He caught a fish in a stream but wanted to keep him as a pet. He kept the fish in a plastic pail outside. The next day the fish was floating and dead. It suffocated. No air could pass through the bucket's plastic. Cloudy thought, that's what living in a house in Westport has done to her—and to us too.

"There's some leftover pierogis in the fridge," she muttered.

"I'm fine, Mom."

"Shirley," his Mom said. "She was in my department. She quit and said, 'You fired Patsy. She did everything you said. I don't want to work for people like you.'" She paused. "Shirley—"

"Mom you told me about Shirley at Clairol."

She her eyes popped open and slurred,"You hate me don't you?"

"No," said an overcast Cloudy, lost in her fading scotch vapor trails.

She went back to sleep. He took the half-filled glass of scotch from the end table. Then he searched and found the second glass under the couch she hid but always forgot about. He put the glasses in the kitchen sink and blasted the water until the entire stench rinsed out. He went up to his room, but he couldn't sleep. He dialed back to how content he was lying in his old bed back in Freehold. In the winter, he'd look out the frosted-edged storm windows and see falling snow illuminated by the streetlights. And in summer, watch the fresh, light breeze softly pull the white curtains against the screen window as if trying to suck him through its thin mesh into the green grass and blue skies of a school-free world of play. But there was no comfort here in *this* room. It was a shelter to avoid his mother when she was drinking too much because she would repeat herself endlessly, bitterly launch into her well-grooved rant about Nana living with them or get into arguments with his Dad. When they lived in Stonehurst, there was only one time Cloudy could recall his mother ever raising her voice at Dad. Clear was in the family room sitting on the couch, cheerfully clipping his toenails and cackling as his snapped nails flew and hit the ceiling with sharp, nicking clicks. Cloudy's Mom yelled, "Stop it! It's gross." He happily kept doing it and laughing.

The Maps of Freehold wouldn't recognize the strangers in this house.

That night Cloudy broke out in hives.

"*D*AR-LINK IS SOMEWHERE ELSE than here," said Penny, who put down two Heineken drafts.

Cloudy looked down at the mug and said, "It's amazing how far you can really go in one place when you don't want to be there at all."

"Come again?"

"I was thinking about my Mom. She never fit in when we moved here from Jersey. It was hard to adjust. She had so many friends in Freehold. We all did. We moved here after I graduated high school. I didn't know anybody. But it was more than that one summer, it was knowing they would all be little like that. In Stonehurst—this housing development where we lived in Freehold—the developer planted saplings along the blocks. When we moved to Fairfield County, our whole family had to start from scratch. I had more noes in me than yeses. There was really no one to walk around and say 'hi' to. I wasn't very good. I really couldn't handle it. All I *could* do was build on everything I was against because there was nothing here I wanted to relate to. Back then, they were called 'preppies' not 'yuppies.' You know, guys who dressed like their fathers in green sweaters and loafers and polo shirts. The girls with plaid skirts and blouses and necklaces with tiny gold hearts because they didn't have real ones. I couldn't date them because I didn't have a referral from one of their friends who I didn't even want to frickin' know to begin with. What these people thought was important meant nothing to me. And even if I wanted to do something by myself I couldn't enjoy the place. You couldn't go to the other beaches to fish unless you lived in that town and had a permit. And neighbors, forget that. Hell, in *Waste*port, we actually lived next door to a guy who was named Harkness!"

"Harkness?" Penny laughed and said, "Ka-yikes."

"I guess that tells you everything you need to know about him and our neighborhood doesn't it? And he was Hark III. His son Tucker was just as bad. One time Harkness asked my sister Wendy if she'd like to come over to make a few bucks doing chores. She figured why not? Harkness had Wendy carrying firewood. She's lugging all this wood to the living room fireplace and she sees their strapping football-player son, Tucker, back from college, sitting in a chair, doing his vocal scales. She was struggling with the wood. He didn't lift a finger. When Dad heard about it. He was mad. He never let her go over there again, and never let *that* slight go." Cloudy paused. "Right then, I should have went over to their house and punched out that longest-punt-kicking frickin' ReRun for treating my sister like that."

"Harkness was the third," said Penny, adding in mock horror, "you think there's a fourth lurking out there that we don't know about?"

"There is!"

"You have a sister?"

"She's a wreck. Battered by her Ex, verbal and I bet, physical abuse but she's ashamed to admit it. She's a recovering alcoholic, which means she's still an alcoholic and everyone else is recovering. My parents had her living with them for six years but it's not helping."

"At least you love your parents. My Mom walked out on our family. We were kids. Dad remarried. Our stepmother was terrible to us."

"And that's a bad thing?

She pressed her lips together, smiled and said, "I think I'd like you better if you weren't talking. I left home at 19. Then when I was 24, I realized my life wasn't working. It wasn't going anywhere." She paused. Cloudy caught a sharp intelligence in her eyes and it sparked him. "I had to change it. Took some community college courses. I got laid off from my last job doing accounting. Been working part-time at the Grind until something else comes up. I'm glad for it. If you're not working all you do is hang out with other people who aren't. Have a job and you connect with people who are and that leads to better jobs."

"That's probably why it took so long for us to meet."

"People are actually pretty good noticing if you're better than what you do. I'm not afraid of my bills so I'm okay. I guess the only thing I dread is holidays and seeing my Dad. After the stepmother died he started living with a woman half his age, she took all our childhood and school pictures out of the house. You'd never know he had another family. And he allowed her do it. One time last Christmas, I drank way too much wine and I said, 'You don't love me.' And he said, 'I do too, in my way.' And I said, 'That's not the love I need.' Then I got up, and fell asleep on the couch."

"Well, I guess you showed him, huh?" said Cloudy, laughing. "My family was great to grow up with and got weird as I got older. I'm not thirsty. Let's go to the driving range and hit some golf balls."

"Whatever blows up your skirt."

THEY HOPPED INTO PENNY'S YELLOW VOLKSWAGEN BUG. Cloudy cleared off several CDs from the passenger seat: Coldplay, Gov't Mule, Jack Johnson, NRBQ, Dave Matthews, Van Halen, Green Day, Tool, Foo Fighters, Radiohead, AC-DC and some early Bruce.

"Nice tune-age," said Cloudy. "I've seen NRBQ forty times. Watched one show where Terry Adams only played the piano with his elbows."

"Toss the CDs in the back seat by my dance-class bag," she said.

"What do you dance to?"

"Everything," she said, shifting. "Radio or a CD?"

"I don't want to hear a song. If I ever hear that tune again, it'll remind me of my mother dying. *That* should never be connected to music. My Mom likes songs that tell stories and that's not a story any song should tell. She enjoyed terrible songs, like 'Indiana Wants Me,' 'Honey,' 'Ode to Billie Jo,' 'Harper Valley PTA,' 'Tie a Yellow Ribbon'—"

"Ka-yikes. Like 'The Night They Drove Old Dixie Down?'"

"Yeah, hideous. But I never made fun of them. How could I? She liked them. As a kid, I'd crank up the music in the car. Cousin Brucie on 77 WABC. She never turned the radio off. She always let me hear my music." His voice cracked. "My Mom always let me hear my music." They drove in silence again. "I'm sorry, I'm not much fun."

"Are you kidding? This is how all my dates go."

"I'm not surprised."

"Maybe I should trade up. What's Harkness The Fourth doing?"

"Probably Harkness The Third."

She laughed.

"My Mom is in pain," Cloudy blurted and ground his fists like pestles into his eyes sockets. "I can't do anything." He sobbed. "I've cried a million different ways and it still comes out the same."

PENNY PARKED AT IRONWOODS. The driving range was dark and dimly lit by the 1⁄16 moon. The stalls were vacant. Bullfrogs croaked from the water hazards, lightning bugs spattered out in clusters and crickets chirred in the rough.

"Looks closed to me," she said as they got out of the car.

"Stupid," said Cloudy, smacking his forehead. "It's a Wednesday. The range only stays open until ten on Friday and Saturday."

"Something's stuck out there," said Penny, squinting at the range's rear netting that prevented balls from flying into the mobile-home park. She reached into the VW's open window and hit the headlights. The beams lit an upside-down owl struggling in the mesh. "That bird's ginormous! Poor thing. She could break a wing. I have a towel in my dance bag and a Swiss Army knife in my glove compartment. Let's free her."

Penny and Cloudy ran past the range's yardage markers, occasionally stubbing their feet on balls embedded in the dried mud. They stood at waist-level to the disoriented bird. It twisted and spun in the black nylon netting and became even more entangled. The terrified owl's beak opened—its gray tongue arched, as if the bird was panting.

"Oh! She's a poor confused thing," Penny said sympathetically.

Cloudy slowly wound the towel around the owl's claws and gently compressed her quivering wings. The owl stirred, then became still.

"We can't release her in here, she'll get confused and fly into the netting and get tangled all over again," said Penny, cutting through the mesh with the knife, freeing the bird. "Watch out for her claws. They're sharp. She's frightened and can't tell the difference between help and her pain. So she'll lash out." Cloudy gathered the bundled owl into his arms. It struggled, but became still again. "She knows we're here to help her," Penny cooed. "You're safe with us little Lady, you're okay."

They walked from the range to the first tee. Cloudy lightly held the owl and flashed to one his early golf tips: lightly grip the club as if you held a live bird in your hands. His fingers absorbed the pulsating creature's soft feel. He gingerly placed the shrouded owl between the tee markers, pointed her at the green and unwound the towel. The owl sprung, unfurled its wings and with two huge sweeping powerful flaps, flew down the middle of the fairway.

"Whoa," said Penny. "Ka-yikes. You're a hoot, little lady."

"Fly, fly, fly!" said Cloudy, crying.

"All you can do is let her go," said Penny.

"Fly!" Cloudy said, his entire body shaking, legs wobbling.

"It's your turn, *dar*-link," she said, hugging him. "My poor guy from Jersey." Penny paused. "I want you to fly too."

Cloudy rapidly planted light kisses over her face and peppered out a barrage of questions, "Why don't I know your favorite food? Why don't I know your birthday, your high school, your perfume? Tell me. Why don't I know where *you* grew up? Tell me why? Why? Fill me up with your whys. Make the whys go away. Make them why away."

Cloudy At The Turn

MOM'S LAST STOP. NUMBER 223. Her Coralton hospice room. The woman who took her family everywhere was at a dead end with no turnaround or ocean view. Nothing prepared Cloudy for the unseen spindle that kept turning and clamped him between two tightening jaws of an emotional bench vise. They were closing in on him. One jaw was cushioned with the framed memory of his healthy, smiling Mom. The other jaw was cast iron with a serrated surface and reflected the inescapable reality of her present condition: a sedated unconsciousness in a dimly lit sterile place, the crook of her left arm was bruised from needles, her hair combed back and flattened and her mouth slightly twisted, lips dry and cracked.

"Mom, you are the most beautiful woman in the world," weakly croaked Cloudy as the vise's relentless grip pressed and squeezed out an endless supply of deep, hiccoughing, wet, uncontrollable raspy sobs. He rested his head on her stomach and draped his right arm across her. She didn't respond. "Anything I ever did that was good was because of you and all the things I ever did wrong were my fault." Each word he spoke felt like a dry hard piece of crystal that scraped his throat. "I appreciate everything. I *know* everything you did for me. Everything. The Elmo Topp Lucky Cakes badge you let me wear in my first-grade yearbook picture. When I had the mumps you got me a Bit-O-Honey candy bar and five packs of *Mars Attacks* cards. My M&M Boys: Roger Maris and Mickey Mantle T-shirt. Taking me shopping for school clothes I didn't want to wear but you thought I looked nice in. My Halloween costumes." His throat tightened, as if an invisible thumb and forefinger was slowly trying to pinch his larynx shut. He kept on. "The cotton candy, caramel apples and rides at the Asbury Park boardwalk. The quarters from the tooth fairy. The pennies to get the Superman ring I wanted in the bubble gum machine at John's Bargain

Store. Money for Toasted Almond ice cream bars from the Good Humor Man who stopped his truck at the corner. On Christmas Eve putting carrots out for reindeer, and when I was asleep you nibbled on them and left marks so I still *believed.* Taking me to the Coca-Cola bottling plant to redeem my Jets and Giants bottle-cap sheets for a football. My Easter baskets. The Butoni Wagon Wheel noodles I liked so much because I could spear five of them on one fork. My birthday presents—Spy's a Poppin', Skittle Bowl, Wham-O Super Ball, Creepy Crawler Thingmaker, Marble Raceway, Rat Trap, Monopoly, Time Bomb, the REMCO Monkey Division rifle and helmet, The Beatles albums." His tongue ached from the weight of each item in the endless inventory. "My models: the AMT cars, Big Ed Daddy Roth's Rat Fink, the Aurora Monsters. My *Mad* magazines and 12-cent Spiderman and 25-cent World Finest Giant comics. Federici's pizzas every Friday. The 'Super' Number 5 and 'Special' Number 4 subs from Sorrento's. Coming back from the shore and stopping at Stewart's for Root Beer and burgers. My braces. The guitar lessons I dropped because I didn't practice. The mini-fridge and clock/radio for college. Leftovers for my lunch at work." Cloudy hoarsely warbled, "The Chocolate Chocolate Chip Häagen-Dazs and Drake's Yodels that were always in the fridge... the life you *gave* me." He sniffed and said over and over gain, "I love my Mom. I love my Mom. I love my Mom..." He stood and collapsed in a chair, depleted, tamped down. He bowed his head, spoke slowly again, the words he formed felt larger than his mouth. "I know you don't want to leave us. But if you want to go... go. I will miss you every day of my life." Cloudy leaned over and rested his right cheek against hers—her cheek, a cheek that would always be smoother than any silk, cashmere, velvet or mink. He let out a dry gasp, then barely added, "Every time I came home you smiled and your face lit up. You saw the best in me. Believed in the best of me, always. The best of me. I will become the best in me. I will be the best for my Mom."

"She can hear you."

Cloudy turned, wiping his eyes, startled by his Dad's appearance. His father stood at the door.

"The nurse told me," said Clear, who jangled car keys in his pocket.

"You keep Mom company for awhile," said Cloudy, grabbing a tissue.

"Mom would have told me to wipe my face and blow my nose."

"She would," replied his Dad. A gust rattled the window. "Storm."

Clear jangled the keys in his pocket again. Cloudy remembered how his Dad hated sacrificing a weekend to visit Mom's family. As soon as they arrived his Dad made a point of having to leave early to beat the traffic. He signalled his impatience by jingling the car keys in his pocket—especially when his wife was taking way too long to say goodbye to her sisters.

A gloomy Clear approached his wife, jingled his keys, shivered from the sound of distant thunder and mournfully bleated, "My lady."

Cloudy slackly drifted down the hospice hallway. A white board on the wall posted the Coralton ward's daily activities: movies, aerobic sessions, sewing classes and daily menus. But no patient in "palliative care" could participate in the events, chew food or possessed the motor functions to leave their room to check the schedule. Cloudy wearily passed each room and stole sideways glances at the diminished occupants. All their possessions reduced to a few photographs on a bureau. They were old, crumpled people. Thin tubes limply dangled from metal stands to their bodies like strings for lifeless puppets. Their heartbeats remixed into electronic bleeps. Machines pumped drugs into them, putting their dying on mute.

"My Mom is one of these people," Cloudy quietly said, weakening, knowing one day he could be lying in these beds looking out instead of in. "Everyone is somebody's somebody. Somebody's me."

Cloudy was surprised by a thin elderly man, who was smiling and sitting in a wheelchair at the entrance of his room. Cloudy stopped.

"The yellow and white angels are painting my room," the man said, his eyes brightening. He pointed his bent finger to Cloudy's mother's room. "And the angels are painting hers too."

Cloudy felt a creepy chill, but smiled and said, "Angels, huh."

"Yellow and white," the old man contentedly said and closed his eyes.

Down the hall, Cloudy spotted the head nurse in her office. Cloudy went past the ward's station. The nursing staff sat and complained about their shifts, laughed, ate snacks, discussed their dates, what they had for lunch and the *Survivor* TV show.

"Excuse me," deferentially said Cloudy, sticking his head into the head nurse's office. "I'm John Map, Patricia Map's son."

"Yes, your mother is resting in 223."

"How long does she have? I won't hold you to it."

The nurse sympathetically said, "Probably a day or two."

"I want to see what Mom has. I have to see it."

"Surely, certainly."

The nurse picked up a file from her desk, removed some papers and slapped an x-ray on the wall's light board.

"Metastatic adonecarcinoma of the lung," she effortlessly said, pointing out several large grayish smudges. "Those are the tumors."

"So that's what cancer looks like," said Cloudy, intently honing in on the deadly smears. He almost teared up, but fought it back with a sharp, hard sniff. "My Mom decided against chemo."

"A very courageous woman."

"That's my Mom," said Cloudy, turning to the nurse. "It's her way of making it easier on us. That's all she ever thought—*thinks* about."

"Here cancer was very advanced."

"What's so advanced about that?" said Cloudy, nodding at the smears.

"Did she smoke?"

"Mom went through three packs a day, easily. When I was a kid, I couldn't even count how many times at 10:30 on a summer night, I'd be laying in front of the TV in the family room and she'd be behind me, standing at a folded-out ironing board, pressing off clothes, folding them, never complaining and watching the show too. Then she'd say, 'I have to go to the 7-ELEVEN, would you run in for me? You can get some ice cream and…' Then I'd rudely finish her sentence, '…*And* two packs of Pall Malls.' She'd get mad. This was back in the days when 7-ELEVEN closed at 11:00. Ten minutes later, she was in her bathrobe waiting in our 1967 Plymouth Belvedere station wagon and I'd come out of 7-ELEVEN with a brown bag of ice cream and two packs of death. She probably smoked a lot more then she said." He paused. "She'd get angry if you got on her for smoking too much. You just didn't go there." Cloudy shrugged. "Well, she won the argument." He looked at the nurse and slightly smiled. "I lost."

"You smoke?"

"Never wanted to. One of my vivid winter memories was heading home after visiting relatives in Lyndhurst. Dad driving. Mom sitting beside him. They'd be yakking about the aunts and uncles—and smoking. Both of them! My sister and me in the back seat. It's freezing so the car windows are shut tight. Smoke everywhere. I'm leaning against the door. Cracking open a window. Pressing my lips against the cold glass and sucking the current of fresh air flowing down it. The air through the crack made a whistling sound. My Mom said, 'A window's open! It'll let out the heat.' I acted like I was asleep."

"Well, it's good you never started."

Cloudy reexamined his Mom's X-ray. He imagined the tumor smudges morphing into the shape of Eggplant's wise-ass smile.

AN HOUR LATER, Clear and Cloudy sat in The Grill Room of the Battleground Country Club. The bar was packed because a lightning alarm summoned golfers off the course. The members griped about the weather which led them to conclude they were being forced to stop playing because of possible lawsuits, which inevitably segued into grousing about the liberal media, government regulations, welfare cheats, until they drifted back into what they knew best: stocks, sports, gambling, sex, beer farts and missed putts.

The TV ran a Fox News documentary *Can 9/11 happen again?* on a large screen. A mob of young Muslims marched through the streets of Baghdad, raising their fists, burning an American flag and shouting about Allah. No golfer was watching the show.

"There's the rain," said Clear, listening to the shower's drumming build on the roof. He nodded. "It won't last. We beat it."

Willie placed a second vodka before Clear.

"So is there any Chilean sea bass, Willie?"

"I already checked in the kitchen, they have some."

"And—"

"I know, no rice or fries, loads of veggies," Willie said, leaving.

"Willie has taken care of me here for 23 years," said Clear, fondly.

"So what's Willie's last name?"

"I don't know, he doesn't talk about his personal life and I respect that distance," said Clear, reflectively stirring his drink.

Cloudy's Dad couldn't deal with a dying wife. In the hospital, he popped in for quick visits and retreated to the club, which was his way of handling it. Cloudy kept him company, let his father emotionally unravel, picked up the slack and tried to stuff it back in, but there was always something leftover and those were stories Cloudy was hearing for the first time.

"In New York, we used to have three-martini lunches at AMF. Worked there for over 20 years until Irwin Jacobs got the company in a hostile takeover. Sold our divisions. Looted our pension fund. I think now Jacobs found Jesus or God or something, like a cannibal finding religion after he eats you. They all do that, it's the next step: philanthropy. Everything except giving back what the stole from what we earned. Religion in business, beautiful. Here's one. I had to fly out to one of AMF's California divisions that wasn't doing well. The CEO running it said he was praying for God to save the plant. God turned out to be a Jewish accountant from New York backdating the division's inventory. Sometimes I wondered what the point of doing my job was. In personnel, no matter what I did, I always felt I got in people's way. How can you really reach people when they hate their jobs? Just looking at them you could see it. They'd all get happy on Fridays." He thoughtfully sipped his vodka. "I did some good things at AMF. I had to go down to the Deep South. We had this plant that made railroad cars in Shreveport, Louisiana. They had separate bathrooms and fountains for 'colored' and 'whites.' And this is *after* the Civil Rights act. And the boss, an asshole, had prayer rooms too. I sat down and told him, 'You have to spend $500,000 to make this right. The black guys working on the line are making 40 cents less than the white guys above them who are in air-conditioned areas and are dropping things down on them. The white guys in those cars are overpaid. The blacks know it. That's why they want a union in here.' Charles Dillard, who worked there, was beside me. The manager said, 'What do you think Charlie?' He said, 'It has to be done.' He said that. Charles Dillard stuck out his neck and backed me. I was scared. Spent most of that night trying to work out what to do, drinking a bottle of Jack Daniels alone in my hotel room. Later those workers shared locker rooms. The white guys started pissing in the blacks' shoes. But the union didn't go in. We won that one. I'd like to think that blacks down there had better lives because of what I did. Charlie Dillard. His wife rang me last year and said, 'Charlie died in his sleep.' Age 76. He got to be a VP. I had my chance to be a vice-president. Rich Sullivan was a CEO. Tom was a kiss-up, kick-down type. He was great to the people who worked for him. He'd do anything for you, but you *had* to work for him. Terrible to his peers or anyone above him. He hated to be equal to anyone. A lot of people are like that. We were at a meeting with a lot of VPs and Sullivan says, 'Great leaders are always successful in business. You can't name one great leader who failed in business.' And without hesitation I said, 'Harry Truman.' I knew right then and there, I'd never become a VP. I wasn't one of them, a lot of those guys saw the job as a license to steal. And it could be anything—ordered supplies for their pools, purchased art to decorate their office and had their company limos take the stuff home. Those guys are bright, but they're only bright at what they want for themselves. That's why Jacobs had such an easy time taking over AMF, he knew those guys would hand it to him as long as they could walk away with something. They were shameless. One time after an employee event, Sullivan went around the tables taking all the apples off them for himself. Apples! Right in front of everybody. Sullivan never promoted me. I stayed in Personnel forever. Took care of me though, I'll give him that. He could be a bully, made fun of people's names. Never did it to me. At a business meeting he called Barry Baben 'Babble'. Ben brought him up short, 'That's not my name. It's Baben, not Babble.' Sullivan never said a word, just sat there. In a cabinet meeting once, FDR said to George Marshall, 'You know about that, George.' Marshall said, 'I'm not George. I'm *General* Marshall.' Meaning you get my advice as a general, we're not friends. I should have probably done that more often." Clear squinted and grinned at his son. "You're going to make a wise crack aren't you? Go ahead."

"At least I don't have to worry about ever being overshadowed by my father's accomplishments," said Cloudy.

"This is beginning to turn into an exit interview," said Clear who sipped his vodka and meditatively added. "We always made fun of Harkness in Westport, but maybe the Grahams had it right."

"It doesn't change the fact that we never treated them the way they treated us," said Cloudy. "Remember when Connecticut had that huge blizzard. In '77 was it? No one could go anywhere. The Grahams were the only ones on our block who had a huge hill in their back yard. We used his hill to go sleigh riding. That's what we did in Freehold, right? If someone had a hill in their yard they let all the kids sleigh ride down it. The following spring Harkness planted a couple trees right in the middle of the hill so it could never be used again." He paused. "No one ever did anything like that in Freehold."

"They might now."

"Well, they didn't do it in Freehold did they? Harkness did it when he got his first chance," replied Cloudy.

"True and says a lot, doesn't it? Maybe all of it. Never could figure Harkness out. Hark knew things. He was a cook in the marines."

"With a name like Harkness, he *had* to become a marine."

"I met Hark's Dad. He was fun, thought his son was a stiff. That was where their real money came from. Had a patent on a tank engine starter or something like that the Army used in World War II. When I met the mother that's when I *knew* why Hark was Hark. A real stern, frigid bitch. She held the purse strings. His wife, Mary Beth wanted to be friends with Mom, with us. Hark stopped that in its tracks. If his wife stayed too long at our house he'd call on the phone. She'd leave like a poor dog on a leash. I went through Mom's photo albums, in Freehold we have pictures with neighbors at parties or you with other kids. But in Westport we don't have pictures of anyone but us. Not a single one with the Grahams. Hark didn't think we were his social equals. His son was the same way—Tucker, the great high school punter. Thing about being a punter is no one *expects* you to score. The kid was dumb too. Just a lucky sperm club member. Hark didn't think we were his social equals. Well hawkshaw, all you can do with people like that is tell them to go fuck themselves." He paused. "I hated the way Harkness said, 'Tah' to me."

"Yeah, I know," said Cloudy, who decided not mention his run-in with Tucker. "Enough of him." He reached into his pocket flicked a wad of cash on the table. "There you go."

"What's this?"

"It's $2,800."

"For what?"

"Money you fronted me to fix up the car. I got it running again."

"Keep it, I can't take my son's money," he replied, pushing away the cash. "I got you back cheap." He looked outside. "The rain stopped."

"Yeah," said Cloudy lowered his voice, "Dad, we don't have to play in the golf tournament here next month. It's no big deal—"

"Of course, we're playing."

"But they have one day where we play 27 holes and you get tired."

"I can do it."

"What if it's hot?"

"So I drink water and park the cart in the shade."

"John," tentatively said a voice laced with stale beer breath.

It was Eggplant. He was in his golf clothes. He was drunk.

"I heard about Pat," said Eggplant, genuinely contrite.

"Thanks, I appreciate the concern," said Clear. "She—"

"If you never married my sister, Mom would be at this table with us," Cloudy said with a calm, contemptuous and menacing edge.

"Put some lavender on it, son," Clear cautiously advised, seeing rage flush across Cloudy's face. "Just a little lavender."

Eggplant quickly returned to the bar.

"Boy, he high-tailed it out of here. He certainly didn't want any part of you," said Clear, impressed.

"When you turn a light on in the kitchen," said Cloudy, reaching for his beer. "And there's a cockroach in the middle of the floor, why does it run and hide? Because it *knows* it's a bug."

"Well, at least he tried to offer sympathy, you have to give him that," said Clear. "My Patsy. For months, she was walking around, hunched over, said her bad back was acting up. She had to be in pain and never, ever complained. Never. How was I to know? You couldn't talk to her. Look how she was about her smoking. I tried to get her to go to the doctor, but she fought me on it. Hell, she was terrible about making dentist appointments for you kids! Had to be on her all the time. Mom came from a Polish family of eleven. There was no money for medical care. She's wasn't sensitive to it. When her mother—your Bobci—had a kid it was probably the only time a doctor ever saw her, although I couldn't prove it. Her poor mother never left the kitchen, on her feet all day on those fat ankles in flat black shoes. Eleven kids. What woman would want to have that many? She was a dray horse. Made a lot of Catholics. One of her own brothers referred to your Mom as 'the worker.' Actually said that straight to my face. A bright young girl like her. The father and brothers treated women in that Polish family like Muslims. They were aliens to me. The brothers went out Saturday nights, got in fights, arrested, drunk. Nana was organized, disciplined. Mom never had that. That's why she resented Nana. Anything Nana did made Mom feel she wasn't running her house properly. I wish my wife would had been nicer to my mom. See your Nana really wanted to *contribute*. But my Patsy denied her that."

"One thing I couldn't stand was how Nana always talked about her bowel movements in the morning when I was eating breakfast," said Cloudy. "I'd be over my oatmeal and she'd say something like, 'It looked like a pile of rocks.' "

"She had that in her to be insensitive," said Clear. "When I was a teenager, Nana made supper and I said something like, 'What is this crap?' And she punched me in the head. With her fist. Knocked me off my chair." He added unconvincingly, "Why not? I deserved it." He paused. "I never touched you kids. Not like that. What do you teach a kid by hitting them? Violence?" Clear tightened the skin on his chin and scratched it. He watched the storm pass. "I told you about my dog Blackie, the dog I had when I was growing up in Springfield, didn't I?"

"Yeah, tell me again. I like the story."

"Blackie use to wait for the red light to change in front of Dundee's gas station, he'd catch the bus, which stopped to pick him up, and go to Harry Gibson's diner. My Dad went in the diner one day and saw Blackie lying on the floor. Harry was cooking a hamburger and said, 'This is for Blackie. He doesn't like them rare.' And Blackie always showed up in front of the school and waited and followed me home. One time, I had pneumonia. Was in the hospital for two weeks. I came home and I was lying in bed, we had these linoleum floors, and Blackie sees me and his legs start spinning. He can't get any traction on the floor, then he runs and jumps over the bed and crashes into the wall. He licked me all over my face. He got killed, hit by a car late at night. The newspaper ran an obituary."

"Poor dog."

"What can you do?"

Cloudy watched his Dad sip his drink and stare at the gray skies. His father read history, followed the news and often pointed out how current events repeated mistakes of the past. But, their old cat Martha scratching his hand, not walking away from Eggplant at Mario's, mentioning Harry Truman at a corporate meeting, and leaving Freehold. Those historic moments held more significance in his life than July 4th, 1776, the Magna Carta and the Fall of Rome.

They sat quietly and watched the 9/11 news special on TV. The planes crashed into the Twin Towers like Eggplant collided into Wendy and cancer exploded within Cloudy's Mom, collapsing the Map family's towers of strength. The club members swirled indifferently around the room and boasted about their triumphs on and off the course. Victories Clear and Cloudy didn't share. The buried pair silently sat beneath their personal rubble and sipped beer and vodka to prevent from choking on the indifferent dust in the air left by others who were somehow better suited for success in the world than they were.

Clear sipped his drink and farted.

"Don't worry, a fart doesn't smell unless it's hot," he said.

"Those are the great words of wisdom you will leave me with forever."

"Yeah, it also has to have a little purple on it."

WHEN THE MAPS LEFT THE CLUB, Cloudy's phone vibrated. His heart jumped. Please, not the call, he thought, not *the* call. It was.

"Yes."

"Your mother's levels are going."

"Dad, it's Mom!"

"Oh, my lady," said Clear, instantly sobering up.

It took 15 minutes to reach the hospice. But that was all the time Patsy Map needed to pack up her soul and leave. She laid like a clay figure in the darkened room. Her mouth slightly opened. Her unique orbit had always held them in a warm ordered solar system of family. But her star collapsed. She was gone. These two men helplessly spun adrift in the flat, dimmed empty and chilly universe of room 223.

"She didn't die alone," softly said the nurse. "I saw her levels dropping. I came in. Her breathing quickened. She opened her eyes and saw me, then she was gone. She wasn't alone."

The nurse's assurances didn't console the twosome. Because when Patsy Map popped open her eyes for the last time she *did* die alone: Clear and Cloudy weren't with her. That means alone. Did she deeply moan in pain? Was she frightened? *Help me, help me.* Was she looking for them? Her brown eyes. Her darting brown eyes. *Help me, help me.* Those eyes. They would see her eyes searching for them forever.

After several free condolence rounds of drinks at The Hugga Mug, Clear and Cloudy were under the weather. A sober son supported his drunk, stumbling and devastated father. The two dragged a heavy lengthening lost shadow of grief behind them. The sky was velvet. Sunlight glared off wet asphalt. They stepped between fat worms in the puddled condo parking lot.

"Your mother let me down," said Clear. "She died."

Cloudy opened the door.

"Oh no," bleakly said his Dad dismally staring into the empty condo.

They entered the settling hollowness. Without Patsy Map's presence nothing linked these men to the furniture, rugs, Hummel figurines and framed paintings. Her pulse of love was the circulating string of warmth that ran through these objects and animated them into the necklace of a home. Without her everything in the rooms was reduced to stuff taking up space—so were they.

"I'll help you upstairs, Dad."

"I don't want to go to the bedroom. The couch. Put me on the couch."His father slipped and fell on the living room rug. "This is so embarrassing."

"No, it isn't."

"Yes, it is," he said, crawling onto the sofa.

"You need a pillow."

"No, I don't," he said, lying down and blankly looking at the ceiling.

"You need a blanket."

"I'm fine."

He gently slid the pillow beneath his father's head, went upstairs, brought down a blanket and tucked-in his Dad.

"I love to be pampered," Clear sighed, closed his eyes and slept.

Cloudy left the sunken living room and went to the dining room table. There was the empty chair where his Mom always sat, drinking her coffee, smoking a cigarette, doing a crossword puzzle, reading the Daily News and commenting on some tabloid murder. Above her chair in the corner was a ceiling air vent—stained golden brown from her smoking. On the mahogany table was an ashtray, crumpled pack of Pall Malls, a small black-beaded purse, fingernail polish, a dictionary without front or back covers, a few scratched-off losing lottery tickets, a shopping list and a coupon for decorative fruit bowls. He pulled a small folder from beneath the dictionary. It contained color pages from the past Sunday sections of the Daily News in a series featuring 'Yankee Greats.' Each page had a drawing of the player, their stats, and a brief anecdote. There was Thurman Munson, Mickey Mantle and Reggie Jackson. She neatly cut the pages out and placed the articles within protective plastic sheets for him! He opened her purse. Inside were articles on vitamins to cure upset stomachs, antacids coupons and three packets of Gas-Tex for heartburn. She knew, thought Cloudy, poor Mom. Maybe, if they never left in Freehold, life could have turned out better. But if they remained in Stonehurst, neighbors would eventually move away, and their Freehold might have left them. That didn't matter. There wasn't another side to this issue. The Maps *did* leave Freehold and took heavy casualties. His mother was one. And now, they all were. Cloudy sat in her chair, placed his head on the beaded purse, closed his eyes and crashed out.

PATSY MAP'S VOICE JARRED HER SON AWAKE with a simple request: *"Help your father with the phone calls."*

Cloudy bolted upright, breathing deeply. His Mom spoke to him! It was *her.* He looked around. It was 6 o'clock. He took the faded address book from the table. His father was fidgeting on the couch.

"Pat, give me some room," Clear muttered, jerking his elbow against the cushions. He stirred and realized she wasn't there. In a dry exhale he moaned, "My lady is gone."

Cloudy said, "Dad? You okay?"

"I dreamed about Mom," Clear sighed, sitting up, hair uncombed. "She walked into our bedroom. I said, 'I thought you were sick.'"

"Dad, we have to let people know about Mom," said Cloudy, handing his father the old Freehold address book that had broken binding and was bloated with torn pieces of paper and business cards of updated information stuffed but never entered into its separating pages.

Clear sighed, put on his glasses and started making phone calls. The task calmed him into a function.

"Hi Helen," Clear said into the phone. "John Map. I'm afraid I have some sad news. Our Patsy left us today. It was for the best. She was suffering. We're all going over the falls. I'm under the rug about it. Our family is a threesome without a fourth."

Cloudy left and decided to spare his father from one unavoidable task.

"I'M JOHN MAP, PATRICIA MAP'S SON," Cloudy said to a nurse at the palliative-care ward station. "I'm here for my mother's belongings."

"Map? Nobody here by that name," said an overweight Puerto Rican nurse, her response felt like a slap to his face. She was feeding a wheelchair-bound elderly man. The patient wore a blue hospital robe. He didn't move. His eyes were vacant lots. The nurse dipped a spoon into a plastic cup. "Do you want pudding?" The expressionless man mechanically dropped his jaw. "That's a good boy." She slowly pulled the spoon out from between his pressed lips. It was stripped clean. "You're eating all the pudding! You like chocolate, don't you?"

"I'm her son, John Map," Cloudy said. "My Mom was in room 223."

"Then someone must have taken her things with them when they saw her the last time," indifferently said the nurse, stirring the pudding.

"What?" Cloudy snapped harshly.

The head nurse heard his raised voice. She came out of her office.

"I'll get your mother's things for you," she gently said, then shot a disapproving glance at the incompetent and rude woman.

"How old was your mother?" said the nurse, who knew she was in trouble and tried to cover it with a belated make-nice.

"Around seventy, I guess."

"So she had a good life then."

"Shouldn't *I* be the one to say that?"

"Well, we're all are going down the same road."

Cloudy retorted. "Really? Then, I'd like to call *you* a cab." He turned and glanced across the hall to the room where he met the old man who spoke about yellow and white angels painting walls. The staff was preparing his room for another occupant. "What happened to gentleman who was in that room?"

"He's in a better place," said the nurse. "Along with your mother."

"When I saw him, he told me there were angels painting the rooms."

"Isn't that sweet?" she replied, smiling and shoveling a gob of brown pudding into the man's mouth. "I'm looking forward to the other side."

"If I ever make it there," said Cloudy, narrowing his eyes and getting right in her fat face. "I'll throw some ice cubes down to you."

The head nurse returned with a cardboard box and put it on the ward station's counter. Cloudy opened the box and pulled out item after item as he whispered slowly, "Here is the bathrobe you couldn't wear. Pink slippers you couldn't put on. The comb you couldn't run through your hair. The thriller novel you couldn't read. Fig Newtons you couldn't eat. The toothbrush you couldn't use. The crossword puzzle you couldn't solve." He blankly stared at her belongings, gasped, then pinched the bridge of his nose to keep the tears in.

"I'm deeply sorry for your loss," sincerely said the head nurse, helping Cloudy carefully replace the possessions and seal the box.

"Thank you," he whispered, composing himself. "What's your name?"

"Brenda."

"Thank you Brenda," Cloudy weakly said.

He turned and shuffled down the ward's white-tiled hall. Ceiling lights harshly glared off the floor and made him woozy. Death put a queasy Cloudy on his mother's bag. He never knew emptiness could be so heavy. He shouldered it, swerved left, slid against the wall for support then righted himself. He felt older, slower. A sudden sharp jab set like a barbed hook into the deep warm folds of his stomach. The pain cast him back into a fishing memory. He and his Dad sat in a wooden leaky rented rowboat at Belmar Basin in South Jersey. He was ten. Cloudy's rod bent and quivered with a fighting life. He grabbed his pole. He thought he was pulling in a big fluke. Instead, twelve feet down in the olive-colored salt water, he saw a struggling eel at the end of his line. A white strip of squid flapped on the silver size-8 hook embedded in the fish's jaws. Unhooking an eel in a boat was always a mess. Thrashing eels left slime everywhere. He didn't want to deal with it. When his Dad wasn't looking, Cloudy cut the line. He watched the angry eel twist and plummet to the bottom, dragged by the weight of the sinker rig. The thrashing shadow sank and blurred into the green murkiness. At first Cloudy thought it was funny, but on the drive home, he felt guilty. He imagined the eel anchored by the lead sinker to the muddy ocean floor, tugging to tear itself free from the tormenting hook, ripping its soft mouth open. It wasn't the eel's fault it was an eel. Cloudy tried to convince himself the eel could bite and snap the line and the hook would rust and drop from its scarred jaws. Today in the hospice, it was Cloudy's turn to be that eel, spinning down into the depths, squirming with pain from the well-set hook of loss. He wondered, does grief rust? Either way, years later, the eel managed to return the favor.

PATSY MAP'S WAKE was held at the Battleground Country Club. The flag in front of the clubhouse was at half-staff. It was one in the afternoon, a beautiful summer day. Cloudy stood where the curved edge of a neatly trimmed lawn met the circular driveway. He wore one of his father's old suits. The vase with his mother's ashes was on the veranda's slate steps behind him. He had been thanking all the departing guests. Most had left. A few Freehold neighbors came, along with some of the women his mother worked with at Clairol, so did Turdle and Schultzie, even several of Cloudy's frat brothers who spotted her name in the obituaries, his father's cousins and former AMF executives and secretaries, as well as Battleground members, and the Polish relatives from Lyndhurst. His clueless cousin Joey inexcusably showed up in bluejeans, T-shirts and orange sneakers, but Cloudy forgave all when Joey hung his head and tears came as he sadly as his voice cracked, "I had to come for Ciotka Anjie… She let me and my brother stay for a week in Freehold with you guys that one summer. That was when my Mom was real sick, before she died. All those meals she made for us, and the ice cream, taking us to the carnival. You had such a nice yard, and Ciotka brought us to the swim club and I'd dive underwater and opened my eyes and couldn't believe how everything could be so clean and deep." They hugged and Cloudy remembered that Joey was dressed the same way at his father's funeral, drank shots at the wake and shouted out "Yee-haa!" like a cowboy. What can you do with that? he thought, people do what they do. Eggplant wasn't invited and fortunately didn't make an appearance. The real offensive no-show was Pudge. He never called Cloudy or visited his Mom in the hospital and didn't attend the funeral. Cloudy couldn't believe it.

Wendy came out the banquet doors to the veranda. She flourished at the wake. It gave her the opportunity to take center stage, pull out her self-pity violin and perform her solo passion play to a captive audience.

"Oy," she said.

"You've been drinking."

"No. It's my medication. If you don't believe me. Smell my breath."

"You're better at lying than I am at finding the truth," said Cloudy, who added in disgust, "Going on seven years of this."

"What does seven years have to do with anything?" she indignantly snarled, stamping her feet and glaring at him.

"It means just that: seven years you haven't shown up for life," Cloudy bitterly spat. "Seven years. Mom's *last* seven years. If you truly wanted to honor her memory you wouldn't be drinking which you most certainly are… I bet you don't even feel remorse."

"I feel horrible!" she dramatically said as if she was performing in the final act of a Greek Tragedy. She pouted. "I don't deserve this. Mom should have taken better care of me. I can't believe Tony didn't come."

"What?"

"I love him," she said, sniffing. "I thought he would be here for me."

"Spare me. You still love him?" said Cloudy, infuriated. "Incredible. Our Mom is dead and you bring up that asshole ex-husband of yours. Tell you what, right now, I'll drive you to Eggplant's house. He'll be so glad to see ya. Welcome you back with open arms. And he'll be the perfect, loving, supportive husband you always wanted and you'll live happily ever after. Come on let's go? I'll take you right now."

Clear came outside. He was tired, drained, hungover with grief. For the first time, he looked older than his years.

"Fuck you!" Wendy growled, brushing past Clear into the club.

"Son, what happened?" Clear asked, hurt, perplexed, A feebleness in his confused eyes.

"What do you think happened?"

"Lavender, son. A little lavender."

"Wendy played us again. The usual."

"Oh no," Clear said, glancing back into the banquet room. "She's been drinking? She told me… "

"Don't worry, she'll behave herself in there. For some twisted reason she actually cares more about what *those* people think of her than us."

"My daughter is a very, sick little girl. She doesn't want to go back to Florida, she wants to stay in the condo and said she'll get a job. I'm not going to give up on her—ever," faintly vowed Clear, looking down at his Florsheim wingtips. "I have to hope."

"Hey, what can I say?" Cloudy replied helplessly. "She's my sister." He shrugged. "Nobody's finished."

"You know," wearily sighed Clear, hands in his pockets. "I don't think she's going to make it." He looked down. "You know, when your Mom was carrying Matthew, she smoked. And I read an article that said, one of the causes of crib death could be linked to women who smoked during pregnancy. I never showed it to her, and I never told her."

His father returned to the banquet room. Cloudy gazed at the rolling serenity of the club's flawlessly green fairways. No one was playing.

"Young John?"

Cloudy turned and politely said, "Mrs. Graham."

Mary Beth Graham was in her seventies. She was pale, a little frail. He hugged her. She felt small and boney in her loosely fitting dress.

"Harkness is at The Cape," she said. "He has a touch of something. Hark didn't want to give you anything he had."

"So you drove all the way down here from The Cape alone?"

"I can't go back tonight. My eyes don't do well in the dark."

There was an awkward silence, but it came naturally to them.

"I have an unspoken regret about your Mom I need to make peace with," she said. "In Westport our maid couldn't come one day. I had all this laundry but I didn't know how to fold it. I asked your mother to help. I watched her fold it for me and I said, 'Oh Pat, you're such a good laundress.' Afterwards, I realized how that must have sounded. But I meant it as a compliment. It was my way of saying she could do so many things I couldn't do for myself."

Cloudy restrained himself from what he wanted to say, and said the truth, "I'm sure Mom knew it was your way of saying 'Thank you.'"

"If your Mom saw me and was heading out she always asked me if I needed anything from the store. When I used the bathroom in your house, she had flowers on the toilet tank. I never thought of doing that! I was so jealous of those flowers, being able to think of that."

"That's right," softly said Cloudy, smiling, "She always had flowers in the bathroom. I took it for granted, I guess."

A valet arrived with the Graham Volvo. She gave him a dollar tip and got behind the wheel and said, "Sometimes, I'd sit on our outside deck and listen to the laughter coming from your home."

"Laughter, we did always have that... with each other."

"We laughed too," she snapped in a defensive tone.

Her quick retort, surprised Cloudy. Maybe, he thought, she sharply responded to paint over how her comment revealed loneliness in a house filled with her son's empty arias accompanied by a ringing phone from Harkness calling to say he was "tired" and staying at their apartment in The City.

"Thank you so much for coming," said Cloudy, closing the car door. "It means a lot to us. I know my Dad really appreciates it. So do I."

"Your Mom had a lot of friends," she said. "A lot of people loved her."

He watched Mrs. Graham drive away, walked to the steps, picked up his mother's vase and said to her, "I do good, Mom? I didn't try to get the last word in."

Cloudy heard wedding music coming across the street from one of the huge residential houses on Country Club Lane. His Mom must have been disappointed she never saw him get married. There was only one time he came close to it. He had been dating in girl in college for three years. His Mom took him to the master bedroom, opened a dresser drawer and showed him a gold ring. She said, "This was my mother's ring, your Bobci's wedding ring. I want you to give it to the girl you marry." He wondered where that ring went, and if he would ever see it again. Cloudy had forgotten all about it, until now.

He went to the Battleground locker room to change from his father's old suit into golf clothes and spikes for his mother's flight.

"MAP TWOSOME ON THE TEE," Buttons announced from the deck, which was packed with respectful golfers from the Ironwoods Mens Club. Cloudy bent over and powdered a portion of his mother's ashes on the teed-up ball. He put down the vase near his cell phone, grabbed his 2-iron and aligned his stance. He waited until the digital numbers on the phone's clock flashed to 2:23, then he swung and launched a shot, scattering his Mom into the blue of the sky and the green of the grass and lost sight of her in the light of the sun.

"Fly, Mom, fly," he warbled, watching the ball land in the fairway. The crowd clapped. Cloudy acknowledged their applause by lightly tugging the brim of his cap with a forefinger and thumb. "At least I didn't turn my Mom into a worm burner," he joked.

The men came over and offered their sympathy and filtered back into the 19th hole. Some of the members were in their late sixties, he realized each one had long ago experienced the loss of someone they loved—and yet, they laughed, joked, worked, played and endured. He never thought of it that way before, or about anyone really. Now, he was a reluctant member in that inevitable club too.

Cloudy heard giggling. He looked over and saw Ernie and Pete on a nearby fairway. They had gotten their clubs tangled in a tree branches again. They were cracking up. The kids were secure and fixed in a world with both parents alive, having no idea how happy they really were. Lucky you, Cloudy thought, lucky you. I had it once too. Enjoy it while it lasts, and remember who gave it to you, dingleheads.

Buttons came over to Cloudy and said, "John, My condolences on your loss."

"Thank you."

"I don't know how much this will help, I've stood over this putt in life too," said Buttons. "I know one thing: love is more powerful than grief. Right now, I know it doesn't seem that way. But your mother will visit you. Her *feel* will never leave you. She will come to you. That's what loves does. It can't be stopped. Ever."

"I'd like to believe that."

"Loss changes things though in ways you can't believe. I knew this one family, and they seemed so perfect," said Buttons. "Everyone was so happy. The mother was great. A saint, really. All the brothers and sisters loved each other and partied together. They had a beautiful place by Greenwood Lake in New York, gorgeous, right by the water. Around the dinner table they laughed and joked. They welcomed me into their home, treated me like family. But when the mother died, they all started fighting in Probate Court over the lake house, money, furniture, her wedding ring, paintings—you name it. Got lawyers. Sued each other over who got the salt and pepper shakers. Blood might be thicker than water but it also *stains.* Ten years later, one brother was dying and still refusing to speak to his sister over the will or money or something stupid."

"I can see that," said Cloudy.

"The Mom kept them together and apart," continued Buttons. "If you want to keep the family your mom made, you have to love what your mother saw in your father, your sister. You have to get out of your own way. You can't *ever* be who you are anymore. Be thankful you still have your Dad. When the last one goes it's tougher."

"Not looking forward to it, no one is ever around long enough."

So, how is your pop holding up?"

"My Dad, he's struggling," said Cloudy. "My Mom did everything for him. He called me one time, crying because he couldn't make the bed right. My sister is living with him, but she's not taking care of him. She's still drinking, sleeps in her room sometimes for three days. I come over and clean up the place. It's a mess. I think he's drinking more, I'm worried about him."

"Well, that kind of thing is everywhere, more than you think," said Buttons. "Hey John, isn't that Chop over there one of your former Vices?" He pointed to the parking lot by the driving range.

Pudge was getting out of a white Camero.

"Yeah, that's my old Vice," said Cloudy, walking away, clenching his 2-iron. "Take care of my Mom for a second, please."

PUDGE PULLED OUT HIS GOLF BAG from the Camero's trunk. He took the small air horn from the bag's pocket and tested it.

BLEEEEEEAAAAAH! blasted the air horn.

"Hey, keep it down to a low roar will ya?" indignantly piped a golfer from a driving range stall. "A little respect for the venue."

"If you don't like it, join a private club," snapped Pudge, who spun and was unexpectedly confronted by a stern, taut Cloudy. Pudge wasn't intimidated. He warmly greeted Cloudy. "Yo Dawg, I'm such a pissah. Wassssup? You come to play?"

"You never visited my Mom in the hospital."

"People get sick in hospitals."

"Do people also get sick going to funerals and wakes too?"

"I prefer to remember people the way they were when they were alive."

"Do you get sick from calling too?"

"I'm different, that's all," he said, grabbed his golf bag and tried to get by. "Peace out, I'm gone."

Cloudy blocked his exit and said, "My Mom fed you. She gave you Christmas presents. You owe my Mom a 'Thank you.' I want to hear it now. And you aren't going anywhere until you do it."

"Wait, you're getting on my case?" snorted said Pudge. "You! Whose Mommy and Daddy paid for his college, insurance, car? You've been given a free ride your whole life. And what did you make out of it? Diddly squat. And I bet you even you feel *entitled* to an apology from me too? No one handed me anything, Dawg." He sneered and slowly spat. "You Westport boys are all the same."

Cloudy detonated.

"*Westport* boy!" lashed Cloudy, his fury hit an octave he never reached before, giving birth to another voice within him that surfaced the bottom of his swing arc. He jabbed the 2-iron's handle butt into Pudge's crotch, jackknifing him over. The air horn clattered on the asphalt. Cloudy dropped the club. He unfurled an uppercut to Pudge's jaw, decking him. "I'm not a Westport boy. I'm from Freehold, New Jersey! Zip code 07728." Cloudy snatched the air-horn and blasted it into Pudge's left ear for a few seconds. "You *hated* your mother. Your father screwed around. My Mom always made you feel welcome in our home. She made sure you always left with something. Get up on your frickin' ungrateful piece-of-shit knees and say, 'Thank you' to my Mom and that you're sorry!"

Pudge wheezed and crawled up into a kneel, wiped blood from his nose and said, "Thank you, Mrs. M., I'm sorr—"

"Sorry ya such a pissah," added Cloudy.

Pudge heaved out breath after deep breath and softly said the words that left blood on his lips, "My bad, I'm a pissah."

A small shadow flickered over the cracked asphalt between them. Cloudy looked up. A low-flying crow had a baby bird clamped in its beak. The struggling chick was plucked from the comfort of its nest. It cheeped, vainly calling out for its mother. Cloudy chucked the air horn at the crow.

He wasn't even close.

Blind Guys Really Can Break 80

"THE MAPS IN THE HUNT FOR FIRST against our the five-time consecutive champion Anthony "Eggplant" Anchor in the final round for Battleground Country Club's venerated Gull Cup," sonorously observed The Judge to Cloudy, who had finished warming up on the driving range and was putting clubs into his bag, which was strapped to one of the many carts positioned along the first tee for the shotgun start. The Judge leaned against the rail of the Pro Shop's porch deck and surveyed the standings on the tournament leader board. The Judge cradled his morning glass of white wine, looked directly at Cloudy and said, "Young John, what do you attribute the Maps unexpected rise to such achieved heights of greatness?"

"We've been losers so long, by now, we should know how to make other people do it," replied Cloudy. "I'm keeping out of the rough. Staying within myself. Let the other guys crash and burn trying to be somebody else."

The Judge leaned on his cane and appraised him, "Young man, your game has truly improved. Quite accomplished. In the past, you hit the ball, but now... you're a *player.*"

Mingle's announcement crackled on the Pro Shop speakers, "Gentlemen, welcome to the The Gull. Players tee off in 15 minutes."

The Judge hobbled away and said, "Go get 'em, Speed."

"Speed?"

"I'm calling you Speed, because you're going *somewhere*," The Judge stopped, turned and added, "Your mother was a wonderful woman."

"Thank you. She always thought you were a real character."

"I am," said The Judge, who nodded, walked away and added, "I see a lot of her in you today."

Cloudy took in the course. Summer was reluctant to hand off its seasonal baton to September. The salt air in the slight breeze from Long Island Sound was warm but had a chilly edge. A sharp, clear blue sky was beginning to emboss the landscape's edges where summer had softened them. The trees were full and rustled but the leaves were green and rimmed with discoloration.

Mingle came out of the Pro Shop and said, "A perfect day for golf."

Lucy barked.

"I thought you said Lucy didn't bark," said Cloudy, perking up.

"Mystery solved," said Mingle, nodding. "She only barks at *him*."

Lucy was on the fringe of the putting green barking at Eggplant. He was trying to pet her, but the dog remained beyond his reach. Eggplant found this amusing and smiled, which made Lucy bark faster—and higher.

"Mr. Anchor is the only person Lucy barks at. She wants no part of him," said Mingle. "And it's weird because he is nothing but nice to her. At first I believed it was a coincidence. But it's not."

"Didn't you once tell me you thought the reason Lucy didn't bark was because she might have been abused by her last owner?"

Mingle tilted his head and said appreciatively, "You remember things people say. Most people don't."

"Lucy knows what's behind Eggplant's smile," Cloudy observed coolly. "She's *seen* it before." He paused. "I wish my sister did. Wish we all did."

"Hit'em straight," Mingle diplomatically replied, walked to a cart and drove off. "I'll be out on the course if players need a ruling."

WHEN CLOUDY STEPPED ON THE FIRST TEE for the best-of-9-hole match, he shook hands with Eggplant and Arax. He warmly wished them good luck. His sportsmanship baffled—no, positively *stupefied* his father.

"Anything to say before we beat your sorry ass, Cloudy?" brashly said Eggplant, loosening up with a swing-trainer club.

"Count the clubs in your bags," said Cloudy. "We're not allowed to have more than 14—"

"Well, look at you, already with the rules," disparagingly said Eggplant. "I have 13 clubs and a putter. Duh. That makes 14 clubs." He held up a ball. "I'm hitting a Nike number 4."

"I'm using a Nike number 3," said Cloudy, taking out a new Nike from the complimentary sleeve of balls given to tournament players.

Clear said, "I'm playing a scuffed Pinnacle 3."

"Donald, what ball are you hitting?" asked Cloudy.

"A Titleist Pro VI with 'Prov: 8:35,'" replied Arax, who picked up the match's scorecard clipped to the base of his cart's steering wheel. He frowned and studied it. "I don't get a single stroke on *any* holes. And I'm giving Cloudy strokes on every hole except the eighth."

"So your game has really improved since the last time we played," said Cloudy. Sometimes ability catches up to your handicap."

"No, some asswipe posted 20 low scores using my GHIN number in the computer," Arax replied. "I complained, but Buttons at Ironwoods confirmed the scores with your club pro."

Cloudy said, "But despite that, you've been able to play to a low handicap into the finals. Think of it as a positive."

Eggplant said, "Your twosome has the honors on the tee. Enjoy it while it lasts because it's will be the only time it's going to happen." He paused. "Just so you know…"

Clear teed up and said, "They lengthened the rough, I'll never reach a fairway." He swung, and somehow popped the ball straight up in the air. It came down and hit the club's graphite shaft, landed on the small Revolutionary Minuteman tee marker and rolled ten feet behind him.

Eggplant found this hilarious. He fist tapped Arax, and said, "It's already over."

"Another great moment of golf," said Clear, shaking his head and laughing. "What in God's name would you call that?"

"I don't know what the Good Lord would call it but in golf I believe it's called hitting three on the tee,'" Arax said.

"Just pick up Dad, don't worry about it," said Cloudy, teeing up his ball and added in a matter-of-fact tone, "You have a 33-handicap. That means you make 33 bad shots in 18 holes. You used up three. What's the big deal? You'll do better on the next hole."

"I should only hit my 3-wood," said Clear. "I hit my 3-wood better than my driver and can reach the fairway more often. My handicap can make up the difference."

"Whatever you want to do Dad, just have some fun."

Cloudy's true strategy throughout the tournament was: 1.) Casually dismissing his father's complaints about bad shots 2.) Ignoring his gripes. 3.) Never questioning his self-destructive choice of club. 4.) Being supportive when he hit a bad or good shot. Those four tactics were based in Cloudy's belief that his Dad was like the Don't Gallery—he came with the territory. Instead getting in his way and taking his father's behavior personally, Cloudy remained safely behind his personal deflector shield: the mental discipline of his game. This had an unexpected and surprising effect. Since they weren't arguing, his Dad's energy was channeled into courteous conversations with opponents and hurt their concentration and oddly improved his father's play. Clear's high handicap enabled him to come in on a couple par-3s, and along with Cloudy's steady play, they were ham-and-egging their handicaps to take a few key holes and win matches.

"I'm horrible," said Clear, heading back to the cart.

"Dad you tried the best you could," said Cloudy, teeing up. "And you missed, so you tried your best. That's all anyone can do."

Cloudy swung and sliced his drive into the rough.

"Outside of that shot how is the rest of your life going?" cracked Eggplant, who put his swing trainer in the bag and took out a driver.

"It's something to do," said Cloudy smiling, walking off. "If you're not looking forward to your next shot you're playing the wrong game."

"Hey, check this out," said Eggplant, putting on a visor with a spiked-orange-hair wig attached to it. He chortled. "Flair hair, looks real too."

Cloudy laughed and said, "That's hilarious."

Arax held out a roll of candy to Cloudy and said, "Lifesavers anyone?"

"Lifesavers? Sure, I love Lifesavers," Cloudy said, snatching the roll, tearing off the wrapping and cramming all the candies into his mouth.

"Hey," said Arax, aghast. "That's my last pack!"

"It's the only way I can taste their full flavor," said Cloudy, crunching down on the candies. "Hey, these aren't Spearmint! I hate Peppermint." Cloudy spit out the Lifesavers.

Arax dolefully stared at the white broken circles of candies atop the blades of grass and meekly whined, "My Lifesavers."

"I can make it up to you, Donald. I have some Altoids in my bag."

"No."

"Donald, I have some beef jerky."

"No."

"Skittles, Donald?"

Arax rounded on Cloudy, "What is it about 'no' you don't understand?"
"Very little, actually," said Cloudy. "It's either the 'n' or the 'o' part. When people put those two letters together I get awfully confused."

The starting horn sounded.

"And don't call me Donald," huffed Arax. He mechanically teed up, swung and hit a monster drive in the middle of the fairway.

"Keep going!" said Eggplant to the rolling ball. "Get legs. Get—"

"Don't talk to my ball!" sternly cautioned Arax. He tapped the crucifix bulge on his chest and smugly observed with his usual self-satisfaction, "I can do business with that."

Eggplant hit his tee shot in the fairway, tapped fists with his partner and said, "Money!" He strutted off the tee and added to Maps, "If you want to play with the big dogs you have to leave the porch."

"Great drive," said Cloudy, applauding. "Perfect tempo. Beautiful."

Clear shot a skeptical sideways glance at his son, pulled Cloudy over and whispered, "You're nice to Eggplant on the tee, and you laughed at his stupid flair hair, and now you're complimenting *him*?"

"Hey, he hit a great drive," innocently explained Cloudy with a slight backspin of insincerity. "After all Dad, golf is a gentlemen's game."

"And why you did do that to his partner's Lifesavers? You haven't eaten Lifesavers since you were a kid."

"People's tastes change over time," said Cloudy, smiling craftily. "Didn't you always tell me that only an intelligent person changes his opinion. So what's wrong with that?"

"Because I know you," said Clear, suspiciously eyeing his son. "You're up to something, hawkshaw."

EGGPLANT TOOK THE FIRST THREE HOLES. Cloudy didn't mind. After he saw Eggplant put the swing trainer in his bag, Cloudy hoped they'd run into Mingle before they started the third hole. When he climbed the steps to the raised tee box of the fourth hole in the match, he was relieved to see Mingle driving a cart in their direction. Cloudy knew his pysch would still work.

"Maps three down after three holes," Eggplant crowed and beamed his wise-ass smirk. "Cloudy, just so you know... after we take the next two holes, that'll make it 5-4. Five holes and with four left to play and you're out of here like you were last year."

Clear studied the scorecard and said, "It doesn't look good for us."

"Ya think?" said Eggplant, taking a practice swing with a 7-iron.

"It's all good," said Cloudy, who sharply whistled and flagged down the pro. "Yo, I need a ruling!"

"What are you doing?" asked Clear.

"A ruling for what?" said Eggplant.

"We haven't even teed up yet," said Arax, confused. "Ruling?"

"A dispute, gentlemen?" asked Mingle, parking the cart. Lucy sat alongside him. "What is at issue?" He strolled over. Lucy barked once at Eggplant. "Stay girl."

Cloudy went to Eggplant's cart and said, "Mr. Anchor has played the first three holes with *15 club*s in his bag."

"Blow me I have 14," Eggplant countered with his usual wit.

"I see 15," said Cloudy, pointing at the swing trainer in the bag.

"You can't count my swing trainer as a club," said Eggplant.

"It's in your bag," countered Cloudy.

Mingle examined the swing trainer and said, "It has a grip. It has a clubface. It has a shaft." He paused. "It's a club."

Cloudy pulled a rule booklet from his back pocket and said, "If I'm correct, according to the rules of golf: 'In match play, at the conclusion at which the breach is discovered, the state of the match is adjusted by deducting one hole for each hole played.' The extra-club infraction results in losing a maximum of two holes."

"Young John's interpretation of the ruling is correct," said Mingle. "How does this match stand now?"

"Anchor is 3 up with 6 holes left," said Cloudy.

Mingle changed the scorecards and said, "With the penalty the score now stands: Anchor twosome 1 up with 6 holes left to play."

"You're shittin' me?" challenged Eggplant, stalking over to Mingle.

Lucy gurrrrred.

"It's gentlemen's game," said Clear. "We don't want to win like that."

"Mr. Map," Mingle authoritatively clipped and climbed in the cart. "It would be unfair to the other players to make an exception. Rules are the game's foundation. That's exactly why golf *is* a gentlemen's game."

"I got your foundation right here," said Eggplant, pointing to his crotch as Mingle drove away.

In the fourth hole of the match, they had to hit from a tee box that overlooked a pond in front of the 140-yard hole. The par-3 had a kidney-shaped green guarded by four bunkers. A cyclone border fence ran along the fairway's left side and wrapped around the green, behind the fence was a recently constructed monstrous colonial mansion that looked like it was on human growth hormones.

"You guys still have honors," said Cloudy.

"A smooth, knock-down 8-iron to the front of the green right at the pin," said Arax, coaching himself. He made a flawless swing. His eyes widened with joy. "I can *really* do business with that." He sighed, clutching the crucifix bulge. "That's a perfect shot."

"In the hole!" Eggplant shouted. "In the hole, beeeee-yatch—"

"Don't talk to my ball!" sharply said Arax.

It was perfect. The shot dropped straight into the hole. The metal cup clanged. Then the ball bounced out and over the 15-foot fence onto the colonial mansion lower roof and rolled into a rain gutter.

"Goes right in the hole and the damn metal cup kicks the ball over the fence!" yowled Arax. "What in God's name do you call that?"

"I don't know what the Good Lord would call it, but in golf I believe it's called hitting three on the tee,'" Cloudy chirped, then added, "Just so you know..."

"The best ball I ever hit in my life is my worst one," vented Arax, who resentfully took out a second ball. He couldn't shake off his frustration. He pulled his third shot over the border fence where it hopped with loud clicks on the asphalt down Country Club Lane. Arax took one step and slammed his iron's blade into the ground like he was trying to split the earth. "Jarred a tee shot and I'm out of this hole." He shook his head. "Shit on my dog. Woof!"

Eggplant teed up. His ball landed on the green rolled past the hole and rested a short distance above the cup.

"Money!" said Eggplant. "Run to the hole, beeeeeee-yatch."

"In the jaws," said Arax. "Own it!"

Clear set up to his ball and hit his tee shot in the water. He chuckled and said, "I'm hopeless. Beyond redemption. I'm in my pocket."

"Dad, it's a lateral and you get a drop in front of the pond."

"It won't make any difference."

"Whatever you want to do that's fine," said Cloudy. He teed up and swung. He dropped his 7-iron, clutched his head in despair and groaned, "Too much club."

His shot sailed over the back fence, hit the mansion's lower porch roof, bounced back and landed on the green above Eggplant's ball.

"Look at you," Eggplant derisively cracked. "Even a blind squirrel finds an acorn once in awhile."

"Well then, nuts to you," countered Cloudy, strutting to the cart.

EGGPLANT AND CLOUDY STOOD ON THE FOURTH HOLE'S GREEN and studied their putts. Cloudy had a downhill ten-footer. Eggplant's ball was between Cloudy's ball and the hole. Eggplant smirked and marked his ball with a silver dollar coin.

"Can you relocate your marker, please?" asked Cloudy. "I can't putt around it."

"My bad," said Eggplant, smirking and moving the marker.

"Thank you," said Cloudy, lining up his putt. "Dad, you want to tend the pin?"

"You won't need it," said Clear, pulling out the pin and walking away. "It's downhill and fast, don't give away the hole."

"Downhill and fast, thanks."

Cloudy stood over his ball and got ready to putt. The Don't Gallery appeared in the form of Eggplant, who intentionally angled his shadow across the line of the putt to break Cloudy's concentration. His slanted silhouette was appropriately positioned so the hole was exactly where Eggplant's heart was.

"*Don't* push it, a lot of meat on that bone," said Eggplant. "If you want to play with the big dogs, you have to leave the porch."

Cloudy closed his eyes, unfazed. How many times had he practiced putting with The Don't Gallery sniping at him? He armored himself against distractions. And one more came. Just as Cloudy's putter face made contact with the ball, Eggplant tugged at his golf glove's Velcro wrist strap creating a tearing sound. Cloudy never wavered. His putter was locked-in the grooved bottom of its arc and maintained a smooth pendulum-like stroke. He remained still and waited.

"Be right," Cloudy said, listening.

The solidly struck ball rattled and filled the cup's metallic emptiness.

"The farther away you are from the hole the better it sounds," said Cloudy, smiling.

When Cloudy walked over to get his ball, he shaped his right hand to resemble a revolver. The thumb was the hammer. The forefinger a barrel. The three remaining fingers curled for a handle. He stuck the forefinger of his handgun into the cup.

"Bang! Bang! Bang!" Cloudy said and snatched up his birdie. He blew imaginary smoke from his finger barrel and added to Eggplant, "Just so you know... if you miss your putt, our match is even."

Eggplant unsteadily circled the hole and studied the break as if he was a surveyor recording readings to build a nuclear power plant on the green. His body language was shaky. He plumb-bobbed his club. Finally, he tentatively hovered over the ball and hesitatingly drew back his wobbling putter.

Cloudy said, "Your putt is good."

Eggplant was stunned and said, "You're giving me an 8-foot putt?"

"I don't want you to lose because you suck," said Cloudy, who walked over, went jaw to jaw with Eggplant and calmly clipped. "I want to win because I *beat* your sorry ass."

Cloudy walked back to the cart.

An amazed Clear sat at the wheel and said, "Who are you? I don't know this son. What are you doing?"

Cloudy narrowed his glaring eyes and said with the firm grim edge of resolve, "Winning."

"BANG! NO BLOOD," said Cloudy, firing his handgun into the match's 7th hole as his third consecutive par putt coiled in the curved rim and drained into the cup. His swing was in a groove, as if his club was an antennae receiving a clear signal of perfection. Cloudy was secure, insulated and protected within the bottom of his swing arc. Nothing could touch him. "You're still only 1-up with 2 holes left to play."

"Wait! We took this hole. I birdied," protested Arax.

"Cloudy strokes here, you don't," said Eggplant, smoldering. "We should have closed the door on them in five holes." Eggplant groused, "I've been throwing up on my shoes since he gave me that putt."

A disgruntled Arax sat next to Eggplant in the cart and said, "I'm getting birdies. Bur Cloudy with his extra stoke has pushed every hole by pulling pars out of his ass."

"If you didn't have to give me strokes, you guys would have clinched the championship on the last hole," said Cloudy, putting the pin back in the cup. "Crazy game, huh?"

Eggplant said to Arax, "Don't worry, he can't keep up the pace. I know Cloudy, his wheels we come off under pressure."

"See you at the next tee," said Cloudy, who got into the cart, nudged his elbow into his Dad's side and lowered his voice, "They're rattled. Let's take this next hole and tie it up."

"You're playing slow," clipped Clear.

"What?"

"You're deliberating too long over shots."

"There is one hole open in front of us and no group is pressing us from behind. So what's the big deal?"

"It's about etiquette," said Clear, scolding him. "We're supposed to keep up with the group in front of us."

"I make clutch pars and you're giving me crap about slow play?"

Clear said, "Today, would have been 52 years I'd be married to your Mom. We were planning to go on a trip."

"What?" gasped Cloudy, distressed. "Your anniversary. Why are you throwing this card down on me now?"

"Son, in the scheme of things, does this game really matter?"

"Yes, but I guess not... to you, it should though, it should," listlessly said Cloudy.

"What should?"

Cloudy's deflector shield lost power. The support at the bottom of his swing arc gave way. Cloudy mentally plummeted in darkness. Completely blind, groping. He desperately reached up and down but all he felt was bottom. And bottom kept coming. Is this what was truly at the bottom of his swing arc? Just bottom? A echoing thump that never ended?

If the game at the bottom of his swing arc couldn't redeem and save a blind man from himself, what could possibly save him now?

THE EIGHTH HOLE IN THE NINE-HOLE MATCH was a 445-yard par-4. A tee shot had to carry 170 yards of marsh to an uphill fairway with an elevated crowned green.

Eggplant smacked two consecutive drives in the marsh, stamped off the tee and said to Arax, "I'm in my pocket. Don't fuck up, partner."

Arax mechanically laced a 300-yard draw down the fairway. "In the jaws," he barked and sharply nipped at the air around him, as if he was gobbling up flying insects. His fist thumped his crucifix and he said, "I can do business with that." He paused. "A lower grooved shot."

"Money!" said Eggplant, giving his partner a fist tap.

"Own it." Arax replied.

"Big," noted Clear, who seemed to dragged himself to the tee. "This hole is always my downfall." Clear stood over the ball. His arms didn't hang, they drooped. He swung. His club hit the ground first and missed the ball. He jumped in pain, clasping his wrist.

"That had to hurt," said Eggplant, smirking.

"Dad!" said Cloudy. "You all right?"

"My wrist is already swelling up," said Clear, walking to a nearby cooler, taking ice and putting it into a golf towel. "I'm out of this hole."

"That's okay Dad, you're in pain," said Cloudy. "I don't want you to feel any more pain than you have to."

"No pressure," said Eggplant. "My partner is in the fairway lying one and hitting two. And this is the only hole in the match where you don't get any strokes because of your handicap." He added in a loud aside to Arax, "Here's where Cloudy comes apart."

Cloudy feebly teed up. His ball fell off the tee twice. He stood over his shot for 30 seconds, hoping for *The Feel.* But his swing arc was gone. He ransacked the shag bag of his mind to regain his focus but found nothing. Sweat dribbled down his armpits like crawling ants. He stepped away and attempted get back in his groove with a few practice swings. But every swing only made his arms and shoulders heavier. The Don't Gallery sensed his weakness, broke through the deflector's shields imaginary ropes, surrounded him and chanted, "*Don't* top the ball into the marsh." In a panic, Cloudy jerkily swung. He topped the ball into the marsh. An unplayable lie. Grief was a ball that rolled nowhere. His game and life had officially bottomed out.

Eggplant said, "Outside of that shot, how is the rest of your life going?" He did his patented mean-puppet chuckle and muttered to his partner. "I told you he doesn't have the game. Only a matter of time. I know this family, they don't have what it takes to win."

"It's not your fault, son," said Clear, sulking in the cart, icing his sprained wrist. "I haven't come in for you on any of the holes today. I've gotten worse. You've been keeping us in this. I let you down. What good am I? Can't even make my own bed right?"

Cloudy's lost heap of father sagged in regret. But within that drained 72-year-old figure Cloudy saw another man rise: his Freehold Dad. In Jersey, every Friday evening around 6:45, Cloudy and Wendy heard the commuter bus drive by their home. They opened the front door and got all excited when they saw Dad walking on the sidewalk through a fading trail of departing black bus exhaust. His tan London Fog trench coat slung over his shoulder, brown hat tilted back and tie pulled down on a sweat-stained white shirt with an open collar. His attaché case banged against his knee. Dad was beat but emerged from his work week with quiet heroic finish. When he saw Wendy and Cloudy at the front door, his face brightened and he smiled and they clapped. How many years had he trekked up the slanted driveway to 223 Stonehurst Way where Cloudy, his sister and their Mom depended on him? And Dad always came through. Yes, he did. Back in Freehold, everything in his Dad's career and their lives held so much promise. And the world around them so vibrant. But throughout it all, even though the future changed, the man sitting in the golf cart never hung up his Dad Uniform and walked off. He worried about his kids. Their problems were his problems. He had every reason not to help but bailed them out time and time again. But now the slumped man in the cart didn't have the strength to make it up another driveway for himself. His wife's love was not at home, mixing a drink, making his dinner. Cloudy knew it was time he got out of his way for the man who came up the driveway.

"Dad, you've *never* let me down," said Cloudy, his voice quavering. "You've always been there for me. The main thing, win or lose, we're here for each other playing golf together. Because if you weren't here with me, this game would be meaningless. Meaningless without you." He paused. "I only have *one* Dad."

"While we're young," Eggplant impatiently said, then smirked and added, "Cloudy, do you realize if you lose this hole the match we'll be two holes up with one left to play. Everything is at stake on this final hole. So the most important thing is to relax and play this next shot like it's no different than any other shot."

Cloudy teed up his second ball. The static was gone. His zone zapped back! He felt relaxed, loose, oily. Then *The Feel* visited him. But it was a loving embrace. A soft, warm amorphous presence pressed like a mist against Cloudy's back soaking and marinating every muscle, joint and bone in his body. *I know who this is*, he thought, tearing up. *I know who this is.* His legs buckled. The driver slipped from his hands. He dropped to his knees. Tears rolled from the pinched inside corners of his eyes.

"Mom," Cloudy barely murmured.

"Are you all right?" said Clear, concerned. "You're crying."

"It's Mom, Dad, she's visiting me," said Cloudy. "I know what this means. She's letting me know she didn't want us see her die."

Clear said, "Is it in the same way she spoke to you the day she left us. You know, when she told you to help me make the calls?"

"Yes," said Cloudy. "She still loves us." He grabbed his club, briskly went to his ball, drew back his driver and pushed off the bottom of his swing arc. The sweeping club's shaft and his spinning body became liquid, and the life his Mom gave him swished, swirled and flew. He watched its force burn down the fairway.

"That's the best in me and it's somebody else," Cloudy said, holding his follow-through and savoring the afterglow of his mother's presence. "The best. And I got all of it."

"Just so you know... in golf it's called 'hitting three, lying four,'" said Eggplant, but without his usual edge.

The foursome drove to their shots.

Arax went to his ball. He was in the fairway. A routine 140-yard shot to the elevated crown of the green. He confidently set up and swung.

"Where did it go?" Arax asked, momentarily panicking. "I lost it in the sun. But it felt good. It felt good."

"You're off the green to the left, I think," Eggplant said, squinting. "Didn't see it bounce."

The Maps went farther down the fairway.

"Look where your drive landed," Clear said excitedly, lightly whacking the back of his good hand against his son's hip. "You nailed that over 360 yards!"

Cloudy stepped from the cart and pulled out his 9-iron. He looked uphill to the elevated green and could make out the flagstick's tip. *The Feel* was still pulsating within him. He was coasting on its throb. He went to his ball, smoothly swung and crisply struck it.

"Pured it," crooned Cloudy. "Golf shot."

"You're on John!" cheered Clear. "That shot put us back on the map."

"I love me," happily said Cloudy, feeling giddy as the ball bounced at the pin. At that moment, Cloudy became what his mother fed him. Her dying eyes—the haunting eyes searching for him became loving eyes proudly admiring him in the same way she saw him at his 5th birthday party and wondered what her son was intended to become as danced naked descending the staircase. Cloudy celebrated his shot by doing the same moves he performed coming down those steps while his young mother smiled. Only this time, he danced with his clothes on—for *her*.

"Have to be the center of attention," his Dad said, amused, shaking his head. "Always on the stage, creating a spectacle of yourself. Your Mom was right about her *sonny*. You've never changed, brat."

"I know, isn't it great?" said an inspired Cloudy, wobbling his head and shaking his dupah down the fairway. "Right, Mom?"

THE MAPS DROVE AND PARKED NEAR THE GREEN. Eggplant and Arax were intensely searching the rough for Arax's approach shot.

"I'd bet any amount of money you landed here," said Eggplant a few feet off the fringe.

"No way am I declaring my ball lost," vowed Arax.

"Hawkshaw, look at your shot!" said Clear.

Cloudy's ball was resting an inch from the pin.

"Pick yours up, that's a gimme, even your Dad couldn't miss that putt," said Eggplant to Cloudy. "You're in with a 5, we're here in 2 hitting 3."

"If you find it," said Cloudy, bouncing out of the cart, walking across the green and reaching down to pick up his shot. "Let—"

Cloudy froze.

He saw Arax's Titleist 'Prov 8:35.'

It was in the cup, snugly wedged against the flagstick.

Arax holed out with a 2. An eagle! The bad guys won. The loss was hard for Cloudy to get his head around. He gave his best and didn't get it done. He failed. He couldn't get past it.

"Donald," said Cloudy. "Your ball is—"

"Found it," declared Arax.

"Sure it's yours?" asked Cloudy. "A Titleist—"

"Without a doubt. A Titleist Prov VI," said Arax as he nodded into the rough, his hands in his pockets. "Who could possibly be playing a Titleist with 'Prov: 8:35' marked in black?"

"I'll tell you who. Someone who played the hole before us," Cloudy said, pulling out Arax's original ball from the cup. "This Titleist *also* has 'Prov: 8:35' marked in black. For some reason they must have left it in the hole. Maybe you both worship at the same church."

Eggplant fired a quick scathing glance at Arax. Cloudy's ex-brother-in-law didn't mind cheating. He hated being caught. But Cloudy wasn't going to go there.

"Proverb 8:35," said Cloudy. "If I'm right, Proverb 8:35 in the Bible says: 'For he whoever finds me finds life and receives favor from the Lord.'" He paused. "I looked it up."

"I'm still here in two. Hitting three," said Arax, who set over his chip shot and gave himself a pep talk, "Back of the ball to the hole. Lag it and tap-in a 4 to take the match."

Arax's chip sped on the green and rolled to the cup

Eggplant clamored in an urgent plea, "Sit, sit, sit—"

"Don't talk to my ball!" hissed Arax, sneering.

The shot stopped a foot short of the hole.

"It's over!" howled Eggplant, fist tapping Arax.

"Putt it out," ordered Clear.

"Blow me. That's a gimme," belligerently insisted Eggplant. "I gave Cloudy his. I thought this was a *gentlemen's* game.'"

"My son told me never give anyone the winning putt. You want to win? Then earn it. Putt it out, Donald."

"It's *Don*," spat Arax, setting up and drawing back his putter.

But when the club's face came into the ball...

BLEEEEEEAAAAAH! blasted an air horn.

The sound startled Arax. His wrists jerked. He mis-hit.

"No!" Arax shrieked with a gasp and recoiled from the sight.

Arax's putt rolled left of the hole and stopped two inches past it.

The air-horn came from a car parked on Country Club Lane by a low stone wall along near the green.

"Republican bastards!" yelled the driver. "I'm such a pissah!"

Pudge's white Camero burned rubber and tore off.

"Hmmm," Cloudy said, appreciating the gesture. Well, he thought, we're even buddy, we're even.

Instead of taking his time, Arax impetuously swiped at the ball. The putter's bottom edge stabbed and caught the green and hit the putt too hard. It fluttered over the hole. Arax was consumed by wonderfully misplaced deep-seated throes of anguish at the malingering ball for betraying his sense of gravity.

"Can't you sink a two-inch fucking putt?" gurred Eggplant, leaning nose-to-nose to his partner. "Now we're *even* going into the last hole!"

"A *six*! I don't get sixes!" a seething Arax keened to the sky.

"If you want to play with the big dogs you have to leave the porch," said Cloudy.

"Woof," added Clear, tapping fists with his son.

THE CHAMPIONSHIP MATCH'S DETERMINING HOLE had a blind tee shot to the green. It was a 345-yard par-4 with a rolling fairway that banked and sloped downhill. Trees ran along the left, separating the fairway from the driving range. Deep rough was on the right for the last 100 yards and was designated as a lateral hazard due to a drainage problem from a broken sprinkler pipe.

"You're on the tee, Eggplant," said Cloudy, who corrected himself. "Oh, I forgot, *we* have honors because we won the last hole, didn't we?"

Clear took the iced towel off his swollen wrist and said, "You want me to take a whack at it, son? I stroke here."

"I'm on your bag, Dad," Cloudy confidently said. "I got this."

"Well, look at you," said Eggplant, hawking a wad of mucous.

Cloudy reached for his trusty 2-iron. *The Feel* was still with him. He teed up and lashed a sizzler down the right side of the fairway. The low shot had a slight draw, perfectly kicked off a bank below a bunker, accelerated and disappeared downhill.

"That's easily going to be in the fairway, 80 yards out," said Clear.

Arax teed up, started his swing, then nervously backed off the ball. He was definitely rattled by his chunking-out on the last hole. He hesitatingly realigned his feet, checked his stance, set up again, wavered, changed his footing and unraveled a blunt stiff swing.

"No!" Arax wailed, wildly whipping his club around him, as if it had suddenly burst into flames and was trying to put it out. He screamed at his tee shot, "Draw! Draw! Draw!"

"Don't talk to your ball!" said Cloudy.

Arax's shot didn't draw—it sliced and splattered in the muddy lateral hazard's rough.

"On the last hole, you hit an abortion like that," angrily spat Eggplant, stepping up to the tee. "That's not why I invited you here as my guest."

Eggplant dug in and struck his best ball of the day. His tee shot was identical to Cloudy's, hitting the bank and kicking down the fairway.

"Run, beeeee-yatch, run," Eggplant said.

"We can do business with that," said Arax, who got into the cart and attempted to tap fists but his partner spurned it.

Eggplant reproachfully glared at Arax and said,"That's how you man up, partner. Let's try to find your useless ball."

When the foursome approached the area where Arax's shot landed, the Maps stopped their cart. Eggplant drove passed them and over the small 'No Carts' sign stuck in the ground. He parked on the wet newly planted sod within the lateral hazard. He pointed at his partner's ball.

Arax got out of the cart, grabbed a club and paced in squishing spikes around his ball, as if cross-examining his lie to find a truth He wiped his goatee and mulishly snorted "Buried."

"Hey, look what I found in my bag," said Cloudy, walking over and holding up a pack of Lifesavers. "I forgot. I had them the whole time. Want one?" Cloudy spit a white Lifesaver near Arax's ball. "A pro told me there was a guy who cheated to win tournaments by using Lifesavers as tee to improve his bad lies. Can you imagine? That would be like dropping a ball through a hole in your pocket so you wouldn't have to declare your ball lost."

Arax looked up and flatly said, "People who lose say a lot of things."

"I bet a Lifesaver would help this shot though," said Cloudy, who reached into his pocket. "Sure you don't need to identify your ball?"

"I'm fine with my lie," Arax grunted. He settled over the ball and coached himself, "Let's turn this around. Short swing. Come down on it. Don't take grass." He savagely swung. Arax yipped in shocked disbelief, "Pulled it." He watched his ball streak over the trees and crash and burn in the driving range. He flicked his club behind him in disgust. The 9-iron clattered against the front bumper of the golf cart.

"That must have been an *upper* groove shot, huh?" said Cloudy.

"Fuckin' O.B.," said Arax. "I'm out of the hole."

"That's not O.B.—it's O.B.G.Y.N," said Eggplant behind the wheel, then added in contempt and pointed at Arax's goatee, "Just because you have hair around your mouth doesn't mean you have to hit the ball like a pussy."

Arax picked up his club and got into the cart.

Eggplant slammed his foot down on the accelerator. The cart's back wheels failed to gain traction. The spinning tires dug deep grooves in the sod and dredged up the plastic mesh beneath it. The netting wrapped around the rear axle and jammed the wheels.

"Caught in a web," Eggplant grumbled, getting out. He pulled a pitching wedge and putter from his bag. "Fuck it, I'll walk from here to my ball."

"I'll walk too," added Cloudy, striding uphill ahead of Eggplant.

"Donald can ride with me," said Clear, smirking. "I mean, Don."

Cloudy was the first player over the rise. He saw two balls in the fairway. One sat up in the grass. The second landed a few yards past it, but rested in a three-inch deep divot, an almost impossible shot to hit.

"Your ball is a Nike number 4, right?" Cloudy shouted back to Eggplant, examining the ball that sat up perfectly.

"Yeah," replied Eggplant behind him and coming down the slope.

"Mine is a Nike number 3," said Cloudy, who kicked the grass. He went to the other ball, stared down at it and disappointedly sighed, "Damn, landed in a divot."

"Outside of that shot, how is the rest of your day going?" smugly quipped Eggplant, smiling. "Since you're so into rules. Just so you know... in golf if a ball lands in a divot you can't remove it." He beamed. "I have a perfect lie."

"If anyone knows how to appreciate the value of a perfect lie, it's you," evenly said Clear walking over from the cart to his son's side.

Eggplant stepped up and made a effortless, buttery swing. The ball floated and caught the edge of the green.

"Get there, beeeee-yatch," shouted Eggplant. "Release!"

His shot hit the fringe skipped and stopped an inch from the hole.

"Money!" said Eggplant, shooting up his arms. "Money! Money!"

"Own it!" roared Arax, who tapped fists with his partner. "A kick-in birdie. We can definitely do business with that. Right in the jaws!"

Cloudy casually assessed the whooping celebrants and said in a low voice, "Dad, you were wrong about something you said to me."

"Which time?" said Clear, chuckling.

"You told me a person doesn't become a man until both his parents are no longer around. That's not true. After parents go, lots of people never become anything or less. You don't become a man when your Mom and Dad are gone. It's when you're *there* for your Mom and Dad. When you're on their bag, that's when you're a man."

Clear nodded, pondered the remark then tenderly said, "Son?"

"Yeah Dad, what?"

"I love you. You don't have to be good at golf to impress me."

Cloudy smiled and said, "Yes, I do."

They laughed.

He walked to his ball, took a deep breath and set over his shot.

"No pressure, Cloudy," said Eggplant, chortling. "It's a routine wedge that happens to be in a divot."

Cloudy stopped his backswing and said, "I can't hit this ball. This ball—it's *yours*."

"Come again?"

"My ball is a Nike number 3," Cloudy calmly explained. "This one is a Nike number 4." He paused. "You played *my* ball."

Eggplant spluttered, "You set me up to play the wrong ball."

"I didn't identify the balls, I only stated what balls we were playing," said Cloudy, pulling out a rule book. "It says here: 'In match play, if a player makes a stroke at a *wrong* ball that is not in a hazard, he is disqualified for that hole.'" Cloudy smiled. "Just so you know... We beat your sorry ass." Cloudy leaned into Eggplant until their noses were an inch apart and added with deep conviction, "From my hands, down the shaft and into your cold black heart."

A rush of elation elevated Cloudy on an imaginary pedestal. His whole body throbbed with haloes of energy powered by the muscles of his dream. So, this is what victory feels like, he thought, no wonder people gladly suffer for it. He joyfully ran and executed a Bruce-Springsteen knee slide on the fairway and stopped at his father's feet.

"Always, center stage," said Clear, beaming.

Eggplant sneered and said, "Clear, your son deceived me."

"Ya think?" said Clear, who tapped fists with his son. "Money."

Arax stormed over to Eggplant and furiously roared, "I've carried you the whole tournament. You hit, what? Two greens in regulation? And we lose because you played the wrong ball in the fairway."

"Why couldn't you sink a goddamn putt?" Eggplant angrily countered. "You never came in when I needed you most."

"You kept talking to *my* ball!"

"Nice match, guys," said Cloudy, standing and extending his hand to the losers, who ignored him. He turned to Clear. "Dad, did you see the darkness, a flashing light and the sound I made just now?"

"What sound?"

"The sound of me pulling my head out of my ass."

"I'm glad my hearing's not *that* good," said Clear, who grinned with pride. His eyes gleamed and held a steady gaze at Cloudy. "Son, without a doubt, you are truly the greatest wet fart of all time."

CLEAR LIPPED OUT A CELEBRATORY SNORT of vodka from The Gull Cup at the Battleground Country Club's member-guest tournament awards evening festivities. He happily watched Cloudy and Penny swing dance to the band playing the 'Tuxedo Junction.' The song ended. The laughing couple smiled and returned to the table, arms around each other.

"You didn't have tempo as a kid, but you got it now," said Clear, who smiled and applauded.

"She gave *that* to me," said Cloudy, reached into his pocket and pulled out a ball. "Here's the game ball from our match that says it all."

"Oh *that* was the game ball in your pants," said Penny. "I thought you were enjoying our dance." She kissed him. "Penny for your thoughts."

"Keep the change," he said, reaching for his beer.

"I admit watching you two puts me a little under the rug," said Clear, looking down and turning The Gull Cup. "Your mother and I danced at all those parties we had in Freehold. And those Polish weddings. You were too young to appreciate them. They were wild. One time your Uncle Bert did a spin, shit in his pants, went into the bathroom, hung his underwear up on a nail and went right back on the dance floor. The Marcufski brothers got into a fight with the groom's best man." He laughed. "Blood and cake everywhere. Women screaming. The bride's father taken to the hospital. That was a hell of a wedding!"

"How's your wrist, Pops?" asked Penny.

"The vodka has taken down some of the sting out of the swelling, cookie," said Clear,. "Fortunately, I can drink with either hand."

Penny sipped her mohito and said, "Wendy seems to be handling her Ex being here okay, given her track record and all."

"Far as I can tell she's behaving, maybe it was a mistake on my part to bring her as my date, who knows," replied Clear, shrugging. "She said she was going for dessert. She's probably smoking outside. Her mother dies of cancer, and she smokes. Smokes in the condo and gets mad when I complain about it. But to listen to her, the things she thinks are important. I can't believe the things she's concerned about. She talks about her hair, her friends, how she doesn't have *fun* anymore. Nothing about getting a job. And moving on with her life. She's like a 16 year-old girl now. The way she talks about her divorce you'd think it happened today. It was how many years ago? And she still gets mail addressed to her in as 'Wendy Anchor.' His last name."

"As long as she lives there, she doesn't have problems because she's your problem," said Cloudy. "Until she becomes her *own* problem she's not going to change."

"Lavender, a little lavender son. I can't throw my little girl out in the street," said Clear. "She'll sleep under some bridge."

"Dad, she still has money from the divorce," said Cloudy.

"You know, I think you're right, I've gone as far as I can with her, and it's not helping," said Clear. "I raised her once, I shouldn't have to do it twice." He stared at his drink. His eyes widened. "Oh, before I forget, hawkshaw, the pro told me your golf clubs are at the bag drop outside."

Cloudy said, "We'll grab them when we leave. So I—"

Someone lurched into Cloudy's chair, pinning his chest against the edge of the table.

"Excuse you," said the bleary-eyed Eggplant. He was drunk, heavily listing. He scornfully added, "I totaled your team scores up. If we played 18 holes you guys would of had a net 78. What do rules have to do with that? How do you fucking justify posting scores like that with your handicaps?"

"Blind guys break 80," replied Cloudy, who grabbed The Gull cup.

"Choke on it, fag," said Eggplant, spinning around to leave.

"Wait, Eggplant, don't go. I have to tell you something," said Cloudy. "No come closer. It's private. Closer. Please." Eggplant leaned over. Cloudy whispered into his ear, "Get the fuck away from me."

"Blow me," said Eggplant leaving. He took a few steps and fell.

Penny and Cloudy looked at each, smiled and said, "That's a shame."

Clear was confused, "What's that mean?"

"Just a private in-joke, Pops," said Penny.

Eggplant stood up and staggered out to the veranda.

Clear stonily stared at Eggplant's exit and said, "I genuinely think that guy believes he did nothing wrong. When Wendy got arrested for her first DUI. He called and said, 'Go get your daughter.' She wasn't my daughter—she was his *wife*."

Penny said, "Hey Pops, how did Eggplant get his nickname?"

"I'm not telling her. It would be in bad taste," said Clear, smiling. He looked at his son. "You've cornered that particular market. You do it."

"Eggplant had a hernia operation," explained Cloudy to Penny. "After surgery, water rushes to the lowest point of the body. In the hospital he lifted up his gown to show his buddies his wang. It was purple and huge. Some guy said, 'It looks like an eggplant!' "

"Can I get you anything, Pops?" Penny asked Clear.

"I'm fine, cookie," Clear said, winking. "Don't need a thing."

"That means he wants something," said Cloudy.

"He said he doesn't," innocently replied Penny. "I just asked him."

"Trust me. Probably wants a bucca."

"A bucca?" chirped Clear. "With a coffee bean?"

"Told you," said Cloudy.

"You're a hoot, Pops," Penny said. "One bucca coming up."

"Hey hawkshaw," Clear said, nodding with approval at Penny as she walked to the crowded open bar. "She's a keeper."

"Yeah, I know."

"Mommy would have liked her. That was something, Mom coming

to you like that on the tee box. In the condo, when I'm downstairs reading the paper, the kitchen floor creaks above me and I hear Mom call me." He paused. "They say that goes away."

"Let's hope not. Mom's good company."

"Yes, she is," Clear firmly said. He weakly added, "At least Mom's no longer in pain. And we don't ever have to wait for *that* phone call ever again. Our only consolation. Not much of one."

A foursome of long-time club members walked past the Map table without acknowledging Clear. They were put-out-to-pasture CEOs in out-of-date suits they once regularly wore to their corporate jobs. One griped, "The latest members are trying to form a building committee to tear down the clubhouse and build a new one. We built this one three years ago, and the bar five years ago."

Clear restlessly stirred in his chair, grimly appraised the group and somberly said, "Tell you what sends a signal, son. I've known that Social-Security crew for over 23 or so years. We were never table-close, sharing drinks. Had back-and-forth hellos, conversations in the Pro Shop. Not one of them ever went out of his way to have the common decency to expressed any sympathy to me about your mother."

"People don't come here to know about someone else's problems," numbly observed Cloudy. "Still, it's unforgivable."

"I still haven't," said Clear. "Someday they'll lose their mate, they'll know. Then they'll know."

Penny returned to the table. She was flustered.

"You okay, Penny?" asked Cloudy.

"That jerk at the bar pinched my ass."

"Which one?"

"The gray haired guy there. Green jacket, yellow tie and white shoes."

"Hey, they all look like that," said Cloudy.

"Your bucca, Pops," said Penny, placing the drink before him.

"What's this?" asked Clear, surprised.

"Dad, you asked Penny to get you a bucca."

"Bucca!" he said like a kid calling a pet. "What the hell, we're having fun. Getting a little cocked on the sauce." He sipped the bucca. "It's so warm in my tummy, eating away my stomach lining." Clear sighed. "I'm ready to fold up my tent like an Arab. Rustle up, Wendy."

"She'll come back to the table."

"No, go and get her. Tell her we're leaving. Your sister gets talking to people she'll go on for hours. Like they're her best friends. Since her divorce, and being out of the club not one of them has called her. I bet she's outside smoking like a chimney."

CLOUDY AND PENNY SEARCHED FOR WENDY. But his sister wasn't among the smokers on the veranda. It was a hard, clear evening. Warm. The course looked like a quiet, dark and rolling sea. The swing band in banquet room was playing 'Skylark.'

"Hey Speed," said The Judge, leaning on the railing, puffing a cigar and holding a huge glass of white wine. "I saw how you handled your inebriated ex-brother-in-law in there. The way you conducted yourself was the mark of a true gentleman."

"Believe me, it's the last thing I wanted to be."

"That's *why* it was impressive," said The Judge. "One of our long-time and distinguished Battleground members, Link Petterini, has a limo service. It's good money. I said you were out of work. He suggested you should give him a call."

"I'll take you up on that, thanks, I appreciate it," said Cloudy. "Have you seen Wendy?"

On the 18th fairway, a woman screeched like an injured bird. It was Wendy. She was fleeing from a dark, lumbering figure.

"Go away!" begged Wendy. "Leave me alone."

"You killed your mother!"

"No!"

"Eggplant," said Cloudy, bolting from the veranda to his clubs at the bag-drop rack. He pulled out a 2-iron and sprinted down the fairway. Penny kicked off her heels and followed him.

"Drama," reflectively said The Judge to himself as he leaned on the railing and sipped his wine. "The stuffing of life."

"YOU FUCKED UP," JEERED EGGPLANT as he drunkenly stumbled in the short grass. "Your mother's dead because of you."

"Noooooo," wailed Wendy, running to Cloudy for safety.

"She'd be alive if it wasn't for you," said Eggplant, struggling to get up. "It's your fault, Wendy."

Cloudy stood in the fairway and looked at his approaching sister. Her dress torn. Blood on her knees.

"He says I killed our Mom," Wendy sobbed and pointed at Eggplant. He was about 50 feet away. "I know I did terrible things. I did! But me, kill Mommy? Not our Mommy."

"You didn't kill Mom, Wendy," said Cloudy. "Leaving Freehold killed part of Mom. Westport killed another part. Getting fired from Clairol killed part of Mom. And cigarettes and whatever was in the bottom of her Scotch glass took away the rest of her from us."

"You're all assholes!" shouted Eggplant, staggering up the fairway.

"Make him go away," said Wendy, cowering. "He killed Mom too."

"Your fag brother isn't going to help you," hoarsely growled Eggplant, hurtling toward them.

"Oh no," she said, terrified.

"Don't worry Wendy," confidently said Cloudy, dropping the game ball in the back of his stance and closing the face of his 2-iron. "I have this shot."

He swung and fired a low stinger that smacked Eggplant in the stomach. He gasped, clutched his gut and dropped like an pig in a cheap suit.

"I can do business with that," said Cloudy.

"You stood up for me," said Wendy.

"That's what big brothers do," Cloudy resolutely replied, marching off, 2-iron resting on his shoulder. "You ought to try it sometime."

"What are you going to do with that club," asked Penny.

"Don't worry, I'm not going to finish him off," said Cloudy. "I want my game ball back."

"Assholes!" blurted Eggplant, coughing and crawling and puking.

"Well, look at *you*," quipped Cloudy, picking up his ball and standing over the fallen Eggplant. "So, outside of that shot, how is the rest of your life going?"

"I love your sister," Eggplant said, gulping air and gagging on the words as he spoke them. "I loved your Mom. Love your Dad. Love you. I love your family. I love them all, love them all."

"Hurts, doesn't it?"

"When autumn came
Freehold will be
a fond memory
touched by today,
the now
influenced by time
different than yesterday."

Go Freehold Colonials!

– 1972 Freehold High School Yearbook

Home Course

PATSY MAP WAS QUIETLY RETURNING TO THE DREAM HOME she first admired in a 1964 Stonehurst development sales brochure from Freehold, New Jersey:

The Williamsburg is the most popular of all our models and is selling for **$25,950.**

A luxurious 2-story home, reflecting the best of American Colonial design. Containing 9 rooms, 2 1/2 baths, full basement, 2-car garage.

The first floor features a large entry foyer and true center hall...spacious living room with wood-burning fireplace and picture-window...formal dining room...17' family-size kitchen with luminous ceiling, completely equipped with **CALORIC** and **HOTPOINT** color-coordinated appliances...separate dinette area...25' 10" wood-panelled family room with adjoining guest powder room. Upstairs are 4 twin-size bedrooms with 8 closets...and 2 baths

Professionally landscaped 125' x 200' plot.

All appliances, including **HOTPOINT** clothes washer and clothes dryer, **CARRIER** year 'round central air conditioning, built-in TV and telephone outlets, are included at no extra cost.

AS CLOUDY STEERED THE LIMO ONTO STONEHURST WAY, the Maps felt like they were safely touching down on a landing strip after a long turbulent flight. The dashboard's digital clock read 2:23, as if it was a longitude and latitude reading. Cloudy timed it perfectly. Earlier, he made mandatory stops at Federici's pizzeria, Sorrento's subs, Monmouth County Peanut Brittle, Stewart's Drive-In and Wemrock Orchards. The limo's interior atmosphere was securely enriched with replenishing comfort-food smells of oregano, onions, root beer, peanuts, apple cider and fresh tomato sauce.

"You know what would be pretty cool, stopping at Jersey Freeze on the way back," said Wendy.

"That's right, I almost forgot," said Cloudy, smiling. "Jersey Freeze."

"No more stops," declared Clear, fidgeting in the back seat and twisting his legs to reposition his feet between wrapped subs, pizza bags and peanut brittle cans. "No more stops. We'll hit traffic coming back."

"What's the hurry? I'm driving. When's the next time we'll ever be here, anyway?" said Cloudy. "I'm off today. My boss is letting us use the limo for free. There's no big rush to get back. Relax." He paused. "Pudge told me the band doesn't have any gigs until tomorrow. We're doing a couple of original songs, just for fun, and the usual classic rock covers."

"My God, look at the trees!" Clear said in disbelief.

The gaunt saplings that lined their old neighborhood had grown into huge maples, their red-and-yellow foliage arched over half the street.

"It's prettier than when we lived here," observed Clear. "Still has those goddamn ugly phone poles."

"Looks like it was a nice place to grow up," said Penny, sitting in the front seat. "Big homes, yards, garages."

Cloudy identified the different houses on either side of the street and explained to Penny, "This first batch of homes were display models. At the beginning of each driveway were little white posts with a shingle hung from them that had the model home's name. That first ranch house we passed was the sales office. Then there's our model home: 'The Williamsburg.' That next house after it is 'The Salem.'"

Clear said, "Your mother and I chose 'The Williamsburg' because it had an extra bedroom, but 'The Salem' had the fireplace in the family room, which I thought was better. We had our fireplace in the living room. But who really spends time in the living room?"

"The California-style home was called 'The Newport,'" said Cloudy.

"Always thought that house was ugly," said Clear. "Still do."

Cloudy continued his guided tour through the past, "That house was 'The Oxford.' And those two different ranch houses? One is 'The Monmouth' and the other is 'The Concord.' I never knew anyone who lived in those, because no one with kids owned a ranch house. Oh, and that bigger one over there is . . . 'The Yorktown'—"

"I can't believe you remember the names of those models," Clear said, shaking his head. "And in high school you got a C in history."

"Back then, every new house had a gas lamp post in the front-yard," said Cloudy "And the lamps burned 24 hours a day. Can you believe that? Looks like they're gone now. Nearly all the lantern tops were knocked off by footballs thrown by kids. Don't think all these homes would have lamps burning gas all the time, now?"

Clear watched the houses go by and said, "Today, contractors wouldn't build a Stonehurst. Instead of the 500 homes with half-acre lots, they'd cram in 4,000 townhouses. Throw in a Walmart, Home Depot and storage lockers. Never would have been our neighborhood. It was all farmlands and orchards before Stonehurst was built. The locals thought we were New Yorkers who ruined Freehold." He paused."Wonder what they're getting for these places now?"

"I checked," said Cloudy. "Our old place went to someone for $280,000. Some are listed for $350,000."

"Isn't that something?" said Clear.

Wendy sat in the back seat, looked out the window and warmly ticked off the names of the neighbors who once lived in each house they passed, "The Ruhls, The Heplers, The Straws, The Perrys, The Harringtons, The Lobiancos, The Berrys, The Flemings, The Louros." She smiled. "We had lots of friends. So did Mom." Clear stirred beside Wendy and uncomfortably looked down at his feet. "I wonder who is still living here."

"No stops," said Clear. He watched the houses go by, smiled and said. "On Friday nights the Stonehurst guys caught the 5:35 bus from New York to Freehold. When we got out of the Holland Tunnel into Jersey, one of us would hold up a finger and say, 'One.' Then he'd hold up a second finger and we'd say, 'Two.' Up came a third finger. We'd shout, 'Three!' And all the Stonehurst guys would pop open their beers at the same time. If we opened them any earlier, we'd get caught short. When we got home, take the wives and meet up at Moore's tavern later. Hell, we were all in our thirties. What did we know?"

"Yeah, Fridays were great for us too, especially if you guys were going out," said Cloudy. "Mom got us Fed's pies or Sorrento's subs. We'd drink soda, eat Charles Potato Chips and stay up late to watch *The Man From U.N.C.L.E.* on TV. You and Mom would come home around eleven, giggling."

"I thought the guy who played Illya Kurakin on that TV show was cute," said Wendy.

Clear said, "In Moore's they had a pickle jar on the bar. If someone wanted a pickle, Jim Carney reached into the jar with his dirty, hairy hand, pulled one out and put it on a napkin. He never charged us for all our drinks." He warmly chuckled. "Jim Carney, one of the great historic figures... Moore's."

"In high school, we'd go in there and Mr. Carney would serve us beers," said Cloudy. "Eighteen was the drinking age back then and we were seventeen. Wasn't a big deal."

Clear said,"The parties we had. Bill Gallagher left so bombed he hit a utility pole with his car and took out all the power in the neighborhood. God, did we have fun! Stonehurst. Eight wonderful years. Memorable times, memorable times."

Penny said to Cloudy, "Being back here, is everything smaller?"

"No, I am."

"What's 'Freehold' mean, Pops?" asked Penny.

"A 'Freeholder' is a term from colonial times, cookie," replied Clear. "It meant you paid your debts and weren't responsible to anyone but yourself. In those days only landowners voted. In college, I didn't agree with it. Makes sense to me now. Hey, I said no stops. Why are we turning in here?"

"We have to check this out, Dad," said Cloudy, turning the limo into the parking lot of the Stonehurst Swim Club. "Too bad it's closed for the season because it's September."

Everyone piled out of the limo and walked up to the chain-link fence that was topped with barb wire. They peered through the turquoise-coated diamond-shaped mesh. The original Y-shaped pool was redesigned and reduced to a smaller O-shape. The high dive and two other diving boards were gone. The deep section was shallower.

"Gez, they ruined it. Now it looks like every other pool behind every motel in any town USA," Cloudy sadly said. "Too bad. The old pool was perfect for everyone. It had deep sections, kid sections, you know, everybody could use it at the same time for different things. Probably took down the diving boards because of insurance so they wouldn't get sued. No one ever got hurt when we were kids. Actually, now it looks more dangerous because it's so boring."

"Sometimes places just outlive their usefulness," said Clear, who shook his head and smiled. "You kids lived here in the summer."

"We'd go skinny dipping on teen nights," said Wendy, giggling. "Ed Menalis did naked one-and-a-halfs off the high dive. He was cute. Looked a little like Illya Kurakin. "

"Now I hear about this," said Clear in mock exasperation. "And I thought I had everything under control. You never do. You never do."

"Yeah, those Teen Nights were great," said Cloudy. "What was I? Fifteen? We'd play keep-away pool games with a ball. Guys against the girls. Cheryl Gettmenoff was near me in the water and I didn't understand why because the ball was on the other side of the pool."

"Gettmenoff was her real name?" said Penny. "Oh, the poor thing."

"Yeah, she had a brother too. I wouldn't want to be a guy with that last name. Anyway, when we were playing keep away in the pool. I'm thinking why is she hanging by me? I don't have the ball. A guy throws me the ball. I catch it, Cheryl jumps me and grabs *my* balls. I held onto the ball as long as I could. She was my first grope." Penny gave Cloudy a playful shoulder jab. "Hey, *she* groped me."

"You just looked too happy when you said it," said Penny.

Clear said, "Every other Friday was 'Adult Night' out by that patio area. We'd have barbecues. Circle lawn chairs in the grass and have cocktails while you kids swam." He paused. "Great summers."

The Maps climbed back in the limo and continued down Stonehurst Way. Most of the colonial houses were remodeled with additional rooms, barn-house roofs, back-yard pools and screened-in patio decks. There were fences separating yards. Almost every place had fences.

"Now that's an true eyesore," said Clear, pointing at redesigned house that had a neoclassical facade with pediments above the windows, pilasters and a colonnade front porch. "Bill Weber would have a heart attack if he knew what his place looked like now." He paused. "The houses that stayed the same look a little rundown, but some of them are still pretty good, really." He smiled. "Some nights Mom and I would go for walks around the block and we wouldn't get home for hours. Somebody would see us, invited us over for a drink, or stopped us to talk. That never happened in Westport, I can tell you that."

"I know what's missing," said Cloudy, rolling down his window, inhaling the cool air. "Voices. Kids riding bikes, playing in the streets. When we were here every house was *alive.* Moms didn't work back then so someone was always home. Rock bands rehearsed in garages. There was always a basketball game in somebody's driveway."

"Places change, people move on," said Clear, shrugging. "I like quiet."

"That has to be the Doyle's old place," Wendy said, pointing across the street. "There's a patrol car in the driveway. Remember young Frankie wanted to be a cop? Bet his Dad still lives here. Their house has the same rusty clothesline in the back yard. Let's say hello."

"No more stops!" said Clear. "We'll be tied up forever."

"HERE WE ARE: 223 STONEHURST WAY," said Cloudy, pulling up to the curb as if they were mooring a boat. The Maps got out and stood like laid-off ghosts on the sidewalk. They didn't look for changes as much as they tried to find what was left. The mimosa tree Cloudy and his Mom planted still stood in the center of the lawn. And the hydrangeas along the front of the house had grown, spread and completely covered the first-floor windows. Gone were the black metal numbers of 223 on the post by the front-steps. The basketball backboard above the garage—removed. But the memories remained and filled in the gaps where the present came up short.

"It has aluminum siding instead of wood," Clear said with a distant tone. "That always takes a certain warmth away from a house." He looked across the street. "The Brunetti's. The religious statues are gone from the front yard! They moved! I never, ever thought that would happen. Gives you hope the world can become a better place."

Wendy said, "When we moved in, the street that went by the Brunetti's house used to dead-end into a farm. It was all fenced off. There were horses there too. Mom gave me apples to feed them. They had these big yellow teeth and would eat the whole apple in one bite."

"The farmer let us build haystack forts and play army," said Cloudy.

"A developer bought that farmland for an industrial plant," said Clear.

"I fought it with neighbors. Some politicians came over to the house to talk to us privately about it. We sat down, then Ed Straw brought in an tape recorder, put it on the table and turned it on. They didn't stay too long. We won. They built homes." He snorted. "My legacy." He turned to their house. "The old homestead."

"Looks like no one is here," said Penny.

"I'm glad," said Clear, holding the vase with his wife's ashes. "I don't think whoever's living here would appreciate what we're about to do."

HERB ALPERT AND THE TIJUANA BRASS MUSIC PLAYED 'Whipped Cream' again for John and Patsy Map at 223 Stonehurst Way from an iPod with portable speakers Penny placed at the base of the mimosa tree where the family gathered in the center of the front lawn.

"Mom and I two-stepped to this music," Clear said, faintly smiling and listening to the tune. "The Tijuana Brass. Brings it all back! Great days. The trees were thin and we were broke and too happy to know it." He wistfully added, "The fun we had, the fun we had. My Patsy loved her Stonehurst house." He turned. "How many times did that New York bus drop me off over at the corner and I'd walk up this driveway and you kids would all be at the front door happy to see me saying 'Daddy's home!'…" Clear's voice cracked. "…and Mom was making dinner. I'd come into the kitchen, kiss her, go upstairs and change and when I came downstairs she had already fixed me a drink and you kids would be eating dinner at the kitchen table and we'd sit in the family room watching the news and talk."

His Dad wiped his eyes, lifted the vase's lid and went to the mimosa. Cloudy expected his father to scatter all the ashes. Instead, Clear delicately worked his fingers into the opening, pinched out a small amount and sprinkled it on the tree's upraised roots.

"I didn't want to lose all of her," Clear haltingly said, turning to his kids. He looked at the ashes, his lips quivered. "This is where Mom always wanted to be." He paused. "My lady is home. She's home."

Tears lightly singed the rims of Cloudy's eyes, he said, "Mom was a song that told a story."

Wendy's face was drawn and bound by furrows of guilt as she stared at the ashes on the roots. "Mommy, I'm so sorry…"

"Uh-oh, Pops," said Penny. "Someone's pulling in."

A thirty-something woman in a white BMW convertible drove into the driveway. She stiffly got out of the car. She was pear shaped, had a Dutch-boy hairstyle, wore a white tennis outfit and was talking on a cell phone. Her body language was territorial and aggressive.

"I'm not getting a lot of warmth coming our way," whispered Penny.

"My Ex has the kid," clipped the woman on her cell phone. "I'll dash over, ba-bye." She strutted over to them. "I'm Ms. Braun and you *might be*?" she asked, her inflection inferring they were intruders.

Cloudy said, "We grew up in this house. Just wanted to take a few pictures of our old place. And be on our way. If it's okay, that is."

"Music, you're playing music?" she suspiciously said.

Wendy explained, "We're scattering our Mom's ashes. She loved—"

"Human remains!" screeched a highly repulsed Ms. Braun. She ran to the patrol car pulling out of the Doyle driveway and stopped it.

"Wendy why did you tell her what we were doing?" Cloudy asked.

"In AA we're suppose to tell the truth."

"Yeah, about yourself not *us*."

"This doesn't look good," said Clear, seeing Ms. Braun cross the street with the cop. "Oh, the hell with it, I haven't heard this music in so long, let's dance Patsy," Clear added and did a jaunty two-step to Herb Alpert, clasping his wife's urn to his chest.

Cloudy, Wendy and Penny encircled and joined Clear on the dance floor of green grass at 223 Stonehurst Way.

"They're trespassing and partying," Ms. Braun spat as she came over to them with the cop, who seemed amused by the dancing and clearly didn't like Ms. Braun.

"What's with this music?" staunchly said Ms. Braun.

"Lady, you're too angry to *ever* hear the music," said Penny.

"I'm turning it off," she said, marching over to the iPod.

Clear blocked her and said in a threatening voice, "Lady, leave Herb Alpert and the Tijuana Brass alone."

A severely miffed Ms. Braun backed down and said, "Officer Doyle, these people—"

"Frank Doyle, class of 72, Freehold Township," said Cloudy, catching the instant recognition in the officer's eyes. Growing up, he and Frank futility tried to catch trout at Lake Topenemus, bowled at Howell

Lanes, skated at Turkey Swamp, rode bikes for Slurpees at 7-ELEVEN then without permission "crossed the highway" for 15-cent hamburgers at Burger Chef. They spent hours in each other's basements listening to the radio and racing slot cars or playing ping pong, Bobby Hull rod hockey, electric football and bumper pool. After the Maps moved, the two friends fell out of touch, but one thing they always had in common was each other. That never faded.

"Johnny Boy!" he laughed and hugged his buddy.

"Doylie!"

"Mr. Map, Wendy Map, and..."

"This is my Penny," said Cloudy as he spun her. "Coin of the realm."

"You're Johnny Boy's girl?" said Doylie, adding with Jersey charm. "So what do you lack in self-esteem that makes him so appealing?"

"The answer is yes and yes," said Penny, smiling.

"I like her," said Doylie. "Feisty."

"Officer," sputtered Ms. Braun. "The dead woman's ashes are right *there*! I can't burn leaves on my property, but these strangers can come out of nowhere and turn my lawn into their personal crematorium?"

"Did you just say you can't burn leaves in your yards here anymore?" said Cloudy, surprised. "You have to bag them? Man, lady that's sucky."

"Ashes?" said Doylie. "Oh no, not Mrs. Map!"

"You're taking their side, aren't you?" accusingly said Ms. Braun to Doylie. She shrilled, "If you're not going to take charge, then *I* will!" She clenched her fists and stomped away. Her tennis shoes squeaked in the grass.

"Whatever blows up your skirt, lady," said Penny, smiling. "And I bet it's a cold wind."

"Mr. Map, I'm so sorry about Mrs. Map," said Doylie, who stood as the dancers moved around him. "When my mother had stomach cancer, Mrs. Map came over and took care of her all the time—she'd take a sponge dip it in cold water and wipe it on Mom's swollen belly to cool her down on a hot summer day. Who does that? Mrs. Map always watched our place when we went on vacation. When we got back it was late at night, my Dad said, 'I could really use a beer. But we don't have any.' He opened the fridge and there was a 6-pack of Ballantine Ale. Mrs. Map put it there, knowing my Dad would really want a beer when he came home. Knew his favorite beer too because he always came over to your guys'z house to—"

"Move!" screamed Ms. Braun, wielding a garden hose. She barreled through them and shoved Clear to the ground. She aimed the nozzle at the ashes covering the tree roots. "That woman doesn't belong here."

"Put some lavender on it, lady," Clear defiantly shouted, springing up and tearing the hose from her hands. He opened the nozzle and fired a blast of water into her face. She retreated to the front steps. "My Patsy belongs! She belongs to everything here. To everything! You leave my Patsy alone!"

"Get her, Dad!" said Wendy.

"Pops is bringing it home!" added Penny. "He's is a hoot."

Doylie lowered his voice to Cloudy, "The broad's always been a real bitch, complains about everybody, no one likes her."

The drenched Ms. Braun screamed, ducked into the house and slammed the front door.

"Now she's a real wet fart," decreed Clear as he swiftly walked down the steps. He shut off the nozzle, flicked away the hose with a flourish, picked up the vase and danced.

"As the officer in charge at the scene, I witnessed Ms. Braun's assault and a clear case of self-defense on the part of Mr. Map," said Doylie.

Herb Alpert's subdued introduction to 'A Taste of Honey' began. The bass drum kicked and the trombone blaaaaaat-ed.

"That song!" said Doylie, his eyes brightening. "Dad came home with a console stereo for the rec room and fired up this tune. He flipped! Said it was the sole reason he bought the stereo. Our old rec room with bullfighting posters, bar, pine paneling, cheesy furniture, ping pong and linoleum floor. I'd trade everything to go back."

"Well Doylie," said Cloudy, dancing with Penny, "right now, we're as close as we're *ever* going get."

Doylie got caught up in the song's rolling, spright, trumpet-laced melody, and did the bump with Cloudy's sister. "It's never left us, Johnny Boy, I was so bummed when you guys'z moved. I was mad about it for a long time. So, Wendy, what are you up to?"

"I'm 90 day sober," she said.

"Around this family that's a lifetime," said Clear.

"And you, Mr. Map?"

"Fortunately, I'm still drinking."

Cloudy cracked, "My Dad has the usual mental deterioration."

"Yeah, it began when I started a family," said Clear, who chuckled, then softly added, "We can still laugh."

"So, Johnny boy," said Doylie. "You ever amount to anything?"

"No!" Cloudy cheerfully said.

"Me, neither," replied Doyle, laughing. "You guys'z gotta come over to Dad's house."

Cloudy looked at his father and said, "Thanks, but we have to—"

"No rush," said Clear, two-stepping with his Patsy.

"We can hit Moore's for a couple of pops," said Doylie. "Only after I'm off-duty, of course."

"Moore's is still there?" said Clear, his face widening in excitement.

"It's bigger, it's changed," said Doylie. "Sports bar thing. They tried to save the 18th-Century bar from colonial days but it just fell apart."

"Patsy we're going to Moore's," said Clear, clasping the vase to his heart. He looked at Cloudy and added, "We'll go, after we make one more stop. I'll scatter some Mom on little Matthew's grave so she can be with her baby too. It's something she'd like." He continued dancing. He held up the vase and sighed,"Look at the trees on our block, Patsy. I can't get over the trees. Herb Alpert. Our home. Patsy, you'd would love the trees!"

"Hey, what dance move are you doing, Wendy?" asked Cloudy.

"I'm flying," she said, flapping her arms. "Mom's wings."

"Penny, I grew up with Johnny Boy," said Doylie, nodding at his pal "Really, how can you love that?"

"Why does a girl like me love my Johnny?" she asked, affectionately smiling at him. "Ka-yikes."

"Yeah, I'd like to know too," chimed Cloudy as he spun her from the bottom arc of a perfect swing around the mimosa tree to the accompanying triumphant pitch of Herb Alpert and the Tijuana Brass' exuberantly bouncy trumpets and became the person his Mom intended him to be. He closed his eyes, smiled and asked her, "Where's the love? Where does all the love come from?"

"*Dar*-link, it's a mystery to me."

Freehold

A life in Freehold, New Jersey
1964 – 1972

MOLLY PITCHER WOMAN'S CLUB
YEARBOOK · 1929–1970
Welcome to historic FREEHOLD
1683
1919
Formerly MONMOUTH COURTHOUSE
AMF
The Spirit
3 Seniors from F.H.S. Win
NEWS
Stonehurst at Freehold
Freehold High School
This certifies that
American HOTEL
RESTAU
CLIFTON T. BARKALOW SCHOOL
FREEHOLD, NEW JERS
1968
Old Monmouth HOME MADE CANDIES
WORLDS BEST PEANUT BRITTLE
Since MOORE'S 1787
Sorrento's SUBS
FREEHOLD, N.J.
Federici's PIZZA RESTAURANT
JERSEY FREEZE

MY PARENTS came to me in a dream and said, "Fritzie, tell our story." And I hope the love and life they gave me shaped their song into a novel.

I left the dream for you.

And them.

Thank you

Mom

Anne Gozdieski Reiss

1934–2005

Dad

Frederick Reiss

1927–2009

More kudos on other stuff . . .

PEN-award-winning novel Surf.Com . . .

"With Gidget Must Die and now Surf.Com, Fred Reiss has emerged as a sort of surfy Hunter S. Thompson, a vicious, merciless, ridiculous social documentarian with a distinct flair for drawing unforgettable characters. Fred Reiss is nuts. But mainly, he is very, very funny."

- Alan Weisbecker, author of Searching for Captain Zero

Gidget Must Die . . .

"Gidget Must Die is a witty, surreal, and insulting text laced with keen perceptions and dead-on portraits of our sport's archetypes. Make no mistake about it, this guy Fred Reiss is sick. I recommend GMD for a hundred or so other reasons.

- Drew Kampion, editor of Surfer's Path

"Fred made me laugh and squirm through the Malibu culturati. I choked on the asphalt fumes of PCH, and breathed the salt spray of the "Bu" again. I'm with him in the pre-dawn perfection, taking off until—but let Reiss tell it. He'll suck you over the falls with his wild surf yarn (Or is it?)."

- John Severson, founder of Surfer Magazine

Insult And *Live!* . . .

"If you've ever been late with a comeback, BUY Reiss."

- Playboy Magazine

PEN-award winning novel

Surf.Com

The dot-commers are ruining Santa Cruz. The only force left to defeat them is a surfer, a dog, and a van. But when the surfer falls in love with a dot-com girl, things get gnarly. **$16.95**

Get the last word in . . .

Insult and Live!

1,000 stage-tested insults. Fred was an insult comic. Appeared on national TV. He identifies every loser in the world. Hot flamers to slam jerks so you can man-up and truly live. **$16.95**

Killer surf novel with a heart.

Gidget Must Die

It's thirty years later, a surf legend from the fifties returns to Malibu to kill everyone in the Gidget movie for ruining his surf spot. **$14.95**

The first sci-fi surf novel based in reality by a writer with a life.

Aliens! Surf! Santa Cruz!

A surfer named Thorn learns aliens are spoiling Santa Cruz so locals will lose their stoke for living. Once aliens extract all the stoke, they can transport a perfect Santa Cruz to their planet. But Thorn's not giving up his stoke and surf spots to a bunch of kook trannie aliens. **$15.95**

Only available as an eBook and phone app.

Insults To Go

2,000-plus insults. Over 1,000 have never been in print form.

Here are over 1,000 more insults. Includes illustrations and slams from the previous book. These flamers were from Fred's act and never put into book form until now. **$9.95**

Purchase First Edition Books (if available) signed by Fred Reiss. Send check to Fred Reiss, PO Box 733, Mount Hermon, CA 95041. Add $3 for shipping and handling. Order eBooks at Amazon, Google, or Apple. Thank you for supporting my work, bad habits, and surf wax.

WAS A REPORTER for 7 years in Connecticut until he had testicular cancer (one testicle plucked, he's now down to five). After being given a second chance, Fredly quit his job, left for California to surf, do stand-up comedy, learn about wine and write. Fredly has performed in Bakersfield, Yuba City and on national TV (see "love me" You Tube). When working, he's a radio talk show host. Fredly grape stomps and gets vertical at the Skov Winery in the Santa Cruz Mountains. He has held enriching dead-end jobs in advertising, a bank, a mental facility, a bed & breakfast, a warehouse, a surf shop, several radio stations, and has been a camp counselor, substitute teacher and tennis instructor. He partially grew up in Freehold, New Jersey. He lives in Northern California with his girlfriend, Laurie, three cats: Groucho, Brooksie, and Bogey. Plus, a dog named Seven (Yes, named from a *Seinfeld* show.).

My Three Greatest Fears:

1.) Moving to Connecticut.

2.) Bass solos.

3.) Hearing Bruce Springsteen sing 'Outlaw Pete' again.

1965

The Stonehurst clown prepares
Freehold children to face the future...